Cogent

Jacob Maxon

Library of Congress Cataloging-in-Publication Data
2022917289

Maxon, Jacob
Cogent / by Jacob Maxon

ISBN : 978 - 195946000 – 8

Part I

Chapter 1

"Is a memory of something that hasn't happened real? I think it is."

My lips hold the strange warmth of a kiss, a feeling of overwhelming love, a hand outstretched to meet mine, only to be ripped away and brought back to reality. It must have been a dream, of course, but it felt real. I rub my eyes, swollen from tears. I need to trust the Mover of Life to guide me through this. Today I join the army.

I don't know how anyone could get ready for a day like this. Sitting up feels like a chore, and falling back asleep seems impossible. The room only grows in chaos with each passing moment.

"Lucas!" someone shouts.

A pillow meets my face with the force of a rocket. I scramble in my bed to see which kid has thrown it. As the eldest boy in the orphanage, this happens often. Someone is always trying to get a hit in. They're lucky I have to leave, and I'm unlucky that I have to.

After tossing the pillow back into the crossfire, I hear a suspicious giggle from the bed next to mine. I'm starting to believe that my friend Justin set this whole thing up. A strange farewell of sorts. He has conveniently wrapped himself in blankets, forming a protective cocoon.

"You know if I get hit, you do too."

He grins, embracing my attack. My projectile pillow is ineffective, though, and he only laughs harder.

"Now!" he shouts.

The room erupts with white as pillow after pillow launches in my direction. With each hit I take, Justin laughs triumphantly. With my absence from this place, he will become the eldest boy, and thus their leader. Rightfully so. I was happy the day he came here. He's been my one and only real friend. I never needed to get close to anyone else—I only needed him.

"It's service day, Lucas."

"I know." How could I not? The weight of it holds me to this bed. "Are you going to be all right without me?"

Justin looks around the room at the storm of pillows, still in chaotic flight. "I think I can manage."

1

"Don't let them win," I say.

"Never."

Everyone should know one person like Justin. Someone you can trust with your life. It will be strange to live a year without him. This is the first time I've ever envied him for being younger than me.

Before anyone can settle, Miss Caroline, our caregiver, enters the room. "That's enough, boys. Let's get ready for the day," she says. "Goodness, what has happened here?"

You've never seen behavior change so rapidly among a bunch of boys. Not because they are afraid of her, but because everyone here owes her their life. She is the reason we have a home.

She takes a seat at the end of my bed. "How are you this morning, Lucas?"

"I'm fine." My efforts to hide my thoughts from her are useless. She knows me too well.

"Look at me, son. You've got this."

Miss Caroline is as genuine as they come, always has been. I find myself admiring the familiar soft yellow glow of her curly hair. It's something unique to her, something I can remember from the day we met.

"You might need my help around here to raise these boys."

She smiles. "I think I can handle it. Here, this is for you."

She leans over and pulls a gray button-down uniform from her bag, then hands it to me. My hand traces the Rockcliff Military Academy Crest. They call it "The Lion on Top of the Wall." The weight of the fabric makes me feel uncomfortable.

"Do you like it?"

I could lie to her and tell her I do. It's nice. Probably the nicest thing I've owned, but I would throw it away in a heartbeat if I could. Instead, all I say is, "I'm going to miss you."

She rubs her nose and looks off for a moment. It's obvious she's holding back tears. I know she wishes I could stay, too. I was the first boy she took in. If I didn't have such fond memories of my mother, I might call her mom.

I was six when my mother was murdered by a Cogent. That day haunts me whether I'm dreaming or awake. Miss Caroline found me and took me in after, and since then, she's tried to lift my spirit. I'm incredibly grateful for that.

2

She still looks as though she wants to cry, but the tears never come. Come to think of it, I've never seen her cry. Today would be a first. She wants us to be tough. When raising boys during war time, it's important to stay strong.

"I love you," I tell her.

"I love you too, Lucas."

Taking a deep breath in, she gently rubs the top of my head. Her hands are warm and full of love. This has been her way of displaying affection since the day we met. There was never a need for a hug or a kiss, just a gentle swirl. Strange to most people, but to me, it's how she expresses her love.

"Don't be afraid of today," she reminds me. "Blaze forward, writing your own future. Stay true to yourself. Remember, you are brave, kind, and smart. And if you should ever have to fight, remember that I love you and I'm on your side, no matter what."

Her words are inspiring, but I still have a sense of dread. I will walk out this door today, but there is a truth that not even she can hide from me anymore. As a boy, I imagined she could protect me from the world, but becoming a man, I know that no one can protect you.

That's the reason for the draft today. Rockcliff needs to replenish the front lines. We are a haven for humanity, but that comes at a cost. It's why every boy and girl is drafted at age fifteen. They need bodies to replace the dead. And even though I know this, it's hard to come to terms with the government controlling my future.

"Why don't you stay for breakfast before you go? I'll have the boys get some fresh tomatoes from the garden. I can make omelets."

She knows I love omelets, but I can't. "I'm going to be late," I tell her.

With a quick glance at the clock, she knows I'm lying. "Okay, I guess this is goodbye then."

I nod and allow her to leave. Justin sits quietly at the edge of his bed. I know if I stay longer, I might cry. I don't want to do that on my last day here—I'd carry that with me everywhere. Throwing on my uniform, I dash to the mirror, running my fingers through my hair a few times. Despite my best effort, nothing will fix it, and it returns to the same crazy position it was in before.

With one more glance back at the room, my eyes connect with Justin's. We prefer not to talk about serious things much; our friendship is one of mutual implicit understanding. He nods as if to say *I'll see you soon.*

3

Outside, I'm met with radiant beams of sunlight rippling across the barrier that sits on top of the concrete wall. It's the city's most advanced defense, apart from our Cogent Guard. They say it's as deadly as a Cogent, with the ability to instantly vaporize a man with a single touch.

The streets are swarming with people on their daily commute. This is normal, with it being a city safe for humans. Living beyond the walls is profitable, but only a money-hungry fool would take the risk—or a forced soldier.

That's how it happened to me. As a boy, I lived in the neutral town of Sincliff. It's right in the center between Rockcliff and Sinder territory. A stupid name for a city, but it was the best way for it to identify itself since no one technically controlled it. The two armies have destroyed that city over and over, but it keeps coming back.

Whenever I think of that place, my mind fills with images of burned buildings, and I can still hear the screams of the people as they take their last breaths. The awful smell of burning flesh is seared into my nose. I never want to go back there again.

I don't know what I'd do if they forced me to return. I fear they will. When I'm part of the army, I will have to follow their rules, no matter what they are. I've thought about running away a time or two, but where would I go? You can't outrun this war. There is no safer place than Rockcliff.

If I lived beyond the barrier again, I would likely die. The Sinder Army has a vast amount of invincible Cogents at their disposal. I have trouble believing anyone likes it there. But we have no choice if we want to live.

I suppose there is another option I've never considered before. Leaving the crowds, I walk to the edge of the bridge, allowing the sound of rushing water to take over. I toss a small rock in and watch as it tumbles and swirls violently until it disappears over the cliff.

This could be my end. I could jump in. Let the water take me out to the cliff and throw me over the edge. It would smash me against the rocks. I'm sure I wouldn't feel pain for long.

Is that what I want, though? I look toward the road that leads to the Military Academy. If I go, I will become a pawn in their war, just like my mother. I can't accept that; I can't trust them. Everyone thinks they can trust Rockcliff, but I know the truth. I know what a life is worth to them. My eyes fall on the rushing water once more, contemplating the decision before me.

They pretend like human soldiers can make a difference in this war. But how can a human be effective in a battle with invincible Cogents? No manmade weapon can kill them, and we know that. Yet they still insist on having a human army. I suppose we are to serve as some sort of distraction, or an offering. I bet they only use us so they can find their suitable matches for the Cogent program. They take two humans every year and turn them into those things.

It makes me sick to think they will create more of these invincible demons, sacrificing humans and claiming that they will protect us. Since the creation of these monsters, the war hasn't ended. What makes them think that will change? They can't save us, and if you're dumb enough to trust in them to save you, then you haven't been let down yet.

"Don't jump!" a familiar voice shouts from a distance.

I step down from the railing I had unconsciously stepped up on. It's Katelynn, the one person who brings me overwhelming joy in life. She places her hands around my waist and squeezes me tight. I hug her back, grasping a strand of her blond curls.

Instantly, I feel lighter. We've been together for a year. Most of the boys in the orphanage don't believe me, and I guess that's to be expected. She is way out of my league, after all. She's the daughter of the hospital chief. Money, beauty, and intelligence are just a few of the things I don't match up with.

I will always be grateful to Miss Caroline for sending me to get medicine. If it weren't for her request, I know we would have never met. I've visited Katelynn every week since, and sometimes multiple times a week. Any chance I can, I've volunteered.

"Hey cutie," she says, placing her hands behind her back and tilting her head just enough for her long curls to fall. "Ready to live together?"

Katelynn is always so positive. She balances me out. I wouldn't say I'm a negative person, but I'm more of a realist. I admit, some days she's the only reason I haven't run away from this place. Her and the fact that I wouldn't make it beyond the walls. If I could stay here and not join the military, my life might be fairly good.

Live together. I suppose she's right. We will be living together. "But you have to promise you won't leave me after you see how messy I am," I say.

Katelynn places her hand on my head and tries to fix my hair before giving up. She laughs and says that messy just might be something she's

5

stuck with. I recall the time we first met; she was organizing medicines. She told me that everything has a place.

At the time, I told her I couldn't live like that. Chaos was what I knew. In the orphanage, you'd be lucky to find anything in the same place the next day. I've grown used to that, so each time I look for something, it's like a mini adventure. Sometimes I find what I'm looking for, and other times I find something new, something I didn't intend to.

"So, what were you thinking about?" she asks. "You looked upset."

"I was just thinking about today," I admit. And it's the truth, but I can't bring myself to tell her about the dark thoughts in my head. I'm afraid it would be too intense for a pure soul like hers. If she knew, it would only hurt our relationship. Mostly because she cares so much about me. It's safer not to bother her with my anxiety.

Her expression brightens as she rises to the challenge of lifting my spirit. "Don't you worry about a thing. The Giver of Life made you and has a plan for you. You can trust in the Giver of Life."

Katelynn has a strong faith, and I admire her for it. She leads the youth of the Church of the Giver here in the city. It is the city's fundamental belief, and I'm no exception. But I struggle with why the Giver of Life would put me through such things. I wouldn't go as often as I do, but it's been an effective way to spend time with Katelynn over this past year. Miss Caroline would only let me volunteer my time for good reasons, not just let me go anywhere.

"Do you think we'll make it?" I ask.

"Where?" Her voice is almost a whisper.

"Through the Academy," I say with a sense of dread.

"Of course!" she says with a sudden burst of energy. "You have to allow the Mover of Life to guide you through. And if he doesn't, then I hope I can find someone as sweet as you." She laughs.

It's times like these where Katelynn's positivity overwhelms me. She is so uplifting, always seeing the best in everything, even me. No matter what I do, I can't seem to be frustrated around her. It's like wherever she goes, the sun is always shining right on her, and all I want to do is stand in her shadow.

I offer her my hand, which she gladly accepts, and the two of us travel through the city arm in arm. I feel like I'm escorting royalty. With her father being one of the richest men in the city, Katelynn is as close to a princess as it gets.

Right before we enter the Academy grounds, she pulls me aside, then holds up a silver necklace with a green gem. Three parallel black lines extend across it. The first represents the Giver of Life, the second is the Mover of Life, and the third is Life itself. "It's the story of us . . . I want you to have it, to bring you good luck and protection this year."

Katelynn pulls her necklace out from under her uniform to show me she has a matching one. It's the nicest gift I've ever received. "Pray with me?" she asks. I follow her to the side of the road, facing the magnificent rippling aura barrier. She kneels, kissing the ground, and begins to pray.

"Oh Giver of Life, make us whole and help us reach our purpose. Mover of Life, guide us through this journey we are about to set out on. For we are nothing without you. Fill us with your love and watch over us till the end. Your words are clear and true."

I echo her. "Your words are clear and true."

Her prayer seems right. If not for the Giver of Life, I wouldn't be who I am today. And if not for the Mover, I wouldn't be here with Katelynn right now. There is nothing more clear and true than that. When we met, I was just a skinny kid with no purpose, but she's helped me see I can become something. By the time we graduate, I hope to be the person she imagines me as already.

"Ready to go to class," she says, swinging her leather bag over her shoulder.

I nod. "Let's go."

The realization that once I go inside, I open the world to an infinite number of possibilities, frightens me. I want to be hesitant. What if the assessment test forces me away from Katelynn? What if she meets someone else? What if they select me to be one of the two soldiers to lose their humanity? Surely, they wouldn't select someone to become a Cogent who doesn't want it.

Near the front of the Academy is an extensive set of stairs. There must be a hundred steps to reach the top. It's an old design for sure. They say it was once a prison for the world's worst criminals. After the war, they killed all of them so they could turn it into a school. I suppose that's why it still looks so bland. The concrete walls and lack of windows make me feel trapped.

Inside the Academy, we receive instructions for the day. Each of us is given a card with a number revealing our homeroom. An assessment test is the first step in the selection process. The result will determine which

7

division we belong to. The most qualified students are selected for the Cogent program. We are scored in three categories: written, biological, and combat. This ensures that everyone is placed in the right division, where our talents can be used to protect our great nation.

Every citizen goes to the Academy for four years, then serves in active duty for the same amount of time. For the first four years, everything is paid for, including your food, clothes, and quarters. Once you become an active soldier, you begin to receive payment. Soldiers are among the highest earners in Rockcliff. For many, this is the reason they stay in. If you're lucky enough to get stationed somewhere relatively safe, like here, then it's not so bad, I guess. Whether you're a soldier or civilian, a Cogent will kill you all the same. So, I guess you might as well get paid for it.

Knowing all of this, I've come up with a plan. I'll make sure my scores point me toward the least risky job. If I score high enough on the written and low on combat, I could work with Katelynn in the medical division. That way, I'm out of danger for my four years of active duty. Then I could retire here in the city and maybe get a job at the hospital. That way, I can stay close to her for the next eight years. I'm not sure it will work, but it's the best plan I've got.

After I walk Katelynn to her homeroom for the day, she kisses me on the cheek and wishes me luck on my test. She's obviously not worried. If I were to bet, I would say her father has already secured her a spot in the medical division. Not that she won't end up there anyway. My point is, her future is already decided, and mine isn't. As I walk to my class, I glance back at Katelynn; hope and joy still fill her face. I do my best to remember that feeling, trying to hold on to it as I enter my homeroom.

The room must have been remade, since it looks nothing like the front of the building. Windows cover the entire wall across from the door. I take a seat in the back of my class, looking out the large grid of glass at the city. My fingers trace the edge of the necklace Katelynn gave me. As more kids enter the room, I make sure I look as uninviting as possible. I'm not here to make friends, and Katelynn is already in class. No need to talk to anyone else.

Isolating myself goes as planned. No one bothers me. I've become invisible to the rest of the class, so much so that I can hear the two boys in front of me talking as if I'm not there.

They brag about how they will be selected as this year's Cogents. One of them, the big one, might have a shot. He's large for a fifteen-year-old and looks like he might be a skilled fighter. But the other boy—I think he's just dreaming.

The confidence they have is hysterical. Before I can stop myself, they hear me laughing at them. For a moment, they ignore me and continue boasting about their abilities. It's as if they forgot there's a written test. The two of them sound about as dumb as they come. And I came from an orphanage. They should know that, beyond the written and physical requirements, you have to be a genetic match. I hate to say it, but I doubt there's anything genetically special about these two.

I think I've heard it all from them, but then the big one says the most ridiculous thing. "Once I become a Cogent, I'll kill Commander Silas and end this war. I'll bring peace to humanity once more."

Again, I laugh, so hard this time I struggle to breathe. It's the most delusional thing I've ever heard anyone say and mean. We all have our jokes, but this guy, he's on another level.

"What's so funny?" the large boy asks.

I do my best to calm myself as he leans against my desk. To most people, he's probably scary, using his size to intimidate, but for me, he's the same kid I saw every day in the orphanage. He's big, but not bright, so I'll need to win with words.

Avoiding him would be easy, but I think I'll toy with him a little. "I'm sorry. I was just remembering a joke I heard earlier."

He looks at me in disbelief. "Really. Let's hear the joke then."

"Did you know even dumb soldiers can make you feel safe, like when you forgot your bulletproof jacket?"

His face squeezes together as if it's hard to see.

"Do you get it? Don't beat yourself up about it, let me."

I know he didn't get it, but he nods like he did. I've beaten his simpleton brain, and now he returns to his desk in defeat. Talking my way out of things is a skill I've honed over many years. It's always good for a laugh, too.

"Smooth," says a girl to my right. "Are you always that good with your words?"

I nod and give a quick, facetious smile, hoping that she gets the message. It seems to not deter her. She insists on not letting me get away with what I just did. She's clearly smart enough to know what I've done, but not a threat that I would have to worry about fighting, given her small stature.

9

"You know, I would have taken him up on that offer if it was me," she says, leaning back in her chair.

"You mean to fight?" I ask with genuine curiosity. I guess I'm supposed to believe this purple-haired, five-foot-nothing little pixie girl is going to take down this guy who's about twice my size.

"Yeah," she says, cracking her fingers. "I could take him—both of them."

This girl is living in a fantasy. I don't want to respond to her. I couldn't be more uninterested in what she has to say. But against my better judgment, I poke at her a little.

"So, what you're saying is you will be our next Cogent? They'll write tales of you and how you helped slay the commander of the Sinder Army?"

This girl's clever. She knows I mean to walk her into a trap. I can tell by her body language as she intentionally accepts my invitation.

"Yes, I will be. And for the record, being a Cogent is the greatest honor one could ever have," she says firmly.

I bite my bottom lip, holding myself back from the argument this girl is trying to drag me into. I know a skilled opponent when I see one. By her confidence, I can tell she means to attack. She intends to call me out for my joke and force me into a fight, while the other guy was too stupid to even get it. For now, I'll just stop talking and force a draw.

I pray to the Mover of Life that this ends soon, and my prayers are answered almost immediately.

"All right, students. Have a seat," an older gentleman says as he shuffles into the room. "My name is Mr. McLane, but you don't have to remember that because this is all most of you will see of me. I am a teacher here; I teach History of the Great War. Understanding the past is important because it helps you to know where you are going. But that is not why you are here now. Today, I will lead your first assessment. Once you've completed the tasks I give you, you can move along to your next assessment. After all assessments are completed, you will get assigned a division in our ranks and study to become soldiers for your division. Your new lives begin here, so do your best."

I wait until the test pops up on my desk screen. They ask several basic morality questions about whom to save in various scenarios. Next, they have a math and science section, which I get through all right. Miss Caroline had a similar curriculum at the orphanage. After an hour, the test asks me about my desired occupation in the military. I choose the medical division and hope for the best.

Only a few people finish before me, including the purple-haired pixie girl. To no one's surprise, the big guy is far behind. Now we wait for the biological and physical assessment to start. After another thirty minutes, everyone has completed the exam, and we line up in the hall. We march toward a medical checkpoint and wait outside the blue screening curtains.

Another thirty minutes pass as we wait in line for our bio screening. The whole time, I've searched for Katelynn's class, but with no luck. When it's my turn, I walk behind the curtain. A team of nurses greets me. They ask a series of standard medical questions and check my mobility. At the end of the exam, another nurse comes in covered wearing several protective garments, like she's handling nuclear materials. She flips over my wrist and jabs me with a needle, drawing blood. I look in her eyes, the only part of her that's visible, and feel instantly calm. Before I can even say a word, she pulls out her needle and another nurse bandages me up.

They send me off, and I follow the arrows to the training room. It's the largest I've ever seen, with a ceiling three stories high and blue hexagonal fighting platforms scattered all around. Crowds of students surround each of the platforms, and a few teachers direct us to get another number card. Mine says "25A." Next, I'm directed just a few platforms down to wait for my fight.

As I approach, my eyes go dark. The thin, soft hands placed over them give away my assailant. It's an easy guess.

"Katelynn!"

"Aww, how did you know?"

"The scent of flowers on your hands. That, and there has only ever been one girl to touch me."

"Aww, you guys are cute," another girl says. "I want that."

"Lucas, this is Niki. Our families have known each other forever."

The two hug as if they're best friends. I'm surprised I've never seen Katelynn's friend before. I suppose I've only ever met with Katelynn during her hospital hours though.

"Niki, you'll have to get your own," she says playfully.

We reveal our cards, and it turns out Katelynn has the group letter "A" as well. It looks like my prayers are finally being answered, and quickly.

"I have to watch," she says. "They've actually only assigned me a number out of formality."

11

My suspicion was right. Her dad has pulled some strings for her so she can go straight to the medical division, no questions asked. It makes sense, though—even if they evaluated her for everything, she'd still end up there.

Before she can finish telling me about what her father has done, the lights dim, and a man appears above us on a balcony. His body emits a glowing blue aura, something like a mixture of flame and steam. There's no doubt that he's a Cogent.

The crowd of students breaks out in cheers as he tears his shirt off. I hear someone in the crowd call him our hero and another call him a hunk. Infatuation rolls over the crowd until they are left with nothing else to do but chant his name: "Marcus—Marcus—Marcus."

I recognize the name, but I've never seen him this close before. He's something of a legend here in the city. They call him the Hero of Humanity, a title he earned years ago by holding off the last Sinder Army attack led by Commander Silas. Many people give Marcus the credit for why they are not enslaved to the vile Sinder Nation.

He plays into this praise and shows his strength. I won't cheer for him, but I'm glad he's on our side. It bothers me that he won't put his shirt back on, but it doesn't seem to bother anyone else. They admire every flex of his muscles. For a moment, I even catch Katelynn swooning over him.

"Soldiers! Welcome to your combat assessment. Please work hard, show us what you can do, and always remember to respect each other. The enemy is out there. Let's not injure anyone to the point they can't fight anymore. Please follow the judge's commands and give us a good show. By the end of today, those feral Sinder Army dogs will fear us even more. Now go get it!"

The teacher in charge of our combat assessment steps up. "Let's begin."

I watch with interest. He calls out two numbers, students who have been selected to go against each other in a practice sword fight. I assume skill or physicality may be the criteria for the pairings. After a few rounds, I look at my potential opponents. My eyes focus on a boy my size with whom I might match.

The groups keep going, one after another. Most of the rounds last just a few minutes. The fights end as you would expect, with one fighter being obviously stronger. It's not a tournament, though, so I wonder how they will compare us to everyone.

"25A and 21A, please," the judge announces.

"Good luck, Lucas," Katelynn says, clasping her hands.

"Lucas Conley versus Bianca Graystone," the judge says, lifting our cards.

I slide onto the blue ring and take my position. At first, I'm confused. They may have called my number by mistake. Across from me stands that purple-haired girl. Her name is Bianca, I guess. I check with the teacher, who assures me this is my matchup. He hands me a practice sword. Bianca removes her uniform shirt to reveal a black athletic tank top. She cracks her knuckles and neck as she prepares for combat. The boys don't seem to like her much, as they mock her unnaturally muscular appearance.

I check once more with the teacher. Without further delay, the bell rings and I'm met with a fury of slashes. I don't want to score high here, but I also don't want to look like a fool in front of everyone, so I stick to evasion tactics for a moment so I can assess her fighting skills. Fortunately, I'm more prepared for this than I intended to be. Back at the orphanage, Miss Caroline would have us spar for about two hours every day. She said boys are destructive and we needed an outlet for our energy, so she taught us swordplay.

I've only ever sparred with the boys at the orphanage. Most days Justin was my training partner, and he was pretty good—he would typically beat me even though I'm a year older. But Bianca seems to be even better than him. There was a time when I would practice with Miss Caroline, who never lost, but that was more for fun. She taught herself—and all of us—everything we know.

"Stop running around!" Bianca commands.

"I'm not running, I'm evading," I explain.

"Then fight me," she says, throwing a kick right across my face, inches from my nose. How does she even get her foot up that far given her height?

I can tell she's skilled in combat. If I wasn't familiar with what she's doing, I would be knocked out in about ten seconds.

Bianca lands an elbow right to my gut. I stagger backward, and my eyes land on Katelynn in the crowd. I have to remember that what I do here will show her what kind of man I am. If I beat this pixie girl down mercilessly, she might think I'm cruel. But if Bianca defeats me, I'll appear weak, and if that happens, Katelynn might believe I can't protect her. Winning is my priority, but in a way that doesn't make Katelynn afraid of me.

I take a couple of swings at her, not putting all my power in them. She swats them away with relative ease. I put in more effort, but nothing changes. With all my power, I lunge at her, hoping to end the fight. My blade slides down hers as she pulls me in and slaps me in the face with her free hand. I reach up to feel the welt she leaves, confirming her hit. It was so fast I couldn't see it.

"Quit playing," she says, landing another stinging open hand across my face.

It turns out she's as skilled with her second hand as the one holding her blade. I'm in real trouble. It's as if her open palm has become another weapon, and I am forced to focus on the new possibilities of her attacks.

Frustrated is only one word to describe what I'm feeling. I hurl myself toward her in a long succession of blows, which she not only stops but predicts. This girl far more skilled than I assumed, perhaps even better than Miss Caroline. Each attack serves as a reminder that I have to come up with something quickly to end this. After a brief calculation, I realize my only advantage is my size. I lean into her next attack and lock my arm in hers. We spin to the ground together as our bodies slam against the ring.

The crowd erupts in shock. To my surprise, it worked. Bianca didn't see this move coming. I have her pinned to the ground in a move I typically used against the boys back at the orphanage. But she's not a boy, and I immediately realize my hand is gripping her chest and not her arm.

She shrieks, "Get off of me, perv!" causing me to tumble backward.

Embarrassed, I pick myself up, but not before she takes a few extra swings at me. If not for the teacher holding her back, I surely would be seeing stars right now.

The teacher promptly calls it a draw. The crowd of students moan in disappointment. Cheers now turn to jokes about our entanglement. Bianca lunges at the crowd as a boy from the back yells "I want a feel next!" She jumps off the stage, violently shoving her way through, but the boy has made his escape before she can reach him.

I search the crowd for Katelynn, but all the faces blend together. She's nowhere to be found. I only hope that she left before she could see how it ended. If these boys don't stop, she may think it was intentional.

Once the fights are over, Marcus calls for our attention once more and directs us to the auditorium. I worry about Katelynn, as I still haven't found her. Hopefully she's not mad at me.

We all file into the auditorium. Large rows of students face the stage in restless anticipation. This is the last event. Once everyone is here, a spotlight appears on the main stage. The anthem echoes throughout the space, and a familiar man comes out to greet us—the prime minister of Rockcliff and principal of this school, Ben Maxwell.

His appearance is one of a different era, and easily recognizable. The prime minister is tall and slender, the exact opposite of Marcus's muscular physique. He makes his status known to us by wearing a premium-fabric black suit, one that could only have been made before the war. His overall sharpness is unobtainable in today's age. With his slick black hair, perfect teeth, and shiny skin, he almost looks plastic.

Prime Minister Maxwell gives an inspiring and bold speech. He works the crowd with talks of bravery and courage. He boasts of our city's strength. It's what everyone enjoys hearing, but not me. I want to hear the results. I'm tired of waiting. I need to know if the Giver of Life has answered my most important prayer. I need to know if I'll end up with Katelynn.

Maxwell clears his throat. "As you know, students, each year we select two of you to join the highest honor of defending our great nation by becoming protectors of freedom, heroes of justice, lions among lambs. For two of you, that means you will make the ultimate sacrifice today. You will give up your humanity so that humanity may live. We don't make this decision lightly. We take everything about you into consideration. Powerful men and women are needed to protect us. And now we will meet our future heroes."

The prime minister lifts his hand, signaling the nurse I saw earlier. She's still covered from head to toe, even now. Gently, she places a card in his hands. No doubt it has the names of this year's Cogents written on it.

With a clasp of his hands, he slides the first envelope open. "Bianca Graystone!"

The crowd of students erupts in cheers as the anthem plays her down. As they get sight of her small stature, their cheers turn to questions. Bianca takes the stage. No one can believe it. I can't believe it. How could she be selected after our fight? Surely a draw is not a worthy score for a Cogent. She must have done incredibly well on all her other assessments.

Our Prime Minister signals for the music to fade as he welcomes her. "Now for our second Cogent—Lucas Conley!"

I frantically begin my search. It's a surprise to me that there's another Lucas Conley living in Rockcliff. I check repeatedly, expecting to see someone rush from the back, but no one ever comes. Again, "Lucas Conley" echoes over the loudspeakers.

"No," I say aloud. "No, this isn't right."

"Where is he?" the prime minister asks as the spotlight searches for me.

I'll just act like it's not me. If I cover my face, they won't be able to find me. No one really knows me. Or so I thought, but someone in the crowd of students abruptly points me out. To my surprise, it's the big idiot from the testing room. I'm not sure how he learned my name, but his revenge is all but secured. More than anything, I want to turn and point back at him—he wants this, after all, and I don't.

The room applauds, but I hear nothing, only my own breath as it slows to a crawl and then speeds up with each thought. A series of strange hands push me forward until I reach the stage.

I pray to the Giver of Life to change this moment, but I fear it's already too late. With each step I take up to the stage, I feel as if I'm inching toward something I already knew was coming. I don't know why, or maybe I do, but either way, I'm here now.

The effects of shock are overwhelming me. My vision is playing tricks. There are no faces in the crowd. The rows of students all look like empty shells, devoid of any expression. Is this even real?

Maxwell lifts Bianca's and my hands with his, displaying us like some sort of champions. I know everyone is excited, but I can't help but look for an exit. My eyes gravitate to a door near the side. Before I can make a move, Marcus steps in front of me, almost making me loose a limb. I won't be able to get away from him without dying. It's as if he knows I want to run.

"This way," Marcus says.

We are escorted off the stage and down a long hall, a walk that goes on for several minutes. The walls are covered in strange markings and symbols from the old world. I imagine this is where they used to take the prisoners who were especially bad.

Marcus stops at the end of the hall beside a metal door. A sense of dread comes over me, followed by shivers, as I enter the cold operating room. It is completely white, apart from the one window that looks into it.

Bianca's seeming lack of concern makes me hate her even more. Doesn't she know what they intend to do to us? With the click of the door

16

behind me, I turn to find the same covered nurse, the one who looks as though she's ready to handle nuclear waste.

"Please step onto the tables," Marcus says.

Looking at the two metal tables isolated in the room, I realize this is my last chance. I can no longer escape. "Mr. Marcus, sir. There was a mistake. I couldn't have scored high enough to become a Cogent," I say.

"Nonsense. You are exactly who we wanted. Now lie back."

Bianca willingly steps onto the table and begins strapping herself down. My eyes connect with Marcus's in the mirrored glass as the nurse tightens my restraints. With each click of the buckles, I can feel my sanity slipping away from me.

With the last strap fastened, reality sets in. They intend to take away my humanity. "I won't be human." The feelings of pain, anger, rage, and confusion all accelerate violently in my mind, like an explosion growing bigger and bigger until it has consumed everything in its path.

"Stop!" I beg the nurse. "Please don't do this."

Her response is strange. She places her palm on the top of my head and gently strokes it as if she is calming a child.

"I don't want to do this," I plead again.

She ignores my pleas and leaves the room. The door swings shut, and my eyes turn to the mirrored observation window. Marcus's aura is so bright I can now make out the faces behind it ever so slightly.

The prime minister and several other leaders seem to be back there watching us. "Please!" I shout out to them. "I don't want to do this! I don't want to be a Cogent! There must be a mistake."

With no answer, I twist on the table, hoping to free myself. With every jerk of my hands, the straps tighten and curl around my wrists like a snake strangling their prey.

"Bianca—Bianca, I don't want to do this. Please. I don't want to do this."

She looks unconcerned. My words don't matter to her. "Relax. It's for the good of humanity."

"No, I don't care if it's for the good of humanity. This isn't right. I can't become like them."

Those final two words echo in my head as I recall the red Cogent that killed my mother at Sincliff all those years ago. I'm haunted by his serrated red blade that took her life. The thought of being like him makes my skin burn. Why do I have to remember? Why now?

I'm beginning to lose hope. It feels as though the Mover of Life wants this. Why else would it keep going? I've begged for them to stop, and yet they continue. Once this happens, I will forever live a life as a demon fighting demons.

A click at the door brings me hope that the Mover of Life has answered my prayers. I'm left speechless in defeat as the nurse reenters the room with two green vials.

Bianca is first. She does her best to embrace it, to accept whatever they do to her, but the screams of pain still manage to slip out. Her discomfort becomes agony, forcing me to turn away. I can't watch anymore, but I can't escape the sound of her cries either. I feel them as if they are my own.

As the pain in her voice subsides, I check on her. My eyes fall on the vial the nurse holds just before she places the needle in my arm. Instantly, it's as if all of my cells have begun separating. I can feel my body being torn apart slowly. My heart races and my tongue swells. I contort my body against the straps in hopes of slowing the spread.

With the damage done, the nurse leaves. The door swings shut, leaving Bianca and me all alone. I continue to shout in pain as my vision blurs and my throat swells closed. I'm on the verge of blacking out. Somehow, I manage to stay conscious while my body goes limp.

I wonder if I even still have a body. The pain becomes so intense I can't feel anything. I can't even lift a finger; I can barely move my eyes. I try to focus, to remember their faces so I can curse every one of them. Then I see something I can't comprehend. Behind Marcus, it appears as if the nurse is crying into her hands. I don't understand. If she's sad, why did she do it? Why?

As she rubs her eyes, she removes her mask and cap. The familiar silver curls with their slight tint of yellow fall to her cheek, making my stomach turn. I can barely bring myself to say her name.

"Miss Caroline."

I want to vomit, but my muscles won't move. I want to scream, but my voice can't be heard. I want to cry, but my tears have disappeared.

I wanted to live, but now I want to die.

Chapter 2

I remember playing human and Cogent once when I was younger. It was our third game in the woods outside of Rockcliff that day. The clouds blanketed the sky, making the afternoon cool and humid. While hiding as the human, I took shelter under some large rocks by the creek. Before I could react, two snakes attacked me. Their fangs pierced my flesh, and the venom pumped into my body. I shrieked in agony as the poison spread like wildfire through my veins. My breath slowed, and I struggled to concentrate.

That's what I'm feeling now. Poison pulses through my body, foreign and reckless.

My eyes open, and I find myself submerged in a vat of water. The glass window before me glows with my reflection. There is a black breathing apparatus around my mouth. Raising my radiant white hand, I confirm my suspicions. I'm a Cogent.

I search for more changes. The only thing I can tell is that I'm underwater and strangely warm. An overpowering sensation comes over my body, and I brace myself against the glass window. But before I can steady myself, I'm flung from the pod and slammed to the ground.

Staggering to my feet, I notice a body-shaped indent, as though someone made a mold of me in the ground. Shattered glass lies all around, but I don't have a scratch on my body. Picking up a larger piece, I press it to my skin, only to see it evaporate into dust against my white aura.

I'm indeed a Cogent.

What's strange is, I'm not wet. My clothes are, but my skin isn't. The white heat is radiating from my pores, forming a barrier around my body. To test this hypothesis, I place my hand in the puddle that has formed inside the crater. My suspicion is confirmed when I remove it and my skin remains dry.

A list of things to check runs through my mind. I don't feel stronger, and my muscles aren't any bigger. Glancing at my reflection in the pod that holds Bianca reveals the same scrawny kid as before. The rumor that Cogents grow fangs suddenly plagues my mind. Running my tongue along my perfectly normal teeth, I exhale with relief.

I take a seat next to my pod and curl into a ball. My mind rushes with thoughts about what happened, but these are quickly pushed out by the feeling of thirst. There's only one water source in this room—the pods. I consider drinking from the puddle, but the sight of glass makes me resist. I'm not sure if Cogents are invincible on the inside.

After a few minutes, I check on Bianca, floating in her pod. Her brown skin is now bathed in a light blue glow. She looks calm and in stable condition. I suppose all the numbers on the pod confirm this, but I can't read them. She doesn't seem as dangerous when she's asleep.

My eyes settle on the red eject button on the side of the pod. I press it. With a loud whoosh, the water drains. Bianca's eyes go wide as gravity sets in on her. The hatch flips open, and she drops to her knees. As she becomes aware, she quickly tears off her breathing apparatus and gasps for air.

"It was Bianca, right?" I ask.

She looks around impulsively, as if to gather information. I try to lift her to her feet, but she takes over, refusing my help. Maybe she remembers what happened in the lab and wants nothing to do with me. She's probably upset that I'm a Cogent alongside her.

"Where are we?" she asks.

"It appears as if we're in some sort of recovery area. Maybe? I'm uncertain."

"You're glowing."

"You are too," I reply.

I pick up a piece of glass like the one I used to examine myself. Bianca holds it for a moment to see her reflection, and then I tell her to stab me with it. Without hesitation, she jabs the shard right into my rib cage as hard as she can. Out of habit, I fall back in shock.

She grins. "We did it!"

I nod, not sharing her enthusiasm. I'm uncertain why she felt so confident about stabbing me before I could even explain. Once she finishes her celebration, I ask her what differences she's noticed. I don't know if all Cogents are the same. My aura appears white, while hers appears blue.

"Do you feel warm?" I inquire.

"I do, like a fever. But I don't feel bad."

My mind wanders back to the moment we were injected. I want to explain myself, explain my behavior. I'm just not sure what to say. Bianca already thought little of me before the procedure, and there's no reason to think that's improved.

"Uh—Bianca. About the things I said before."

"Look—Lucas. I don't know why they chose you. If I were them, you would have been the last on my list. I don't make the rules, I just follow them. If you're looking for pity, you won't find it with me. This power is mine, and with it, I will be the one to end this war. You should stay out of my way."

She walks past me and presses the intercom button. If I'd been a bit more observant, I might have caught that device. Regardless, now all I can do is wait as she informs them that we're awake.

A minute later, the large metal door to the room slides back, squealing to a halt. Marcus, who is shirtless again, walks in and calls for military attention. I follow Bianca's lead and stand straight as he walks over to examine us. He starts with Bianca, walking around her, poking her sides and arms with his index finger.

"It's been a day—how do you feel, Bianca?" he asks.

"Great, sir. Ready to go kill some Sinder scum."

He seems pleased by her words. I'm confident that's what they're hoping to see from their Cogents. So why did they choose me? I know I didn't score high on all my tests. The fight with Bianca was definitely not a win. So why me?

When he inspects me, Marcus is most curious about the color of my aura. I ask if the white glow is normal and if I'm okay.

"I've never seen a white aura," he says.

It becomes hard to keep focus as he pauses in front of my face. Did he even want me as a Cogent? I still don't understand why I was selected.

"Are you stable now?" he asks.

"Yes, I think so. My aura seems to be okay."

"No, I mean, are you done whining about becoming a Cogent?"

His tone isn't sarcastic. I suppose, in a way, he's genuine. To him, I'm just another student. He probably wants to make sure I won't try running. I could freak out, but I'm not going to.

"Sir, I—I didn't want to do this. Why did you make me? I don't want this power. I don't want to be like you."

My questions seem to annoy Marcus. "What's wrong with being like me?" he asks.

Being like Marcus is fine for most people. Desired, even. He's considered the Hero of Humanity—who wouldn't want to be like him?

The answer is me. He couldn't protect my mother when I was a boy. While everyone else loves and admires him, I know the disappointment of a hero. Beyond that, I know that the reason they select two new Cogents every year is because they need to replace the ones that have died.

"Look, kid. There's more to this. I don't make all the decisions either. The nurse will check you now."

Miss Caroline? But it's not her, it's just some regular nurse who comes in. She scans our foreheads with a large wand that lights up green after a quick pass. After confirming that we are stable, she exits the room. Disappointment washes over me. I was hoping to confront Miss Caroline. I know it was her; I know what she did. I just want to know why. She knew I didn't want this lifelong commitment to the military. All I wanted was to serve my time and live a life of peace. Now I'm a target, almost guaranteed to die at the hands of the same people that killed my mother. I thought she loved me like a son. I thought she would protect me. She said she would always be on my side. How could she betray me?

"You've got holes in your uniforms," Marcus says. "Put these on. They're more resistant to heat. They are made with tantalum carbide fibers to keep your aura from burning through them so fast. This stuff costs a fortune, so try to take care of it. It's a bit on the itchy side if you ask me, though."

He drops the uniforms in our hands. I notice a new symbol along the pocket. It's no longer a single line signifying our private class. They've added a shield with a lion. It must be the symbol of the Cogent branch. I've never seen it before on any soldiers around the city.

"Meet me outside when you're done changing," he says before walking out.

Bianca clutches her uniform to her body, as if she's calling me a pervert already. It was just an accident that I grabbed her earlier. I try to apologize and reassure her I'm not some perv, but I don't think she believes it.

"Turn around, idiot," she says.

Promptly, I comply with her request. Sliding on my clothes, I can't help but wish I were stupid, like the big oaf I met on selection day. If I were like him, I wouldn't be worried about all the danger in store for me when I walk out this door. It sounds blissful to be unaware.

We follow Marcus through the campus, making our way down long, busy halls. The swarms of student's part around us as we pass through. It's as if we are infected. A smile comes over me—the idea of never being bumped into again sounds pretty nice, to be honest.

As we enter the main courtyard, I stop to take in the large fountain up ahead. Two imposing lions stand atop a rock cliff with water shooting up behind them, almost creating an aura around them.

I've never seen a real lion—we were told they don't exist anymore. But they've become something of a legend since the Great War. Most large animals don't survive after a thing like that. Now all we have are pictures. I suppose they could be fake, a made-up story, but they remind me of enormous cats, and there are plenty of those roaming Rockcliff.

I have fond memories of sitting on my bed and listening to Miss Caroline talk about the old world. She said it was like a dream, but better, because it was real. I

22

particularly loved the stories of people who would travel all around the world freely—they would eat as much as they wanted, and they never feared death. It sounded blissful, and I wish I could have lived there.

It's sad to think that because war reached perfection—in the form of these beings—it will never be like that again. And now I'm a part of that story, but not the part I ever dreamed of being. I'm a Cogent, an invincible war machine.

Miss Caroline told us how this all started. In that old world there was a Cogent soldier who abandoned America. With his newfound power, he wanted to make a new world. He took the Cogent formula and created his own followers. America had no choice but to launch seventeen L3 nuclear bombs to take them out—but it didn't work. They didn't kill him or his followers, and that man became Prime Minister Silas.

Once they knew that even L3 bombs couldn't kill Cogents, our leader, Prime Minister Maxwell, took charge and retreated to Rockcliff. He would work with the few Cogents who joined him to preserve humanity. He created the barrier to protect us. He is the lion that stands above the cliff, protecting the pride—or so they say.

After walking through the courtyard, Marcus takes us to our barracks, where we'll sleep while in training. Upon opening the door, I see it's even more depressing than the orphanage. I know Miss Caroline must have tried her best, but this level of emptiness seems intentional. The room is filled with gray beds propped up on concrete blocks. The only unique feature is the double bathroom at the end. Oddly, there are twice as many beds as there are Cogents. Probably because the rest died.

Marcus explains that our belongings have been moved to trunks at the ends of our respective beds. I rush to find mine and open it up. On top lies the necklace Katelynn gave me. A bit of joy comes over me as I examine the three lines once more. I pray for clarity and purpose to be revealed in the coming days.

"It's not much," Marcus says. "The beds may be stiff, but that's because the tantalum fabric needs to resist your auras. There are fresh sheets and clothes stacked in the corner. Speaking of which, Lucas, hand me a new one."

I toss him a shirt and look around the room once more. "Why is everything so gray?" I ask.

Marcus smiles and slides on his shirt. "Because it's easy. Anyway, now that you know where you'll sleep, it's time we go catch up with your class."

I follow Bianca, who stays close behind him. We're taken back through the courtyard and walk for several minutes until we come upon a large glass structure. There aren't many places like this around here. The building is one giant room with one side covered in windows three stories high, as if we are on display for the whole army to see.

We watch from outside for a moment, seeing the six Cogents training inside. Each of them radiates a vibrant, colored aura. I'm not scared of them—I'm intrigued. There's no looming death in the air. I almost feel like I'm back at the orphanage, watching the others train.

Inside, the Cogents stop their exercises at once to stand at attention. With a quick salute, they greet Marcus. Bianca stands at the ready as well, though we are behind him. Feeling lost, I mimic her posture. Seems like she knows what to do in these situations.

Marcus dismisses the Cogent students, and they return to sparring practice. "I'll introduce you to everyone soon," he says. "For now, it's best if we go through a brief introduction."

He walks us over to the edge of the room and asks us to wait. While I stand with Bianca at attention, I notice how the fighting rings are similar in style to the ones we took our aptitude tests in. The only difference is that these are made of concrete. Upon further observation, I notice a very odd, large container by the side wall. It looks to be filled with a massive amount of water.

From the corner of my eye, Marcus's blue aura shines as he returns to us. He carries something I've seen a lot around here—a large rifle. Without explanation, he cocks it and points it at Bianca. A thunderous clap rings off the large windows as he takes his first shots. I instinctively tackle her to the ground and cover her until the violent pings turn to clicks.

"What are you doing?" I yell at Marcus.

"Get—off!" Bianca says with a shove. "Why are you always touching me, perv?"

Her brows are scrunched, and her face is full of disgust. I look at the holes in her shirt as she lifts herself back up. Seeing she's uninjured, I feel a bit like an idiot. She's fine. I'm fine.

Laughter echoes in the room, but Marcus promptly silences everyone. I don't know why I did it. I mean, I already knew Cogents can't be killed by weapons. My body just moved before my mind could process it.

"Well, now you know what it's like to be shot," Marcus says. "It's time we talk about what you don't know."

"Could've just told us," I mumble.

Marcus clearly hears me, but he ignores it. He tosses the gun to the side with no respect, as if it's a toy for children.

"As the leader of this city's army, I am here to educate you, to train you in everything you need to know so that someday you can protect us. I won't be around forever, so we are going to need powerful men and women to do the job of keeping humanity safe. We've discovered over the years that the only way to beat a Cogent is with another Cogent. Since you two are now Cogents, I'm here to set the record straight on what you may have heard about them."

Marcus takes a step forward, then continues.

"The first thing you may have heard about Cogents is that they are immortal. We are far from that.

"Second, that glow around you is not just a pretty color, it's a part of you. It's your cells at work. Your sweat glands now break down hydrogen in a way that produces an enormous amount of heat. This heat is equivalent to a hydrogen bomb consistently exploding around your body. The colors that surround a Cogent are the burn process at work. We call this your aura."

Marcus takes a step back and closes his eyes and strikes some sort of strength pose. His hands make fists, and it's as though his body becomes stiff. A few seconds later, an even stronger flash of blue light pops and illuminates off his body as if a bomb has been released. The sheer energy radiates as his skin crackles with power. Arcs of light beam off his chest, shredding through his shirt until there's nothing left.

After showing off, he relaxes the intensity of his aura back to a normal glow. "Your aura is like a dry heat burning through everything." He demonstrates by picking up the rifle he threw down, burning through it simply by applying pressure. "At your aura's base intensity, you can hold things and move objects without destroying them."

What's left of the gun drops in two pieces to the floor. While I've always known that a Cogent's power is destructive, seeing it up close is surreal. Marcus has such control over his aura, I almost forget about how it ends up being used. But the smell of burning flesh won't let me. No fancy light show will deceive me into thinking it's okay what Rockcliff has done to me, what Miss Caroline has done to me, and what this means. I will always know what being a Cogent really is—an abomination.

"Listen up. This next bit is important," he says. "If your aura runs low on hydrogen, your glands will search for it elsewhere in your body. This dehydration of your aura can consume you if it's not taken care of. Your skin cells will burn up, your aura will move to your organs, and you will disintegrate into nothingness from the inside out. It's not a good way to go. It's best if you stick to the twenty-four-hour rule. You need to drink your body weight every day, and even more if you have exerted yourself in combat."

Marcus walks over to the blue containers of water on the side. "If at any point during your training you feel you've overexerted yourself, please dunk your head in here and drink as fast as possible. Getting water inside your body is the most important thing to keep yourself from this tragic fate."

I glance at Bianca, who looks unfazed by this revelation. How can she be okay with this? We were just told our bodies could eat us from the inside out until there's nothing left. After everything they've forced us to do, why doesn't she have a problem with this?

"Now watch this," Marcus says.

With his right hand, it's as if he reaches into his other hand and pulls out an impressive long blue blade. It happens so fast. He presses it against the top of his arm, and blood comes rushing out, boiling and burning off. His wound closes, leaving a faint line. That's when I see that his entire body is covered in thousands of faint scars.

"Third thing to know, the most common way to kill or be killed is by another's aura. Since modern weapons can't penetrate our skin, Cogents have developed blades like this one, formed from our auras. Think of it like a focused jet engine swirling in your hand. It requires a great deal of your body's hydrogen, but with these blades, Cogents have been able to kill each other. As you just witnessed, minor cuts are manageable. Large cuts can be survivable even, but deadly blows to the head or any other vital organ could send your body into an instant shutdown. Your aura will turn inward and consume you."

He knows he's scared the soul out of me. "Go get some water and come back," he says with a grin.

As I'm walking away, I overhear Bianca compliment Marcus's teaching abilities. She mentions a brother that serves under him. Her adulation makes me submerge my head in the container of water until I can't hear her.

I keep my head under for as long as possible, hoping that when I come up, this will all be a dream. It isn't, though. Nothing changes. I'm left with no other option than to take a breath and expose myself to conversation.

"Don't forget to breathe—or do," Bianca says as she joins me at the container.

"Lucas, come here," Marcus calls to me.

I accept this escape from Bianca and walk over to him alone. Marcus places his large hand on my shoulder and brings me in close. He's about a foot taller than me, so I'm left uncomfortably staring into his bare chest.

"Lucas, are you all right?" he asks.

I nod, hoping to end whatever I've found myself in.

"'Cause you've had some concerning moments, and, well, that's not who you are?"

Who I am? How would he know who I am?

"I want you to know, I see a lot of potential in you. Now, I know that change is scary. I know it is. But I also know that you're going to be an excellent defender of the people. I want you to give it your all here, okay? Forget yesterday—just focus."

I stare back at him, holding in my every thought. I want to scream at this man, but that won't fix anything. My life is over. The good things I had going for me are all being ripped away. He doesn't know me. I'm not like Bianca. I won't so willingly give my life to this city.

Marcus calls an end to the break. The Cogent students return to sparring while Bianca rushes over to us. He leads us to a door in the back corner of the room. Inside is a large pool with solid white walls, the Rockcliff crest etched into the base.

"This is the summoning pool, where you will craft your weapon for the first time. Normally, this process would take years to refine, but the pool is incredibly forgiving, allowing you to mold a weapon freely. Once it's formed, you will be able to recreate it through a thing I like to call aura memory."

He continues to demonstrate methods of summoning in the pool. Apparently, it helps if we visualize and mold our blade until it takes shape.

"So, who's first?"

After a second, Bianca steps forward. "I am."

No surprise that she volunteered, only that she allowed me a brief window to step up. As she steps in, her aura rapidly heats the water until the pool resembles a large boiling pot. Once the water is to her elbows, she pauses, closing her eyes to focus.

Marcus gives her advice. "Visualize every inch of your blade." After a minute, the steam generated by her aura creates a cloud above her. She lowers herself deeper into the water until she is no longer visible.

After some anxious waiting, the intensity of the cloud subsides, revealing her position. Bianca approaches the steps in the pool and energetically reveals a blue blade. Although it's not large, Marcus seems impressed. But I'm not—it doesn't seem hard to envision something much larger than that. Several of the other students were sparring with larger blades. I can easily do better than her. My

27

confidence is short lived, though, as she pulls a second blade of equal size from the water.

"Dual blades!" Marcus touts. "That's a rare talent, to produce two quality blades like that."

His applause echoes in the room as he admires her creation. A smile stretches across her face as she displays them by moving them back and forth. He allows her a moment to get comfortable with them.

"Well done, Bianca," Marcus says. "Like all great weapons, it's common to give them a name. I call mine Motif. What will yours be?"

Examining her blades, she responds, "I believe this was meant to be—and I've trained this long to get here. I'll call them Fate and Devotion."

"Very fine names. You may release them now."

She opens her hands, dropping Fate and Devotion, which shatter into tiny light particles as they hit the ground. Marcus again points out that the blades are a manipulation of her aura. With concentration and some movement, she can now recreate them at will, without the summoning pool.

Marcus lifts her hands outward. She makes two fists and places them next to each other. He reminds her to see the blades and then steps away. As she pulls her hands apart rapidly, she reveals her dual blades once more.

"Incredible. Just an overall great job, Bianca." He smiles, then turns to me. "Now, Lucas, it's your turn."

I take a deep breath and step into the pool. The feeling is bizarre. I'm dry even though I'm halfway in. The water boils so quickly I can't feel wet. I recall the feeling of being in the pods this morning. Come to think of it, this is the coolest I've felt all day.

Once I reach the center of the pool, I turn and plant my feet. I can still see them through the cloud of steam. Clearly I should mold my blade, but I'm not sure what to bring up. My mind is blank as it runs in circles, trying to come up with an idea.

"Focus and visualize," Marcus calls to me.

I look down at my hands and try to push all this aura stuff into one point. Should I make a blade like Marcus's? No. I need to come up with something original. If I pull up a blade like his, they'll just make fun of me and call me a copycat or something. I need to get inspiration. I think of all the blades I've ever seen in my life, but this becomes a problem. Then my mind focuses on the one that killed my mother, and I can feel it as it forms in my hand.

With a quick jerk, I release any minimal focus I have and slip into the pool in frustration. The thought of pulling out that serrated blade causes me to panic. The rows and rows of teethlike points pierce my mind.

"You doing okay in there?" Marcus shouts.

I scramble to my feet once more and slide my hand out. I'm afraid to look down. Afraid to see the monster's weapon in my hand. With haste, I make my exit.

"Let's see it," Marcus says with a bit of excitement.

I close my eyes. Anxiety weighs my hands down as I fight against gravity to present it.

Marcus lets out a curious, "Hmm."

Opening my eyes, I see I have not created my mother's murder weapon. The rough, jagged blade is nowhere in sight—instead, what I'm holding looks like a stick.

"Is that a practice sword?" Marcus asks with concern.

I nod, both to him and myself. It is. It is a practice sword. This looks like the ones I used back at the orphanage when I would train with Miss Caroline and the other boys. I'm going to be a laughingstock if I present this edgeless blade to the other Cogent students. Recklessly, I release it and summon it again, hoping a sharp edge will appear.

"It's still the same . . ." I drop it and summon it once more. Time and time again, I get the same result. My blade has no edge—nothing to cut with.

Marcus grabs my wrist. "Lucas, relax. In time, an edge will appear. This process took me five years to perfect when I started. Most of the other students took weeks to get it right. Bianca here is just a natural."

His words are supposed to be supportive, but I couldn't care less. Bianca stands next to me with her impressive dual blades, and all I have is this stick. I'm definitely going to die as a Cogent.

"Lucas, I almost forgot. You need to name your blade."

I'm not sure what to name a blade like this. It's not what I want to end up with. How am I supposed to turn this into what I want it to be? Observing it, I notice it's white, almost clear, actually, with an immense light evenly reflected throughout. Maybe I could name it something around how bright it is? Illumination? No—that sounds stupid. There was a word I heard Miss Caroline use once. She used it to describe the barrier when the light hit it just right. She said it was not diffused or distorted, it was— "Lucid."

"Lucid—I see. A good name for your blade. I'm sure one day Lucid will have an edge. Now, it is important to hone your blade. A Cogent's weapon is much like a fingerprint, unique to oneself, fabricated in both mind and body by the user. It reflects one's soul."

I want a do-over, but Marcus insists that it's enough for today. When my mind and body align, an edge will manifest, he assures me. I'll have it figured out in the next four years of training.

Bianca and I leave the summoning pool and return to the large open sparring room. Marcus dismisses us to the mess hall for dinner. With a quick salute, he leaves. Before everyone goes running out the door, they make their way to the wall, where they pull new uniforms from the stacks of clothes.

Looking down, I see that I too have burned several holes in my clothes. I suppose this will be a normal occurrence, to change so frequently. Sliding on a fresh shirt, I look around to see where we are going next.

My eyes connect with Bianca's as she's midchange in the corner with the other girls. I quickly pretend to check my clothes again for more holes, but it's too late. Bianca has already called me a perv.

With everyone's attention on me now, I jog out the door and around the corner before anyone can tease me. Once everyone has left, I make my way through the halls and into the courtyard behind them.

That's when I see her. Her blond curls wave in the wind as she sits reading a book on the fountain's edge. *Katelynn.* I stand there for a moment, not sure what to do. I don't know what we are anymore. *It can't work,* I remind myself. A human and a Cogent can't be together. I want to say goodbye, but she probably wants nothing to do with me.

Chapter 3

Her blond curls fall across her book. I can't help but notice the beautiful yellow bow in her hair. Even wearing a gray uniform, she brings it life. I admire that about her—how she loves to find joy in the small things. More than anything, I wish she could find something joyful about our situation, but she can't. It's impossible.

"Katelynn," I mumble.

Her eyes widen as she looks up. The book she's reading practically falls out of her hands. I don't blame her, though. It must be terrifying to see me like this.

"Lucas!"

Her arms reach out for me, but I know the danger. Retreating from her, I shake my head. If only I'd known yesterday would be the last time I could ever hug her. I would have held her a little longer—a little tighter.

"Are you scared?" I ask, breaking the silence.

She shakes her head. "I was worried about you. I prayed all night."

I need to find the courage to accept that it's over. I'm a bit frustrated with the Giver of Life right now. This wasn't supposed to be my life. Now Katelynn's trembling in front of me because she needs to end it, but she can't, because she fears me—fears what I am.

I clear my throat to push out the words I need to say. "It's okay, Katelynn. I know it's over."

With one hand, she squeezes her wrist. "Over? But why?"

She must know. So why is she asking for an explanation? This is already hard enough for me. "It's just not possible."

Katelynn steps toward me until she's a foot from my face. "I'm not giving up on you. Don't make me."

Is it the nurse in her, this refusal to give up? Every attempt I've made to let her down she has matched with a perfect counter. Us being over doesn't seem like a conclusion she's willing to accept.

"Listen," she says, running the backs of her fingers carefully down the outline of my cheek. "I'm not sure how this affects us. But I'm not giving up on you . . . I won't give up on us."

Her words are overwhelming. How can she be so perfect? Even now, despite what I have become, she wants to make it work between us. I don't understand. I've become a monster overnight. If I could cry, I would, but the tears would just burn away in my aura, and Katelynn would never know.

"I won't give up on us," I say to her.

She picks up her book and clasps it tight. It feels like her way of hugging me in this moment.

"We'll figure this out," she says. "I promise. Just meet me here tomorrow after classes finish. I have to go see my dad, so I'll catch you tomorrow. Don't disappear on me."

Watching Katelynn leave reminds me of how much better I feel every time I'm around her. Her mere presence gives me hope. I don't know if I'm lucky because I have a girlfriend like her or unlucky because they forced me to become a Cogent. Either way, my stomach grumbles and reminds me that I better eat and drink to keep from exploding.

Inside the mess hall, things are chaos. Students fill every inch of the place. It's so loud I can't even hear my own thoughts. Every one of the metal tables is packed full of soldiers. The food lines are just as bad. As I approach, people jump out of the way for me. I suppose they don't want to bump into a Cogent by accident. They could lose an arm, after all.

Grabbing a red tray, I slide through the line, picking a few edible-looking things, including some fruit and a sandwich. I avoid the suspicious-looking foods. It's sad—Miss Caroline served better meals at the orphanage.

That reminds me that I don't have my normal spot to sit and eat. Glancing around the room, I

find the one place in the mess hall that's glowing with colorful auras. Despite it being the Cogents' job to protect others, it seems they sit above the humans at a special table. Maybe it's for their protection, or maybe they think they are superior.

Upon approach, I notice the overly patriotic background behind the table, an oversized Rockcliff flag with our lion. It makes me sick to see this obsession everywhere around here. Everything is military, all the time.

Standing at the end of the table, I wait to see if anyone still has a comment about what happened earlier. Fortunately, it seems like everyone has moved on, and their banter intensifies as I take a seat at the end.

One of the Cogent girls gets up and moves down to sit in front of me. As she walks over, I notice she's wearing a gray skirt over her military pants. It seems like she's the only one with a modification to her uniform.

Her hand extends across the table and hovers for a moment. "Hi Lucas, I'm Brooke."

She introduces the girl next to her as her aura partner, Jean, who gives a friendly wave before proudly showing me a ring she made from the same heat resistant metal as our uniforms. It has a mounted piece of glass that amplifies her green aura against her dark skin.

I nod and tell her it's a clever design. There's no telling how long they'll want to talk to me, so I continue with my meal as if they aren't there. Hopefully after a while, they'll get the hint, much like people did at the orphanage.

Without warning, a hand reaches over my shoulder. A boy with an orange aura and shaved head leans in. "So, I heard you felt up your aura partner, the little purple-haired pixie, on the first day? Nice. How was it? Doesn't look like there's much there, but you know . . ."

"Don't answer that," Brooke demands.

I try to explain myself, but he doesn't buy that it was an accident. Instead, he pulls me in tighter and whispers, "I'm Liam. We'll talk details later. So is she your girlfriend or something?" Clearly, he's trying to turn this into whatever sick fantasy he has going on in his head.

With a loud screech of her chair, Bianca gets up from the table. She storms off without looking back. Brooke and Jean scold Liam. He tries to calm them down, but these girls already know his tricks.

Brooke lands a punch on his shoulder. "Don't be such a pig, Liam. Lucas is dating someone already. I saw him stay behind at the fountain. She's the daughter of our hospital chief, right?"

I nod, afraid of how much she already knows about my personal life. She's figured out who I'm dating from one conversation that happened a few minutes ago. I doubt there are any secrets in this group with Brooke around.

Liam leans back in his chair. "Oh, the pixie is his side chick. It's good to have options. I'm an options man myself."

"Her name is Bianca," Brooke corrects him.

Another boy promptly slams Liam forward, sending the chair to the ground. "Is this guy bothering you?" he asks.

The boy is definitely the oldest here. He looks like a mini version of Marcus, but with a yellow aura. I'm sure all the girls love him, too. At least he wears a shirt, unlike our fearless leader.

33

"Lucas, it's nice to meet you. Sorry, my partner here is a bit . . . eccentric," he says, glancing at Liam to keep him in line. "I'm Brock. We are fourth-year senior officers, or just fourth years."

I don't know how he does it, but somehow Brock's presence seems to keep Liam in check. He commands a more serious tone from everyone. It's surprising how opposite they are. It might be a good idea to know where he is if Liam gets out of hand.

"It looks like you've met almost everyone. I'll help you out with the rest. The two quiet ones at the end here, that's Cameer and Ryan. Cameer won't talk to you until you've been here a while. Ryan, the guy next to her who looks like he could bench-press a truck, he'll give you a great fight if you're ever looking for one. We're all excited to have you. This is my last year before deployment, but I hope it will be enough time for us to get to know each other. We may very well fight side by side on the front lines someday."

Liam laughs. "You didn't hear? There's no edge on his blade. I wouldn't expect him on the front lines soon, unless it's to be a punching bag."

I wonder if Bianca's was the one who told them about my blade? It must have been her. Just as I'm about to respond to him, Brooke reaches across to smack Liam upside the head. "We're all in this together, moron!"

"If you want to put your hands on me so bad, you just have to ask," he says. "I know a place we can be alone."

Brock clearly knows Liam has reached his limit and drags him off. Ryan and Cameer seize the opportunity to go as well, leaving just Brooke and Jean. Everyone knows each other so well, I'm not sure how I'll fit in.

"Don't worry. We're all nice once you get to know us," Brooke says, as if trying to read my mind. "So, what's it like to be dating the girl at the fountain? What's her name?"

"Katelynn," I respond.

"Right, Katelynn. She seems nice. Do you love her?"

"Love? I haven't thought about it like that."

It really isn't a word I've considered using yet. My hands shake, reminding me that I haven't eaten enough food yet. I stuff my mouth and continue chewing so I don't have to answer. Eventually, Jean notices that I don't want to talk about it and drags Brooke off by the hand.

The mess hall is almost empty now, allowing me to relax and enjoy my food. Come to think of it, I don't know why I let Brooke bother me at all. Back at the orphanage, I wouldn't let any kid get away with that much conversation. It makes me uncomfortable, like I have a sister snooping in my life. I'll give her credit, though—she has a skilled approach to getting information.

"Hey Lucas," Brooke says, sitting back down.

How did she get back here so fast? She left a few minutes ago and now she's back with two yogurts. I try to refuse, claiming I'm full, but she insists there's always room for a snack. I can tell if I don't take it, I'll never hear the end of it, so I give in.

"You know, the first day I became a Cogent, I ran away. I thought the school was a prison. They claim it was once, you know. Anyway, I thought they'd made a mistake picking a girl like me. I got to the edge of the territory and then I realized—if I go, I will have no one to support me. I hated the need to be here, but I didn't want to be alone. So, I came back."

"What changed?" I ask.

"Nothing. I think I was just more afraid of being alone than I was of letting everyone down."

Her response isn't what I expected. She seems so open about herself, and I've only just met her. At first, I thought she was a little over the top, but I can see now she has a big desire to have friends. Like it keeps her sane.

"Thanks," I say, lifting the cup of yogurt. Honestly, I want to say more. It feels nice to think of her as a friend.

Brooke talks with me all the way back to the barracks. She's especially interested in my relationship with Katelynn. It feels a bit too involved; I've only ever known Justin as a friend, and now her. But the conversation doesn't feel bothersome like with everyone else.

We arrive at the barracks still in full conversation. I haven't talked like this with anyone in my life. I'm not trying to impress her, and I genuinely believe she wants to help me. Liam gives me a mischievous look as I make my way to my bed. The fool probably thinks I've got another side chick, as he called it.

Opening my trunk, I find Katelynn's three-line necklace. She's the real prize. A smile comes over me as I recall our talk before dinner. I hold on to that joy and focus on it until I fall fast asleep.

During the night, I dream of Katelynn in the middle of a church of shining stained glass. For a moment, it's peaceful, but then it's abruptly stripped away.

"Get up," someone says. "Get up."

My eyes snap open. I'm being shaken back and forth. As soon as I'm able to focus, I can see Liam's shiny orange bald head. Why now? Does he want to know what a boob feels like that bad? That can't be it.

I jump to my feet. "Are we under attack?"

He shakes his head. "Follow me."

Something isn't right. The vibrant auras I fell asleep to no longer paint the walls. No one is here. And if the clock is right, only a few hours have passed. Where has everyone gone?

Following Liam outside, I see a group of brightly colored auras in the distance. He signals for me to move with haste, and I comply. At the edge of the school, a staircase leads to the wall that holds the barrier. They're trying to be covert for some reason. But why?

Answers don't come as we make our way down the wall. Looking around, I get my bearings when I see the bridge I crossed on my way to the Academy. Brock's fist shoots into the air and holds firm, halting the group.

"You all ready for this?" Brock says.

"For what?" I ask.

"Tonight . . . is initiation."

It looks like they want Bianca and me to prove ourselves worthy somehow. But that still doesn't explain why we're here. And I don't get why I have to prove myself. I didn't want this—I still don't. What's stopping me from turning around and going back?

Before I can threaten them with my escape, Brock nods to Liam, who appears overcome with excitement. I watch with curiosity as he bounces toward the barrier. He lifts a large concrete block from the wall and throws it in. Instantly, it's vaporized.

Earlier, I gave Brock the credit for being the sane one in the group, but I'm starting to have my doubts.

"Have you heard of a trust fall exercise?" he asks. "Well, this is it. Run through this barrier and jump."

They've all lost their minds. This doesn't look safe in the slightest. And the most important part—I don't have to do this. This is stupid. I'm not about to run through a barrier that's on the same level as my aura.

"Come on, who's first?" Liam asks, still bouncing. "We've only ever seen one person get ripped apart."

The sad part is, I don't know if he's joking. For all I know, someone did run through it and get vaporized. It could send my aura into a shock.

Brooke nods, encouraging me to try it. I trust her, placing my hand on the barrier. To my surprise, it feels solid. With a little more pressure, a jolt of light sparks off and sends me staggering backward.

Our stealth mission goes out the window as everyone laughs. Hopefully they enjoyed their little prank. Liam doesn't give up, though—he continues to claim it can be done. After he regains his composure, he explains how it works. "The trick is to use your blade to break the surface tension and then slide on through. So, let's go!"

I pace back and forth, wondering if he's serious. While I'm deep in thought, a gust of wind rushes by me. Bianca just summons her blades and slams it into the barrier, sending bolts of aura shooting out like lightning. In a flash, she reaches the other side and instantly disappears over the horizon.

"She did it!" Liam screams. "Now why didn't you go first?" he scolds me. "You're her partner, and that's not the way to earn points with your side chick."

"Stop teasing him," Brooke says with a little push.

I try to explain myself, but Liam doesn't care to listen. With no more hesitation, he runs through the barrier and disappears into the night. One by one, everyone jumps after him. Brooke stays behind for a second.

"You got this!"

With another quick flash, she too disappears. I can walk away here, and no one can stop me. Sleep is appealing right now. After about ten steps, though, I realize what will happen if I leave. They may never accept me. I'll never be part of the group. Then I remember that's what I want, and I keep walking.

Once I've reached the stairs that lead back down to the school, I notice an active duty soldier on his late-night patrol. I'm starting to think the stealth was to avoid these guards. If I'm caught doing something reckless like this, I could get in a lot of trouble.

With only a few minutes to spare, I decide it would be better to get caught with the group than without. I take off running toward where the river goes over the cliff. There's a reason they jumped from that spot, of all places. As I cross the wall, I see a few men along the bridge. Before they can see me, I summon my blade, close my eyes, and slam into the barrier as hard as I can.

Light flashes all around me, sending shocks of heat surging through my body. It's not right, though. I don't feel the sensation of falling. I open my eyes and see nothing, just an empty void. My lower body burns in agony as I look down to find myself trapped in the wall.

Sparks fly violently as I wiggle to get free. If I don't break through soon, it could cut me in half. I drop my blade and press against the barrier as hard as I can.

Then it happens—I made it. The sensation of falling brings a moment of relief.

With little time to maneuver, I come crashing down into the cliffside. My body burns through the rock face until I'm flipped around. Five seconds, maybe eight—that's all it takes until I hit the water.

My body slices through at a rapid speed. I'm carried downward for some time until I become weightless. The water around me boils immediately, carrying me to the surface. It's invigorating, I have to admit. I look up at the wall, barely visible, and can't believe I did this.

The shore dances with auras on each side of the river. I'm not too far behind them. I can see Liam waving me over and shouting. Upon exiting the water, I discover I'm completely naked. The only rational conclusion is that the impact ripped my clothes apart. I shouldn't be surprised though. Shirts can barely stay on Marcus even without him diving off a cliff.

Liam jumps back in the water and splashes about. He's too amped up for me. "You did it!" he says. "You sounded like a missile hitting the water! So cool!"

He places his hand around my shoulder and walks me out. Embarrassed, I cover myself up as he walks me over to a tree. Beneath it, they've created a storage area for extra uniforms. Clearly, they've prepared for this.

"That was awesome," I admit. "I can't believe we all just did that."

Only at this point do I realize one of us is missing. Liam confirms it too. Ryan, the tough guy in the group, doesn't hang out with them much. Too serious for Liam and his games. I may have that in common with Ryan; I too see little point in group activities. Tonight is different, though. I have to give them a pass.

"You did good, Lucas," Brock says. He throws up a high five. "You know, the first time we jumped, Liam pissed his pants on the way down. Of course, I was the only one who knew, which makes it more disturbing."

My brain bounces around with what that means. If he'd wet his pants, no one would know because his clothes would have disappeared. So how does Brock know? I shiver at the realization he peed on the way down. "How gross."

Brock pats me on the back. "Yeah, always keep your mouth closed when jumping—wouldn't want to swallow a bug on the way down, or anything worse."

Liam jumps on Brock's back and swings him to the ground. "How long you going to keep telling that made-up story?"

"Until it stops being true."

The two of them manage to get a smile out of me. I didn't think I would ever smile again after becoming a Cogent, but they seem like good friends, and they remind me of hanging out with Justin. This is their last year. I suppose they want to enjoy it before being deployed. Who knows what next year will bring?

I misjudged them. I've been telling myself they don't know what's going on, but that's not true. They know exactly what's happening to them, and they're each choosing to handle it in their own way. Despite our differences, we all have one thing in common: we are kids forced to be soldiers in a world that doesn't want us to enjoy it.

Chapter 4

When I wake, I feel uneasy. Maybe because there are no pillows being launched from the other side of the room. Instead, I see the others promptly making their beds with new sheets. I decide to follow their lead, rushing to catch up. As I'm making my bed, I bump into Bianca, who looks through me. Is she mad that I didn't jump with her last night?

"Attention!" Marcus calls as the door swings open.

Everyone stands at the ready as he paces the room. He stops for only a moment to inspect our beds.

"I have some important business to handle today. I know it's a bit early for our new recruits, but there is no option. That means, Brock, you will be in charge today. No one gets hurt. Understood?"

Brock gives a firm, "Yes, sir!"

With this confirmation, Marcus leaves the room as fast as he entered. Interestingly, everyone stays in formation as Brock takes control. Liam doesn't even give him a tough time. This must have happened before, with Marcus being both the teacher and commander of our army.

"You heard the man. Let's get to it," Brock says.

Everyone rushes out the door as if nothing has changed. We're only allotted ten minutes for breakfast. After scarfing down the food, we go for a run along the wall. The pace they keep is overwhelming. I wonder if Brock would be this hard on us normally or if he's trying to prove something.

After a few miles, I'm almost certain I feel my body ripping apart from the inside. Abruptly, I make a detour to the fountain, where I dunk my head and drink without reserve. After making it to the training room, Brock only allows us a short break. I don't think it's even two minutes before he starts us onto the next thing.

"Today, we will show you some basic sparring," he says to us.

Bianca steps up to the platform and enters a fighting stance. She looks more like a veteran than a recruit. I have some knowledge about fighting, but not like her. Upon entering the ring, I give her a smile, hoping to ease her aggression. It seems to send the wrong message though, as she changes her guard to her chest. I'm almost certain I hear her call me a perv once more.

"Start by taking a stance like this," Brock says. "We will start with the basic strikes: above, across, below, thrust. Once you understand these, all others will be variations."

We practice strikes for an hour before Brock asks us to practice on each other. Not a round goes by where Bianca doesn't best me in combat. She's obviously too good to be a first year. At this rate, we'll graduate early. I have to stop her; I have to hold her back somehow. If I don't, she'll get us both killed.

"Okay, you two go again," Brock commands. "More speed this time."

Bianca takes his words to heart and at the start of our round slides in with several cross strikes from Fate and Devotion. It's unfair having to fight both her expertise and her dual blades. I'm only able to survive because I'm so skilled at evasion.

Brock gets on me for this. "You're supposed to be defending, not avoiding!" he shouts.

I'm distracted by his words, missing my chance to dodge her last attack. I'm too late. My legs lock up as one of Bianca's blades comes inches from taking my head off. "Stop!" I yell, before tumbling backward off the stage.

"Lucas! Get up!" Brock shouts with little empathy.

I liked him a lot more yesterday. What happened to the fun guy leading us to the edge of the wall to jump? I keep waiting for Liam to lighten this place up, but he never does. I wish he would. I'm not sure what Brock wants from me; this is only my second day, and I'm outclassed in every aspect of this fight. They made a mistake choosing me to become a Cogent. I can't even summon an edge on my blade. What's it going to take for them to realize this?

"Can I fight her?" Liam asks. "She looks fun."

Brock looks at him with disapproval. "They aren't ready."

"She looks ready," he responds.

Bianca jumps to the opportunity with a firm, "I am."

The three of them look at each other and size up the moment. After careful consideration, Brock decides against it. He claims it's for Bianca's safety, but I'm wondering if it's for Liam's pride. It would be rough if on the first full day of training, a fourth year got beaten by a first year.

"No more sparring for you two. I want you to focus on stance and strike until lunch. And Lucas, take some time to see if you can make that stick a weapon," Brock says.

We spend the better part of the morning quietly practicing our strikes. I still can't summon my blade, and I'm not sure how to feel about it. Without an edge, they may not pass me, which would be nice, but there are also a lot of negatives. I become a target of both real and verbal attacks. It's easy to pick on the guy who can't stand up for himself.

I must be smart about this. I'll need to have some sort of grasp of my partner if I'm to survive. Training every day is risky with a girl as skilled as her. And who knows what will happen to me if she really doesn't like me?

"Hey Bianca," I say, trying to end the silence between us. "We'll be partners for the next several years, so we should probably talk and like, get to know each other and stuff."

This goes against everything in me, but I know it's to my advantage to understand how she works. If I want to keep my head these next four years, I'll need her to like me enough to not kill me. Right now, there's no hope of that happening. It doesn't have to be real, but I need her to believe it.

"So last night was crazy, right?" I ask her when she doesn't respond.

She glances at me midstrike and then rolls her eyes. Looks like she's detected my strategy, just like the day we met, when she called me out about those two boys. I have to remember that she's just as clever a mental fighter as she is an actual one. There's no getting past her with basic tactics. I'm going to need to go all out if I'm going to fool her.

"All right, everyone, time for a water break," Brock says.

Now's my chance. If I'm to make any progress with Bianca, I have to corner her and find a topic she can't resist. I set my trap by the water container, patiently waiting for her head to emerge. Then with precision, I pounce into conversation.

"So, I heard your brother got our vice commander injured in a skirmish by the neutral town a few months ago. What's that like?"

Bianca looks at me like I have three heads, and I know I'm in. "What are you talking about? That's not true at all."

"Oh, you have a brother, right? Isn't he stationed in the south near all the fallout dead zones?"

"Not even close. He's at the farm town in the north, and he's gotten no one injured. Get your facts right."

"Oh, my bad," I say. "Must have heard the wrong name."

I have her now. From the moment we met, I could tell she likes being right. She can't stand someone telling her bad information—especially when it's about her family.

"He almost died at Sincliff a few weeks ago," she says. "There's been some trade issues going on lately, and they asked him to step in, but the Sinder Army sent a Feren Guard, one of those Sinder Elite Cogents, to counter our support. He almost lost his life."

Her words stun me. I almost died there too. It sounds like my life. I hate Sincliff—that place brings me so much pain. More than anything, I wish to never see that stupid serrated blade again.

"Hey, are you okay?" Bianca asks.

"Yeah. Sorry. He sounds important. Are you guys close?"

Her story again sounds like mine. She misses her family, and is upset she couldn't be there to fight alongside them. I notice her hand tighten around her arm as she thinks of her brother. They must have a deep bond, much like me and my mother.

"I hope you can see him soon. Genuinely," I say.

"Thanks."

This conversation didn't go how I thought it would. I wasn't expecting to have anything in common with her. I envisioned a girl overconfident and brainwashed into loving her country, but she seems to have more depth than that. Maybe there's hope for us after all, and just maybe, I'll get to keep my head.

After lunch, we return to the training room once more. This time, we are observers. Brock says watching someone fight can teach you a great deal. Combat skill comes from combining what you see with your own style. His lesson is inherently true. I too have done this back at the orphanage. There were many days I would watch the other kids, study their attitudes and fighting spirit. This helped me keep my dominance as the eldest boy. Without it, I surely would have been dethroned by another, more ambitious, boy.

Brock stands at the platform and speaks directly to us. "Each year of student will spar in a no-rules fight. This will give you some idea of how you may improve over the years. Do not be deceived into thinking one could not beat the other. After all, any opponent can beat another in the right situation. And you should underestimate no one."

The first fight is between the second years, Ryan and Cameer. I know little about Ryan other than that he's incredibly strong. His partner looks mouselike next to him, small and quiet.

As Ryan enters the ring, he removes his shirt in a display of power. His red aura ripples off his black skin as he prepares for combat. He wields an oversized blade he calls Dissent. It's at least six feet long and one foot wide. It's hard to believe he's only sixteen. Cameer looks outmatched in every way.

She doesn't back down, though. Cameer swirls her brown hair around her finger and ties it into a knot. She summons her dual daggers, Pain and Purpose—small, like her. Seeing them makes me feel more confident about my edgeless blade. There is no doubt in my mind that Ryan will win.

Brock starts the match, and no one moves. To no surprise, Brooke and Jean cheer for Cameer. I still can't see this going well for her, but then she does something impressive. She closes a ten-foot gap like it was nothing. Sliding to Ryan's right side and avoiding his blade as it strikes the ground, she slashes at his legs as she rotates away. Ryan tries to regain the distance he needs, but Cameer rushes forward, whooshing past his forward thrust and following with rapid strikes. Ryan drops his blade and defends himself with his fist, matching her blow for blow.

They're each skilled in their own style, using their blades to their direct advantage: speed for Cameer and size for Ryan. This isn't over, though, far from it. Ryan dips his shoulder, charging into Cameer and sending her flying back. She counters by springing forward, sliding down his blade and into his chest. But he is ready—he releases his blade at the last second, grabbing her wrist. His head becomes a battering ram, knocking her to the ground. His blade returns, inches from her neck. She can't evade. He's won.

"Excellent fight!" Brock says. "There was a lot to notice there. They each used vastly different styles that matched their weapons. Both used their knowledge of their opponent, and most of all, used a means beyond their blades to win."

Brooke and Jean take the ring next. I can't help but cheer for Brooke a little. She summons an elegant blue rapier she calls Sapphire. It's a long, thin blade. Her stance is graceful as she stands up straight with one arm behind her back. Her friend and partner, Jean, wields a green falchion called Emerald, a notched blade. Jean's stance is very loose as she sways from side to side.

44

Brock calls for the fight to start. Jean runs to the outside, then slants inward using her whole body to strike her opponent. Brooke counters almost without moving, shifting just slightly to redirect her attacks. The dramatic motions of Jean keep Brooke on the defensive as she counters with short combos. It almost looks like a dance, both of them moving with such purpose and poise.

This goes on for several minutes. Things change when Brooke feints a large attack. During her strike, Brooke switches her blade hand. For a moment, she has it, but Jean bends at the last minute, wrapping her hand and twirling around her opponent. In the end, Jean stands behind Brooke with the blade to her neck.

"No fair!" Brooke complains. "You know I've been practicing that move."

I think she's right. No regular opponent would have seen that coming. It's impossible. The change of dominant hands would be awfully hard to counter midfight. I suppose there isn't much you can hide from your partner if you train with them every day. Surely her move would have defeated everyone else here.

"Wonderful," Brock says, clapping them off. "Great stuff. I think the thing to take away from that fight is the purpose of your movements. You notice they chose what their balance looked like and fought accordingly."

"You ready, old man?" Liam asks, interrupting his lesson.

Brock looks annoyed. "You're only a month younger."

"Yea, but a whole lot better looking."

"You're bald," Brock counters.

"Bald and better looking, what's your point? Haven't you heard? Bald is beautiful."

I can hear the girls groaning at his overconfidence. Brooke even reminds him he's not that cool, which he ignores, calling all of us haters.

"Are you ready, then?" Brock asks.

Liam doesn't respond with words, only action. He dashes forward, summoning his blade, Mischief, at the last possible moment. His blade is similar to a military-style sword. It's balanced in size and form. Brock counters with his yellow great sword, Dignity, a long blade with a commanding appearance, much like one a king would wield in a fairytale.

We watch as their fight moves at an incredible pace. Fourth years have a great deal of skill. Their styles match their personalities, as Liam bounces playfully between strikes while Brock takes a serious, analytic approach.

After several minutes, Liam bounces away with a suggestion. "Hey Brock—let's make things interesting. A wager. If I win, you have to let me lead the rest of the day and call me great teacher."

"And when I win?" Brock says with a smirk.

"In the unlikely event that happens, for the rest of the week I will be your servant. You can command me to do anything."

"Confident, are we?" Brock says, returning to his stance.

"Great, then I'll stop fooling around," Liam says, leaping forward.

Liam's fighting style shifts drastically as his focus wraps into his strikes. Blow after blow, he moves in with speed and precision. Brock does his best to keep up with this new, calculated style, but quickly realizes he must change as well. We watch as he becomes the springy counterattacker that Liam once was. Brock's movement now becomes hard to predict as he makes additional pointless moves for the purpose of confusion.

This goes on much longer than expected, as each style has its advantages. Liam finally gains the upper hand, smashing his head into Brock and following up with a combo of blunt strikes.

Brock staggers back, resting on his longsword. He smiles, then with a quick burst throws his blade in front of Liam, running up it and jumping over him. He lands, summoning his blade again and placing it against Liam's back.

"I got you," Brock says, that big smile stretching across his face.

I'm glad he's loosened up. The fight pulled him out of the teacher mode he's been in all day. "That was great," I say.

"Amazing!" Brooke and Jean shout.

"This sucks," Liam complains. "A bit of a cheater, don't you think?"

"How so?" asks Brock.

"You used my style to defeat me," he says.

"And you used mine to try to defeat me. Now go fetch me some water, servant."

Liam drags his feet offstage—he knows he can't do anything. The fight was fair, excellent even. And if it hadn't been, it still wouldn't matter. In the real world, people don't have to fight by the rules.

"So, while my servant gets me some water, what did you think?"

Bianca responds, "Liam was sloppy as he imitated you. He should have won, but he couldn't stay consistent in his striking. He let up when he should have pushed forward. He got cocky."

Brock nods. "You noticed that too, huh? Don't tell him—it will go to his head."

As Brock gets his water from Liam, he tells us all that training is over for the day. Without a moment of hesitation, I'm out the door and on my way to the fountain. There isn't a second I want to waste without Katelynn.

This is the moment I've envisioned all day, seeing her here, waiting under the lions. The low sunlight gives her blond curls a bright, golden appearance. She quickly notices me and forms a soft smile, pressing her thin lips together.

My mind goes to all the questions I've been thinking about since we last spoke. I'm not sure it's better. Someday, I will be stationed far away from her. I don't know how to handle that, or us, right now.

"You just going to stand there?" she asks, approaching me, her hands clutching her book.

Her tone reminds me of the playful person I knew before all of this. I hope we can get back there somehow, back to what we were. Katelynn is perfect in every way, and I don't know how I'll ever do better.

She tilts her head, letting her hair fall. "You there?"

"Yeah, sorry. Just a lot on my mind."

"No worries. How about we go on a walk and talk about it?"

I agree. There are still a few hours left before I have to be back at the barracks. It might be nice to see the city again. We start near the school in the north part of town, staying on the main road as we walk near the Rockcliff suburbs, a pleasant part of town reminiscent of pre-war housing. The rich here are far from the orphanage in the southeast neighborhood. As we walk by, she mentions missing home.

The market square nears, and the crowds of people grow. This time, however, everyone makes a path for me. After a while, Katelynn reaches for my hand as if I'm normal again. I pull away in fear I might hurt her. Brooke told me the other day that we can gently touch people, but that depends a lot on the pressure and intensity of our auras. So, for now, I think I'll avoid all contact out of fear I might burn her hand right off her body.

Katelynn is upset at first, but she quickly understands why. We walk in silence until we come across the hospital on the lower west side of town. When we get there, we find the bench we always used to hang out at.

I can tell we both have a lot on our minds. At least this whole time, I've been trying to figure out what to say to her. What words could fix this situation. Things have changed, but I don't know how to fix them. I'll be a Cogent forever.

The hospital is a busy building. It's the one place that doesn't look like it belongs to the rest of the concrete structures around here. I suppose it's the white paint they've plastered over it. Maybe it gives people hope. I could use some of that right about now. Instead, dread seems to come in waves. I forget about it from time to time, but it comes back to me and reminds me something isn't right. I know what it is, too.

"I need you to talk to me, Lucas," Katelynn says, pulling me out of thought.

Her hands clutch her gray military pants, and she doesn't make eye contact. I can tell she's upset, though. I haven't seen this face before. She's always so happy. I'm not sure what to do.

"I'm sorry," I say, hoping to fix whatever is bothering her.

She turns her whole body toward me and scolds me. "I don't want your apology. I want you to talk to me. I miss you. I'm worried about you."

I can see the concern in her eyes as she holds back tears. She really is concerned about me. It's strange—just yesterday she was so optimistic, and now today she's worried. Maybe she's been like this the whole time, but able to hide it better than me.

"Lucas, please talk to me. I want to know what you're thinking." She reaches for my hand again, but I pull away. "Lucas, I know this is hard, but I need you right now. I'm worried about us."

"I'm worried about us too," I assure her. "I wish more than anything that I could hold you, but I can't. My body is a weapon. I don't know how to stop worrying about us."

She sighs. "Me too. I couldn't sleep last night. I couldn't stop thinking about you. About us." She grabs a blond curl and wraps it around her finger over and over while looking at the ground.

"What are you worried about?" I ask.

Katelynn looks at the gray-blue sky and says everything I've feared myself. "Do we have a future? You know, as a human and Cogent. What does that even look like? I don't want them to send you away someday. I'm just struggling to make it all make sense. My feelings for you are real, but this—this is something I've never thought about. Then there are the questions I hate even thinking about."

48

The city's aura illuminates her face, revealing her tears. "Do you still want to be with me?" she asks.

"Of course I want to be with you. I won't ever give up on us. I promise," I tell her.

She forces a smile for a moment, trying to be the strong, confident, beautiful girl I've only ever seen her as; she wipes her tears away quickly, hoping I won't notice.

"Don't worry about it," I tell her. "I'm not going anywhere. I'll be right by your side, and we'll figure this out together. Besides, what happened to the upbeat girl I saw the other day? The one ready to take it all on?"

Katelynn tries to fake a smile once more for me. "There's something else I have to tell you. I've already moved up in my division. My father had me tested so I could advance a year. He wants me to finish as soon as possible so I can come work for him. But that means I'll be serving my field time a year early as well. I'm excited for it, you know that. I feel a great deal for those in need. I'm struggling, though. With the timing of it all."

Becoming a field doctor has been her passion ever since she was a little girl. Heck, it's the first thing she told me about herself when I met her at this very hospital. I can see this has caused her some discomfort, to say the least. She's always seemed like the kind of person who has to stick to the plan, or it eats at her.

"Don't worry about that. You still have plenty of time until you're deployed. We'll just make the best of it now, and we can figure the rest out when we get there," I say, trying to calm both of us down.

"You're right," she says.

Eyes wide open, she leans in for a kiss. I don't pull away. She carefully hovers just inches from my face before taking the leap. I embrace her, anticipating the soft touch of her lips, but it never comes. Instead, I'm met with the most vile smell imaginable, followed by a quick retreat. My stomach turns as I realize the smell is that of her burned flesh.

"I'm sorry!" I shout as she covers her mouth.

"No, no," she says, trying to gather herself. "That was me. I just couldn't help myself. I wanted to kiss you, and so I did. It's my fault."

"I'm sorry," I say again. "What can I do for you?"

She shakes her head and tells me to stop worrying about it. But that's not possible. How can I stop thinking about this? I just hurt the only person I care about.

"I can't stand this—I wish this never happened to me," I say.

"Don't say that, Lucas. I know this is hard for us. For you. But I believe you were chosen by the Giver of Life. I know we don't understand it right now, but I believe it's all by design. You are meant for bigger things. You are. I struggle with it, but I know it too. So please, don't be upset with this."

I don't know if she's right. I don't care. I only care about her. Somehow, I'll make this right between us. I'll find a way for us to be together. There has to be a way. This can't be the end of our story—surely the Giver of Life's plans aren't to make me suffer for the rest of my life.

Chapter 5

The old lady snips the flowers and arranges them in a beautiful bouquet. It's exactly what I wanted; vibrant red wildflowers pop out at me with the same intensity as my love for Katelynn. "She will love these, thank you."

"You'd better be careful with them."

She wraps the base of the flowers in a thick metal cloth before handing them to me.

"Thank you," I say again.

This city has changed for me over these last few weeks. I know I'm being treated differently. People respect and fear me at the same time. Before, I was something less than, a result of loss, damaged goods.

I'm still that same broken boy on the inside, but for a moment, I can feel the value a stranger like her sees. It's nice. Regardless of what I am to her or anyone else, today I only want to be one thing—the best boyfriend to Katelynn.

This date is going to be amazing. I can feel it now. Brooke has outdone herself, finding a historic church in the south, just an hour or so away. Katelynn's going to love it, and I hope as our first official date, it's one she can remember forever.

With the flowers in hand, it's time to meet up with her. She's waiting for me at the east bridge. Brooke secured us a vehicle in the cargo bay. I know Katelynn learned to drive last year with her father's ambulance crew—hopefully these military trucks aren't too different.

She's there, looking over the bridge, breathtaking like always. I don't know how to thank her for these past few weeks. I'm hoping these flowers can show her how I feel. I want her to know I see a future for us, despite of how impossible that sounds.

"These are for you," I say.

Her eyes light up with excitement. "I love them. They're so beautiful."

I would say step one was a success, and we are on our way to making memories. My goal is to carry this rush of excitement with us. Now, we only need to make it out of the city undetected by the city guard.

"Are you ready?" I ask.

"Mm-hmm!"

Arriving at the cargo bay, I wonder again how Brooke pulled this off, but then I remember she's probably got dirt on someone. I've never known her to have bad intentions with the things I tell her, but maybe that's how she gets you. I wonder if someday she might ask me for a favor, knowing I won't be able to refuse. The sign of a true master. If everyone is in debt to you, you never have to worry about anything. Clever.

At the truck bay, we do our best to keep a low profile. It doesn't take long for us to find the truck with "34" written on the side. Sure enough, the keys are snug behind the visor, as promised.

I hide under a blanket in the passenger seat so it looks like Katelynn is doing a solo delivery. If they'd been a bit more thorough, they would have checked her rank and maybe caught us. I should be thankful they didn't.

I haven't been beyond the walls like this since the day I lost my mother. *Take a deep breath*, I tell myself. This time will be different—it will be better. I'm off to have a magical date with the girl of my dreams. Truth be told, I'm not sure which part I'm more nervous about, the date or leaving the walls.

"I know you said we're going south, but you still haven't told me exactly where we are going," she says.

In the glove box is the map Brooke left for us. It's a bit silly when I see it. It looks like a kid put it together with wax sticks. There's a cliff with a lion, a bunch of hastily made trees, a long, winding road that stops at a toxic symbol, and an arrow pointing to the symbol of the Giver of Life.

"Don't worry—once I figure out how to read this, it will be easy. For now, just stay on this road. We turn when we get near the first dead zone sign."

She looks at me, highly suspicious. "Okay. Don't let me miss it."

The ride is maybe an hour long. Rockcliff's countryside is foreign compared to the city. The fields are filled with various crops and wildflowers. Colors live vibrantly out here, unlike inside the walls. I guess you could say beauty is dangerous.

It reminds me of the stories Miss Caroline would tell about the old world. Back when people could go anywhere they wanted, they often lived in what she called "exotic areas." I'm still not sure what that word means. My guess is they were places of happiness, with pure freedom to do anything you wanted.

"Almost there, I think," Katelynn says, turning before the dead zone.

Sometimes I get the feeling the Giver of Life wants me to cherish these moments. They feel slow and precious, somehow. My eyes can't help but admire Katelynn as she focuses on the road. I study her soft cheeks as her curls bounce against them.

She catches me staring but smiles it away. "Tell me about your classmates?" she asks.

"Let's see . . . Brock is kind of like the leader of all of us. He's in his fourth year. Nice, but also serious about everything, as I guess he should be. He reminds me of a dad, but our age. I suppose he looks like one too, just a young one. And then there's Liam, the other fourth year. He's the guy with the shaved head who's like the joker of the group. He can't stop messing with everyone. The other day, he dug a hole in the ground with his aura just to have everyone fall into it as he led us around the campus on our daily run. He got a kick out of it."

"That does sound kind of funny. What about the others? Aren't there some girls in your group?"

"Oh yeah. There's Jean, who's friendly with everyone. Then Brooke, who I've told you about. She's become something of a sister to me lately. You know she helped me plan this for us. She likes you a lot."

"I like her."

"Yeah. Then there's Cameer, who's a little timid for a Cogent, but she still manages to fight well. She doesn't like to talk in the big group, but I get her, because that's kind of me too. She's matched up with Ryan, who's pretty serious most of the time. I never see him joking around. I think that's all of them."

"What about that one girl? You know, the one you're paired with. What's her name again?"

"You mean Bianca?"

I find it strange she's forgotten her name. I mean, I know I've mentioned her plenty of times. Given that I train with her every day, naturally she comes up.

"Is it stuffy in here?" Katelynn asks. She cracks the window, which sends her hair streaming across her face. She struggles to remove the strands from her mouth before rolling the window back up again. "Oh yeah. How's she doing?"

"She's good, I guess. She's a little annoying from time to time as she's always talking about our responsibilities at Rockcliff and living the values of our nation. But other than that, we've learned to put up with each other."

"I heard she doesn't believe in the Giver of Life."

"I honestly don't know. I haven't brought it up. Maybe."

Katelynn lets out a bit of a sigh and stops the truck, clicking it into park.

"We're here. Wherever that is, anyway," she says.

I pull up the map once more. "This should be it. Now we walk."

When we start our journey, I can't help but notice the almost-completely-gone remnants of civilization. Lush greens thrive over stone. Even the road we walk on now is barely visible. I can only imagine what these cities used to look like.

"This way," I say, summoning my blade to clear a path for us.

While my weapon may not be the best for killing, it can remove the overgrown vegetation just fine. Maybe if I can't ever get an edge for my blade, they'll reassign me to the capital lawn crew.

"Is that it?" she says with pure joy.

Up ahead, it pierces through the trees and vegetation—a white steeple, a beacon of the Giver's love. Katelynn takes off running to get a closer look, forcing me to keep pace. We stop in front of the arch, which bears three parallel lines. Above each of these marks, the words "Giver of Life", "Mover of Life", and "Life" are etched.

"It's beautiful."

"I wonder how it's been kept up for so long," I muse.

"By the Giver's grace, I'm sure."

"Want to go inside?"

But the door is stuck, and will need a bit of force to open. I kind of laugh, because I end up forcing her to open it for me, which takes a few good pushes. It's worth it though. Inside, we are met with the most magnificent view, a church from the old world. Color splashes vibrantly through the massive stained glass and onto the wooden pews. Concrete beams spiral up with elegant designs, each one hand carved.

The words "serenity" and "bliss" come to mind even though I've never used them before. All I know is that I feel something here. The opposite of weight. A connection to something.

I lift my hands to the ceiling, reaching out to give thanks. *I know you are there, Mover of Life. I can feel you.* "Thank you for bringing me here."

"What a miracle," Katelynn says to me. "What a beautiful miracle this place is."

At the altar she falls to her knees, kissing the ground. I join her in admiration and respect. After a moment of silent prayer, I look to the candles on the side, which are somehow still lit.

"What do you make of the painting?" she asks.

I look back toward the altar. The wall is filled with faces, stories, images of a world we don't know. "I'm not sure, but it's beautiful."

"It is," she echoes. "You know, when I was a little girl, my mother would bring me to church every Sunday. She used to say church was a place that connected souls. I think she was right. I know I feel connected right now."

I know there must be a reason behind all of this, a connection to me being selected. I pray to become what the Giver of Life has designed me to be, to reveal my purpose and to help protect the ones I love.

I want to kiss Katelynn, but the smell of burning lips hasn't left my nose. Instead, I offer her a seat next to me in the front row. Together we sit in silence, the good kind, the kind that brings you closer without effort.

"Um . . ." Her hands clench her clean military pants, making wrinkles spring out in all directions. "Hey Lucas, I know it's a few months away and all, but . . ."

"What is it?" I ask.

Her eyes meet mine in a sudden burst of confidence. "Please join me at the Military Ball this fall?"

She searches my face trying to decipher my answer before I speak.

"Yes . . ." I say. "Yes, of course."

Her shoulders drop, and she sinks back into the pew with a long exhale. I smile. I'd thought she wanted to talk about something serious. But I guess it was. I mean, I have just committed to her that in a few months we'll still be together. Plus, everyone in the school will see us on display. I wonder what they'll think. It doesn't matter, though. None of that matters. What matters now is being by her side.

"Katelynn, I'm excited to go with you. Thank you for asking me."

Chapter 6

This date couldn't have gone any better. I believe we connected on a spiritual level, allowing us to grow deeper together. Her asking me to the dance makes me feel confident that we'll make this work. We can get through anything.

"Do you like music, Lucas?" she asks. She shuffles through a few of the radio stations broadcast by Rockcliff.

"I do, but don't expect me to know anything current from the city. I only listened to whatever Miss Caroline would play around the orphanage. It was always old songs from before the war. Most of the time I had no clue what they were singing about."

"Something like this?" She pauses on a station.

I nod. "Yeah."

She turns it up slightly, until it drowns out the rumbling engine. The familiar tunes are relaxing, almost lulling me to sleep as the truck rocks back and forth.

This whole time, I've felt a sense of belonging and calmness, but suddenly, I'm met with confusion and chaos. My body shifts with an abrupt force as the truck turns sharply to the side. I'm forced to watch in slow motion as I brace my hands against the door, only to go through it.

I'm flung to the ground, spinning and tumbling rapidly until finally coming to a stop. I brace my hands against my legs, trying to steady them, only to be met with the horrific sound of metal crunching as the truck hits a tree.

"Katelynn!" I scream. "Katelynn! No. No. No."

Rushing to the truck, I see the frame has twisted into an unrecognizable shape. I call her name, hoping to hear her under the wreckage, but she doesn't answer.

Where could she have gone?

Then I hear it—the sound I've been craving. "Lucas! Over here. Come quickly."

I pinpoint her voice behind me and take off running. She's only a few feet away, lying in a ditch. I raise my aura to see her better only to be met with the sight of blood all over her face.

"Katelynn! Are you okay?"

"I'm okay, but she's not."

I look down and see that she's holding a badly injured woman. "Did we . . ."

She shakes her head. "This wasn't us."

We didn't hit this woman. But if that's the case, why is she like this?

Her blood-soaked clothing looks like something a farmer would wear. Whatever happened to her, it doesn't look like she's going to make it. Katelynn is trying everything to help her.

"Are you still with me?" she asks the lady.

The woman's head rolls uncontrollably as she tries to focus once more.

"Are you okay, miss? Do you understand where you are?" Katelynn asks.

The lady stabilizes herself by grabbing Katelynn's face with her bloody hands. "Please. Please."

"You're going to make it, don't worry."

Katelynn shouts for me to check the truck for an emergency med kit and water. To my surprise, the items she's looking for are exactly where she thought they would be. Her recall from her medical training is perfect.

I slide back to her side with the supplies in hand. "Is she going to make it?" I ask.

Katelynn cleans the woman's wounds with water, then follows up with the bandages. Everything I can see seems fine, but then she lifts the woman's shirt to find a large gash across her stomach. Having run out of bandages, Katelynn tears off the sleeve of her military jacket to improvise.

"I need you to hold this here," she tells her.

"Thank you," the woman replies.

Katelynn meticulously cleans the woman's face, examining her for any other unknown injuries. As far as we can tell, it's just the cuts and burns on her body that she's suffering from.

"You . . ." the lady says, wincing in pain. "You are soldiers. From the capital. Please. Help. Our farm. The Sinder Army. They are—attacking. Please. Save my daughter."

Her words move me, or maybe it's the connection I feel to the Giver and Mover right now. For some reason, I promise to save her daughter. That's not what I should do—I should go get help—but I feel compelled to. Katelynn can stay with her; that way, I know she's safe.

"Where?" I ask.

"Just over there," the woman gasps.

I nod, ready to take off running. "Keep her safe, Katelynn. Call for help."

I don't know if it's adrenaline from the car accident or the Mover of Life, but I know what I must do. My legs propel me through the fields, faster and faster. I know this will be dangerous, especially without an edge on my blade. I don't need to fight, though, I just need to get the girl out. I'll be careful.

A billow of smoke comes up from the town, marking the location. I wait by the crop line for a moment until three soldiers walk out. Black-and-gray camo, rifles, and a fiery red Sinder patch. These are the soldiers. Seeing they are only human, I step out slowly, then faster and faster, until I'm sprinting straight for them. One of the men takes aim at my chest and fires a hail of bullets.

This is my chance, my chance to do something here. I grab the soldier's gun and burn it into nothingness while the other two get away. He falls back, begging for his life, fear shining in his eyes. It's unsettling even for me.

"Go!" I yell. "Don't ever come back."

I sigh as he disappears into the tree line. This could have gone so much worse. Now I can find this little girl. Thinking of it now, I wish I had asked for her name. Calling out for a little girl seems wrong for some reason. Hopefully, she'll recognize the uniform.

I try the barn first. A trail of blood leads into a stall. To my relief, it belongs to a cow that's been shot several times.

"Little girl," I whisper. "Little girl. I'm from Rockcliff. You can come out if you're in here."

There's an eerie creak of a gate, and out walks a little girl. Her face is covered in dirt and blood. She must have been hiding behind the dead animals. I kneel to her level only to be met by a face completely disconnected from everything that's happening around her. I see myself in it.

"Don't worry, your mother is alive. I'm going to take you back to her, okay? She's alive."

"Where's my daddy?"

Her words come with such weight. "I . . . Um . . . I will look for him next, okay? For now, I have to get you to safety."

58

In the stall next to hers lies a corpse—a man's corpse. He must have sacrificed himself to keep her safe. I reach over and pull the gate shut so she won't see. "I'm sure he's around here somewhere. We'll find him."

She doesn't respond.

"Hey, I'm Lucas," I say, trying to get something out of her. "What's your name?"

With her eyes trained on the floor, she whispers, "June."

"That's pretty. Well, June, I need you to stay close while I take you to your mommy."

Leaving the barn, a surge of dread consumes me. Three Sinder Cogents stand twenty feet from me. Their auras are something beyond red, orange, and blue. They carry an intense malice. I tell the girl to run, but the blue Cogent cuts her off.

"I wouldn't run," she says.

June takes a step back toward me. She can't escape, and I can't either. The trio begin to circle us slowly. I wonder for a moment if I could make it if I left the girl. A terrible thought, but one I have to consider. She wouldn't be fast enough to keep up with me. It's better if only one of us dies. Right?

"You're not the one we are supposed to meet, are you? You have a white aura," the man with the orange aura says.

I shake my head in confusion. "Meet? No."

"Interesting. Looks like you're a bit upset with what we've done here. It was a simple misunderstanding, you know. We didn't mean to kill these people, but they got suspicious and, well, we had to make it look believable, so we . . ."

He shrugs his shoulders as if it's no big deal. He killed the people here and wants to call it a misunderstanding. Give me a break.

"You killed these people. And you enjoyed it. I've seen monsters like you before."

"I just told you, we had to. It was an unfortunate event."

"You're disgusting—vile demons."

"Woah, woah, woah. What's with the name-calling? I think we need to start over. They call me Hatcher. Next to me is Bear, and behind you is Hara. We came to meet a Cogent, but you don't match the description. So, I'm not sure what we should do with you. Have some fun, I suppose."

"If your business is with me now, then let this little girl go," I say.

Hatcher looks into my eyes, seemingly playing with the idea of releasing her. He knows he has me right now, so he doesn't need the little girl. With a wave of his hand, he releases her. At first, she seems unsure about leaving.

"Don't worry, June," I say, "there's an army at the road up ahead. They're on their way here. Just go in that direction until you run into them. Your mom is with them."

Hatcher smiles with glee as the girl runs off in distress.

"You guys are sick," I say.

The guy named Bear approaches me. I look up at him, a beast of a Cogent, covered in hair like some sort of wild animal. The protrusion of his brow makes me think he's taken a few hits to the head. Regardless of how ugly he is, I remain still as he sniffs me.

"He's not the one," he grunts.

Hatcher laughs. "I already knew that, Bear. I told you I don't have to rely on your sense of smell. It's not needed for someone of my caliber. Now just stand next to me and be quiet."

I stand firm. "I guess you didn't hear me. There's an army on their way."

"He's imaginative, isn't he?" Hara says, mocking me.

Hatcher calls my bluff. "That badge on your shoulder, it says you're a first-year private. There's no army where you go, boy. I bet you're out getting into some of that teenage trouble. Well, you found it. We're here."

"You're wrong. They'll be here any minute."

They laugh and mock me. My life is a joke to them. I have to change their minds quickly. Instinctively, I summon my blade, ready to strike them down. It quiets them for a moment as Hatcher examines it in disbelief.

"Oh. There really is no edge! Now what are you going to do with that, poke me to death?"

I swipe at him quickly to end his laughter, but he moves away with ease. I swing again, over and over in rapid succession, but he's too skilled.

"Stand still!" I command.

To my surprise, he stops dead in his tracks, and my blade connects with his shoulder. He just stands there, no more laughter, no smile. He looks me in the eye, unhurt and unafraid of me. Then, in an instant, he sends a powerful fist into my chest. A shockwave of pain shoots through my body until I collapse.

60

I gasp for air, rolling on the ground, pounding on my chest to get my lungs to work again. It was just one punch, but it had such force behind it. I've never felt anything like it. Finally, relief springs through my body. I can breathe again.

Hatcher kneels beside me. "I like your spirit, kid. Stay in school. Train up. When you're ready, I'll meet you on the battlefield and we can see what you've learned at that prestigious academy of yours."

I lie helpless on the ground, watching them walk off into the fields. My physical pain is now gone, morphing into mental agony instead. I was useless. They could have killed me if they wanted. I'm pathetic. I feel exactly like I did when my mom was killed. I shouldn't be alive. My mother would be ashamed if she saw me now.

I lose track of time lying here on the ground. Slowly, I can feel the earth swallowing me. This is becoming my grave, and I'm okay with that. I should be dead.

Barely a moment before I embrace my resting place, I'm lifted to my feet.

"You okay?" Marcus asks.

I want to answer him, but the answers are all horrible. "I shouldn't be a Cogent. I told you."

"Why is that?"

"I don't belong. My blade, my skills. I'm useless."

"Maybe . . ." he says.

I don't know why, but I'd hoped he would say I wasn't useless. I suppose even he can't deny it now. This was a mistake from the beginning.

"If I remember correctly," he continues, "belonging wasn't a requirement in our selection. Your blade will form when the time is right, and your usefulness comes from you. It's your effort, and you can always put more in. If you don't like who you are today, you can change it, be somebody else tomorrow. I didn't get here because I was perfect, I got here because I try, relentlessly, each and every day. And if it's worth anything to you, I believe in you."

His words weigh on my mind as I ride back to the capital. I'm not sure I believe in myself at this moment. If Katelynn saw what happened, if she saw how useless I was . . . she would stop believing in me too.

At the hangar, I'm escorted out. Katelynn waits in the hall, but I'm not allowed to talk to her. I've been summoned for a full report of the incident, and I assume I will face whatever punishment they deem fit for me. I should be preparing my defense, but then again, what's the point?

Marcus stops before the door and allows me to enter first. Inside the room is a large table surrounded by our top military officials and members of the Palis Guard, the Elite Cogents that protect our city. My eyes quickly spot Miss Caroline's familiar gray curls. She stands up, looking like she's about to cry. She tries to hug me, but I promptly stop her.

"I was so worried. When I heard you were out beyond the wall, I thought I had lost you," she says, looking me over. "Did they hurt you? Are you okay?"

"I'm fine, I—"

"Have a seat, Lucas," a deep voice says from across the large wooden table.

"Prime Minister Maxwell."

"Please, sit," he says, gesturing with his hand.

Marcus sits next to the prime minister and looks on with a firm expression. There's no way this is a good meeting. I'm not sure if I should look at him or look away. I haven't been this close to the prime minister since the selection.

The men and women that surround the table appear to be part of our Elite Cogent Guard. I've never seen the symbols on their uniforms before. Collectively, this group makes all the decisions for the city.

The prime minister leans forward, placing his elbows on the table and clasping his hands. "Lucas, do you love your country?"

I search the room for a moment, trying to make sense of his question.

"Yes, sir."

"Are you grateful to be living in this capital?"

Again, I find myself searching to understand this bizarre line of inquiry.

"Yes, sir."

"Do you love your leaders?" he asks.

"Yes sir," I say, trying to keep pace with his questions.

"Do you love humanity, and will you do anything to protect it?"

"Yes, sir."

He leans back in his chair, tapping his fingers together before pressing them to his lips.

"Good. That makes this easy. Then you owe me an explanation as to why you went beyond these walls even though you were specifically told not to. We could have lost you, a valuable asset to Rockcliff."

"I don't understand, sir."

"Tell me why you were beyond the walls."

I study Marcus's face, looking for clues as to how I should answer. Do I lie, make something up? Do I tell the truth? I don't know.

"I was, umm . . . I was on a date."

"Interesting. A date. Because I have intel that tells me otherwise. Intel that tells me you're a traitor. You've been leaking information to the enemy—admit it. You've been reported for sneaking out past curfew on multiple occasions and somehow managed to obtain a vehicle. You can't hide behind this lie that you're somehow dating Terry's daughter. I know the truth. I know you're threatening her life so she goes along with this little game of yours, and it's time you confess. You're a traitor. You want to see us all dead?"

"No, sir."

It wasn't me. But I can't convince him of that. There are no words that will change this man's mind. It's made up. He thinks I'm using Katelynn to be a spy. He thinks I've threatened her life to be with me. I'm at a loss. They'll probably throw me in prison. I'll never be let out again. I'm through.

"Max . . . Prime Minister, sir," Miss Caroline butts in. "I can assure you he is an honest young man. I can vouch for him, as he has been close with the hospital chief's daughter for some time now—"

The prime minister glares at her with a powerful look of annoyance, silencing her plea. "Lucas, I will watch you. If it weren't for the fine lady next to you, you'd be dead by my hands already. So don't think I wouldn't have you killed at a moment's notice. I would do anything to protect humanity, anything."

His passion is overwhelming. I was just threatened with death by the prime minister himself. I make sure not to move as he stands up and leaves with his personal guard. The rest of the leaders follow, leaving only Miss Caroline.

This is the first time we've been alone in a room since I joined the Army. The tension from my conversation with Maxwell doesn't even compare to the tension I now feel with Miss Caroline.

The words I want to say boil inside me until they overflow. "This is all your fault, you know!"

She recoils in disbelief. My eyes quickly bounce back and forth as I search hers. "I want the truth," I demand. "I know that was you on selection day. I know you were the nurse. You did this to me. You turned me into this monster."

Her silence pushes me to continue. "You fed me lies! You ruined my life, and you have nothing to say about it. I never wanted this."

She looks as though she might cry, but she can't even muster a single tear for me. "Why don't you care about me? I used to love you. You were like a mother to me."

I don't even want to hear her answer. Nothing she could say would remove the pain I'm feeling right now. Forced to be a Cogent, treated like a criminal, and threatened to die by my own country. If she loved me, there's no way she could have done this to me. She knew how much I didn't want this.

"Keep your excuses."

I stand up and slam the door, removing the doorknob with it. I'm so tired of this. Tired of the military. Tired of the war. Of being a monster. The Sinder Army wants to kill me, and now my own prime minister does too. What kind of life can I even have now, with everyone out to get me?

Chapter 7

My dreams are haunted. I stand before a council of shadowy figures, each with a smoky aura. I turn to run away, but I'm met by the Rockcliff Palis Guard. They raise their hands and strike me down. Katelynn screams for me. From within our own ranks, out walks the Cogent that slew my mother. His red aura burns with despair, and his serrated blade presses against my neck. I'm unable to move, paralyzed by what I know about him. He's the right hand of Prime Minister Silas, the strongest of the Feren Guard. Even in my dreams I am no match for him, as he ends my life without effort.

Morning comes, but my nightmares haven't released me. I lie in bed motionless, like the day I was selected. Fear has crippled my body and my mind. I am alone, surrounded by people.

My stomach grumbles as I watch everyone leave for breakfast. I can't go, though. Marcus made it clear that I would be on rations for three days. One meal a day would be fine if my body wasn't a literal nuclear reactor. He assured me I wouldn't die, but he also said that to be safe, I'd better drink twice as much.

I can't stand to watch them eat, so I run ahead to the training room. It hasn't even been an hour, and I'm determined to find a way to cheat. This whole thing is stupid. I didn't do anything wrong. They should reward me for what I did.

Liam is the first one to arrive after me. "Oh, look who it is! I hear there's a new baddy among us."

Like the day we met, he slides over to me, placing his hand on my shoulder. "You know, as the previous holder of the title, I think it's important we stick together. What do you think? Partners in crime?"

I hesitate. "I'm not sure."

"Sure you're sure. Hear me out—one time they made me run two days straight because I carved a very provocative body part into the ground by the water fountain. It was high quality, to say the least. But I was ratted out by someone here. Talent like us needs to stick together. So, remember, I got your back, and you got mine."

With the arrival of the rest of the group, Liam winks at me and walks away. "Just remember, I got you."

His proposal isn't something I'd normally go for, but I wonder if it would play to my advantage to have him on my side. If he thinks we're friends, that could come in handy someday.

"Attention!" Marcus says, entering the room.

He looks serious today—maybe because he has a shirt on. If I were to bet, I'd say all of this is because of last night. It comes as no surprise that he scolds the group, but they all know he's really talking about me. They know I'm being punished. I might be afraid of him if I hadn't met the prime minister last night. That guy brings serious to a new level.

"I want everyone to remember: what we do here matters. Your effort here, it makes a difference out there. Someday, you will see the fruits of that. So, I need all of you to take this seriously. Let's do our best. Sparring drills to start, strike patterns next."

Bianca steps into the ring with me, already looking annoyed. I know what's bothering her—my run-in with the prime minister will be troublesome to her progression. She won't be able to join the fight early like she'd hoped.

"Let's go," she huffs.

Summoning her blade, she strikes with little hesitation. Each blow gets progressively stronger. Over and over again, she restarts without waiting. It doesn't take long for her to cross the line from practice to serious. Her blade bounces off my counter and cuts into my arm. Yelling at her doesn't seem to slow her down. She swings at me again, this time almost taking my head off.

"What's your problem?" I ask.

She counters, "What are you even doing here?"

"You almost killed me."

"Oh, sorry. I guess I missed."

Her complete disregard for my life has me worried. I've been trying for a while now to make her at least tolerate me, but that doesn't seem to be working out. Each round we go back and forth, and each time we end up back where we started.

I don't know why she doesn't understand me. She knows I didn't want this life. If I could have chosen to not be a Cogent, I would have. So why is she always taking it out on me? I already know I'm a failure at this. I'm a failure at everything—being a boyfriend, being a Cogent . . . even being alive.

"Look Bianca, you're mad at the wrong person. I didn't do anything. I tried to save a little girl and almost died, so why are you trying to kill me? What did I ever do to you?"

She proceeds to throw the hardest combo she can at me, each hit more intense than the last. With her final strike, she knocks the blade from my hand. Taking advantage of the opening, she rams her shoulder into me, then quickly slams her head into mine.

"Act like you don't know—"

"I don't know. I have done nothing wrong. My personal life is my personal life and doesn't affect you. If anyone should be upset today, it's me. I'm the one who has to eat rations for three days, the one that almost died the other day, the one who can't summon an edge on my blade—"

"That's it! It's all about you. You don't think of anyone but yourself. You're always focusing on you. I hate to tell you this, but *everything's not about you!*"

Her words eat at me. I know it's not about me, but I'm having a hard time today too. I didn't try to kill her just because I was upset. Bianca doesn't understand me. I'm not gifted like her. Her aura amplifies who she already is, while mine shines a spotlight on who I'm not. Not the hero they want, not the human boyfriend I need to be, not the boy who could save his mother.

"Lucas, there's a war going on out there. We have people to protect. You don't take this seriously—you haven't since the beginning."

Her blue aura pulses with anger. She wants an answer, I'm sure, but I don't have one. In a way, she's right. I haven't taken this seriously because this isn't what I wanted to do. Everything has been messed up since it started. I don't have my best friend Justin with me, I don't know why Miss Caroline betrayed me, and Bianca wants to kill me. The only thing I have going for me is my relationship with Katelynn, and that's slipping through my fingers.

"Say something!" Bianca demands.

"Just forget it. You wouldn't understand."

"I wouldn't understand? Understand what? The fact that you're too selfish to think of anyone else? The fact that you don't want to be a Cogent? The fact that you'd rather be anywhere but here? We know. We all know. You should grow up. Life's not fair to any of us. So quit being a baby, and do what's right."

She's had enough, and so have I. With nothing more to say, Marcus calls for lunch, trying to defuse the situation before he chases after her. I guess he feels the need to tell her how great she is.

Once everyone's gone and the door closes, the training room becomes a glass prison. I'm trapped here, alone with my own thoughts, the worst thing to be stuck with. Maybe Bianca's right about everything. I don't know where to even begin, though. How can I become the person I want to be tomorrow if I don't know who that is?

Am I really selfish? If so, is that even a bad thing? It's kept me alive this long. No one will look out for you but yourself.

Ah. Why do I allow her to get in my head so much? It's like sparring with her shadow, and she's still winning. If only I could have told her off somehow. I wish I'd asked her how putting Rockcliff first is going to work out for her when they leave her for dead. We're just assets, after all.

I've seen firsthand how loyalty like hers gets rewarded. It gets you killed, just like my mother. Devoted to our country, our people, our land, and our leaders, but none of that matters if it takes your life.

Feeling defeated and empty, I drop to my knees, ready to receive my finishing blow from her shadow. "Kill me now." A surge of pain shoots through my body and my aura flickers. "Stupid rations."

With a quick dunk in the water bucket I can finally not worry about bursting from the inside, at least. Now's the time to rest. I lie on the platform, looking at the ceiling. Why does what she thinks even matter to me? I wish it didn't.

From the door comes a slow squeal. Brooke pops her head in and glances around. "Lucas, hey, do you care if I join you?"

"Sure."

She takes her seat right next to me where I lie motionless in the ring. I don't know why she's here; maybe she wants to make fun of me too. Maybe after all this time listening to me, she's ready to dish it out like Bianca.

"I just wanted to come tell you I'm sorry," she mumbles.

I sit up, completely taken aback. "For what? You've done nothing wrong."

She grabs her long blond braid and strokes it as if to calm herself. "I did, though. I recommended you take her there. I was the reason you almost died, the reason you had an unauthorized truck. You didn't tell on me at all. I feel so bad. This is all my fault."

"Don't be silly. I asked you for ideas—and besides, the date was amazing. How were you supposed to know there would be an attack on a nearby farm?"

Brooke leans back, steadying herself with her hands. "I'm still sorry. I don't want anything bad to happen to you."

"I'm fine. Hungry. But fine."

"Was it scary?"

"Yeah, it was the second most terrifying day of my life."

Her hand rakes through her hair a few more times, then suddenly halts. "I would ask what the first was. But I have a feeling I already know. We've all had something similar happen to us, haven't we? I lost my parents to the Sinder Army as well. I'll never forget that day . . ."

Sometimes I forget how similar we all are. How we all have something or someone missing from our lives.

"I'm hopeful, though," she says. "Much like your partner, Bianca. She wants to protect people. Like me. To protect humanity. I may not be as strong as Marcus, Ryan, or Brock. Or as skilled as Jean, Cameer, or Liam. But I have hope that I can do something good if given the opportunity."

"I don't know how you do it," I admit. "How you and the others stay so positive and hopeful. The world we live in is dreary and awful. Everyone wants to kill you and tell you what to do."

"There's always a way to stay positive. It might just take more effort."

"Effort." I never thought I would hear that word so much. It seems like everyone keeps telling me that if I try, I'll somehow remove all my problems. I'll somehow magically find a way to become human again, marry Katelynn, end the war in our country, and live happily ever after—whatever that means.

"Try it," Brooke says with a playful nudge.

I contemplate her words. I know she only means to help. And to be honest with myself, she's more of a friend than I deserve. I constantly misjudge her.

"Okay. Here goes."

Back on my feet, I pat my face and shake my body. I need to break free of the hole I've been sinking into since yesterday. I know I can say something nice about her. Something positive.

"Thanks to you, I now have a date for our Military Ball."

Her eyebrows rise, and a big smile takes over. "Aha! I knew it was going to be good. I did it, I did it!"

"I'll give you credit, your date was a hit. Katelynn loved it. Now, in a few more weeks, I can take her to the dance and have another amazing date."

"I'm glad to hear it," she says. "I was hoping that would happen for you. Now if I could just get—"

"You're the best, and I bow to you, oh great matchmaker."

"Stop." Brooke giggles. "Oh, speaking of being the best, look what I have." From behind her, she reveals a half loaf of bread that she snuck in.

"What! Why didn't you lead with this?"

I want to yell at her and hug her at the same time. Instead, I stuff that bread in my mouth so fast I have to dunk myself in the water a second time. I even have to beat my chest a bit to clear it out.

"Thank you. Thank you. I can't tell you how much this means to me."

She smiles, and I feel myself smiling too. I don't know how she did it, but she pulled me out of my funk. Maybe it's time I admit I have two real friends in my life. Who knew that friends could do this for you?

"I guess Liam was just a bunch of talk. That guy said he had my back, but you're the one who's really been here for me. I don't see him showing up with any bread during rations."

Brooke lets out a laugh. "He's a good guy though, once you get to know him."

"I guess." I shake my head.

"All right, I'm going to head back before people realize I'm not in the bathroom."

Brooke returns an hour later with the rest of the class. Bianca remains distant and quiet while everyone else seems to avoid him. Marcus does his best to keep the rest of the day on track.

"Okay, listen up everyone. We're coming up on finals in a few weeks, so let's try to finish out strong. As a reminder, this will be an opportunity to move up ranks in our army. If you want to be one of our Elite Cogent Guards someday, you're going to have to do well here."

I considered failing this assessment when I first heard about it. If I wanted to, I still easily could. That would be a sure way to put me somewhere safe. Each year, I would just have to convince them of how terrible I am. But everyone is watching me now, and that includes the prime minister. It would no doubt look like I'm intentionally trying to get placed in a position inside the capital. That would only make them certain I'm the spy.

"Excuse me," I say, ready to shock everyone. "How will we be rated? I need to know what I should work on."

Marcus nods to me, perhaps to encourage my question, but Bianca doesn't look like she believes it.

"Good question. So it'll be three categories: aura strength, field exercise tactics, and combat readiness. Then we have a bonus category, which is potential fighting power. Essentially a guess of what you will look like when you complete your training here."

"Why'd you bother asking?" Bianca says. "It's not like you'll do well. You'd have to try, and we all know you don't do that."

I don't know what comes over me. It's possible all the rage I felt when arguing against her shadow comes back. My heart pounds, and my aura intensifies. Without thinking, I snap back at her, "You'll see! I'll outrank all of you in our assessment."

Not a single one of them believes me, except for maybe Brooke. I'll do it, though—I don't care how crazy they think I am. I'll get the top score, and then they'll respect me. I may be a joke, but this is me standing up for myself. This is me putting in effort.

"You'll see. You'll all see."

Chapter 8

The tomorrow I've been waiting on has finally come. I stride into the testing site on the edge of campus with my head held high. I'm the first to salute Marcus and the other leaders present to watch our midterm assessment. This is my chance to prove everyone wrong. Nothing will hold me back. I've worked too hard for this.

No one thought much of me, but since my fight with Bianca, I hope they see I'm at least serious. I'm not sure when my blade will have an edge, but that doesn't matter. They can doubt me, think I'm a spy, but today I'll show them I'm for real.

There's little chance I'll get the highest score, but that's not the real goal. The trick is to make everyone see me give it my all. That way, when I take fifth place, they won't care. They'll just say, *Wow, great job. Looks like you do care.*

More than anything, today will be a day where I beat at least one person. Today I beat Bianca's score. Hers is the only score I actually care about topping. I want that Rockcliff-anthem-singing, do-gooder pixie to eat my shorts. It's going to feel so good holding that over her.

"Attention!"

The prime minister joins Marcus at the front. "It's time to see some progress, ladies and gentlemen. I hope you've all come prepared." His eyes fall on me. I remind myself to not look away. He'll be convinced when this test is over.

"Welcome, everyone," Marcus says, taking the lead. "Today is your midyear assessment. Beyond the basics of testing, this is an opportunity to show the improvements you've made. As you know, I've given each of you several areas to focus on to prepare you for the real thing. This is your chance to show me what you can do. Don't hold back. Give it your all, for country and humanity."

The first test is a simple aura-strength test, the second a field exercise simulating a real scenario. Our third and final test is combat readiness. This happens to be the most interesting, as we will fight alongside our partners against Marcus himself.

They call my name, and I make my way behind a small cinderblock wall. Now's my chance to outperform Bianca. The leaders of our military look down from their raised seating at the edge of the testing site. The prime minister doesn't look all that interested for someone who's made such a big deal about what I do.

"Okay Lucas, are you ready for your first test?" Marcus asks. "This one gauges your aura strength. While it seems simple, it reveals the natural bond between your aura and your blade."

This very well may be my worst score, since I can't summon my blade with an edge. I can't do anything about it, but that's okay. My goal is to show Bianca and the others that I'm a better fighter.

"You will summon your blade and place it here on this concrete block, releasing it from your grip. Once the weapon is not in your hand, a clock will start. The longer it can stay in form, the higher you score. Twenty seconds is the time to beat."

As I approach the table, the idea of failure sets in. This is a first for me. I've usually expected failure, embraced it even, but now I don't want that. I want to win.

Okay, focus, I chant to myself. *Summon and release.*

I examine my palms, visualizing my blade. With a deep breath, I close my eyes and pour my aura out into my hand. Now would be a good time to make that edge—I can only hope it works.

I give it my all, running my fingers down the blade, pressing it into an angular shape. Then, without opening my eyes, I place my blade on the concrete block, giving one last push of aura before releasing it.

"Very good," Marcus says.

I hear a gasp from the leaders. This prompts me to open my eyes. To no one's surprise, my blade remains without an edge. I'm disappointed. After all this time, I have yet to make my blade worth anything.

"That's a record!" Marcus says.

"A record?" I ask. No one looks like they believe it, not even me. Maxwell stands up to verify moments before it disappears. I must admit, I don't get it. Why is this important?

"One minute!" Marcus says. "Very well done. That's the longest ever. Congratulations, Lucas. If your blade Lucid had an edge, you might have the strongest weapon in Rockcliff."

If, I think to myself. "If" is the sound of failure. Like, if you were strong, you could have saved your mother. If you were wise, you would have run away on selection day. So this "if" means nothing but failure.

"Still a very good attempt," Marcus says, trying to play it up. "No one has ever made it that long before. Now, if you would follow me."

73

"Great, now after they kill me, they can look at the stick I tried to fight them with."

Marcus shakes his head and chooses not to respond. Instead, I follow him past the table to what looks like a series of wooden rooms. "This is a traditional military training course. You will run through the course, striking down all enemies marked as such. Spare all the innocents you come across. Don't forget it's timed, and if you kill any innocent people, it adds five seconds to your time."

Now that I'm in the start position, I see the times of the others. Bianca finished in two minutes and thirty-six seconds.

"When you're ready, Lucas."

This is my chance. I can't fail. My eyes now focus on the countdown above the first room. At the sound of a sharp beep, I sprint inside. There, three wooden cutouts that resemble Sinder soldiers stand armed and ready. I summon Lucid and strike them with ease.

The second room has five soldiers, plus one that pops up behind me after I enter. A quick spinning slash takes care of them as well. Next is a long hall. Assuming it's made to slow me down, I sprint all the way through it. Moments before I reach the end, a civilian cutout springs out from a false door. Without thinking, I twist my body, sending myself crashing through the wall next to her.

The third room is strangely full of civilians. I double-check to make sure there are no hidden soldiers behind them and then quickly make my way out the back. At the door, I'm met with a brightly painted Sinder Cogent. This one has a blade and swings it for my chest. I evade and cut through him, running through the next room.

The clock buzzes as I slide to a stop. Panting, I search for my time— two minutes and forty-two seconds. I'm crushed by the realization that I didn't beat Bianca's time. I'll never hear the end of it when she sees me.

It takes an hour for everyone to finish the first part. When everyone is done, we move to the other side of the training course. It's an arena about twice the size of our training room and with only one dedicated fighting platform. This platform is also three times the size to simulate a normal environment.

This is my last chance. Bianca's ahead. My only hope is to keep her from scoring more than me in this fight. I have to find a way, or I'll be a joke to them forever.

"Listen up!" Marcus shouts from the center of the platform. "This is your last test. It is a way to gauge your fighting skills both as a team and as individuals. I am your opponent, so don't hold back."

Everyone moans in discomfort. I hear whispers about how it's impossible and that no one has ever won. Hearing them, Marcus reminds us that there's always a first for everything. He says we should win, given that the numbers are in our favor.

No one here is dumb enough to think that two or even all eight of us together are strong enough to take down the Hero of Humanity.

"Now, just a reminder of the rules. Everyone will be given a red plate to wear on their chest. This plate represents your life. If your plate is broken, you lose the round. Don't worry though, points are still awarded based on your improvement. However, to the person who breaks my plate, an automatic maximum point value is given. Each team will get five minutes with me to show how you've improved."

Marcus attaches the red plate to his chest and calls out Brock and Liam to fight. As fourth years, they have the best shot at winning. They secure their plates to their chests—it's now time to see how two fourth years compare to the Hero of Humanity.

I wonder if they have a strategy for beating him. Brock is smart, and he knows how to lead people, so I'm sure he can work with Liam after all these years. I've never seen Marcus fight. It could be over in an instant or drag on. It may not even be possible to beat him.

With a crackling gunshot, the round begins. Brock and Liam hold their positions, not ready to charge in. Liam boosts his aura's intensity and summons Mischief.

"I've got this, Brock, don't worry."

"Don't rush in, stick to the plan."

"Your plan sucks."

Liam charges toward Marcus with a forward thrust. Marcus sidesteps past him and strikes him with an elbow to the back. Liam recovers, bouncing around him, striking from weird angles. He's intentionally not going head-to-head. Clearly, he knows he can't win against Marcus's strength. But what's the plan? Why isn't Brock fighting alongside him, and why is he going against Marcus alone, knowing he's outmatched one-on-one?

To everyone's surprise, Liam is doing okay by himself. He hasn't damaged Marcus's plate, but he has control of the fight. The man is dedicated to countering his wild strikes.

"This is getting old!" Marcus shouts, striking a preemptive block that trips up Liam. "You should fight together instead of on your own."

Liam lifts himself up, grinning from ear to ear. "But we are!"

Realizing it's a setup, Marcus turns, anticipating Brock's attack for his plate, but it's not there. Brock is flying through the air above him. With no time to react, Marcus grabs his blade and slams Brock to the ground. Liam sees a second chance and storms in with a side slash. Marcus counters by striking his wrist and disabling his blade. With Brock back up, he throws Liam into him with a fierce boom.

"That's a match," Marcus says.

Everyone is stunned. We missed the moment in which he broke both of their plates, but somehow, they're nowhere to be found. What a fight, though. That blind aerial attack would have defeated anyone else.

"Keep fighting like that, and someday you might take my place," Marcus says with a smile.

Even though Brock and Liam say they're grateful and thank him for the fight, I can tell they're disappointed. I'm sure they've been trying to beat him for years. They used both their styles together very well. Liam was a great distraction in such a well-executed blind attack.

"Don't let us down," he says, bumping fists with Brooke. "Go take him out."

I suppose none of us believe we'll win if Brock and Liam can't, but at the same time, we want to see it. At the sound of the gun, Brooke and Jean have their chance. Their approach is their own. They fight like one unit; Brooke is the blade striking from behind and Jean the shield catching and countering.

With their combined ability to strike fast and together, they slowly begin to overwhelm Marcus. At any moment, one of Brooke's precision strikes could take out his plate, and it's clear he knows it.

Their technique works so well, three minutes flash by in an instant, each attack inching them closer and closer to Marcus's plate. *Could they do it?* I wonder. He doesn't seem able to strike back against this style. *They might do it.*

Everyone leans closer in anticipation. Brooke extends into an opening, ready to remove the plate. It's perfect, but for whom? Marcus releases his recently countered blade and grabs Brooke's wrist, pulling her over Jean. With them separated, he summons his blade again.

They know they have to move back together, but Marcus won't allow it. Instead, he keeps himself positioned in between them, bouncing from one attack to the other. Then, with a swift motion, he twist the two girls into striking each other. They let out a frustrated sigh of defeat.

"No way did that just happen," Liam says.

"They had him," Cameer says, disappointed.

Marcus allowed them to be successful with their own fighting style, waiting for the strike he knew would come so he could execute. Still, a well-done fight by everyone. It's truly impressive to watch him fight.

Brooke and Jean salute Marcus, thanking him for the fight, before hugging each other and walking out of the arena. Marcus calls for a time out to change clothes. It seems Brooke really put his through the shredder.

With that out of the way, Ryan and Cameer join him in the ring. Ryan stands next to Cameer as if she's a small accessory. Their ability to fight together seems complicated, as their physical sizes don't properly match up.

They start their approach much as expected. Ryan is big enough and strong enough to go head-to-head, while Cameer runs to the outside. Ryan's oversized blade, Dissent, is a perfect match of power with Marcus's.

After a minute, their plan starts to become apparent. Cameer has gone around the ring several times, burning the ground to create a haze that she can move freely in while Ryan does his best to keep Marcus's attention.

"Very interesting. They might be able to do it!" I hear Brooke say.

The fight becomes difficult to see, and we're left with only glimpses of Cameer as she jumps in and out of the smoke, striking. Then with a loud boom, the haze is forced away. It seems Marcus has eliminated their cover using some sort of special technique.

But it may be too late. We watch in awe as Ryan is the first person to disarm Marcus.

"They have him," Brooke says.

"Not yet!" Marcus cries out. His hands become his weapons, as blow after blow he defends himself against their advances. Every move he makes is so calculated and refined, it only takes thirty seconds for him to disarm Ryan and Cameer.

"They need to summon their blades," Liam shouts.

"They don't have the time," Brock responds.

Before we can judge them further based on what they should be doing, their plates shatter with Marcus's punch, Ryan's first and Cameer's quickly after. They couldn't do it either, but they may have been the closest yet. I see that their power comes in many forms, both direct and indirect.

Marcus is visibly worn out for the first time, and it comes as a surprise when he asks for a five-minute break before our turn. Now that I've seen everyone fight, I need to consider what they've done well and why they lost.

I just need to remember to keep Bianca from gaining any points, and I'll have a chance. This is the moment when everyone will be watching. Knowing Bianca, she'll come out aggressive, trying to take control and score the most points before being defeated. I think it's a safe bet to say he'll beat us, but that's okay. So, my only choice is to be faster than her if I want to get on the board.

"All right, Lucas and Bianca. Let's do this," Marcus says, stretching as if he's just starting for the day.

My throat tightens, and my legs shake a little as I step up on stage. Marcus is a much more intimidating foe when facing him directly. All that charm and showmanship from when he's teaching and leading is out the window. He's serious, and he takes his enemy seriously.

"I hope you're ready," he says.

I look to Bianca, who seems confident as she takes her position. My eyes fall on the arena and all the markings of the past battles. This is going to be a challenge, but I want it. I'll make my statement here. To Marcus, Bianca, the leaders, and everyone else here. I'll show them I'm serious and that I'm in control.

My body matches the speed of the gunshot as I shoot past Bianca with a thunderous clap. I move forward with one goal and one goal only—stay in front of her. At full speed, I charge a bright blue Marcus and take my first strike against him.

His counterattack is effortless, and uses less strength than I thought. He redirects me past him, taking advantage of my momentum. Stumbling, I turn to see Bianca, now enraged. I can't allow her to fight him by herself. She'll gain to many points. I force myself between them, always stepping in front of her.

It doesn't take long for Bianca to realize what I'm doing. She tries her best to slide in, but I stay consistent in taking the lead, never allowing her to get more than one attack in at a time. Marcus seems to be allowing us to fight. I'm sure he doesn't want to end the round too quickly, or he may not be able to assess us.

Marcus loses his balance for a moment, and that's when Bianca manages to take over. I can't let this go on for too long, so I jump in even when there's not a spot for me. I almost lose my head to Bianca's attack, only to be met by Marcus redirecting my blade across her chest. The two of us twist together and crash to the ground.

"You've got to be joking!" Bianca yells in frustration.

I look down at her chest to see her plate cracked in two and then quickly glance at mine to see it's still whole. I'm the only one left now. I have to score more than Bianca right here.

It's my time to show them. I know Marcus won't actually hurt me, so maybe I can use that to my advantage. If I can get a few points off before he defeats me, that's all I'll need. It's time to use every attack he's ever shown me as quickly as possible. They don't have to be powerful, just fast, because I need to score before he takes me out.

Charging in with a cross slash, I follow up with every angle. I throw in every spin, feint, and counter he's ever thrown at me. Faster. Faster is my only goal—*don't worry about defending, he'll hit you anyway.* Each attack grows in speed until I hear it, the slight crack. Marcus's hand stretches out and launches me back into the air, my plate shattering from my chest before I hit the ground.

His fist is so powerful he didn't even need his blade to take me out. My chest throbs from the force of his punch. Then I see it—his plate sliced in half by the thinnest crack. But did it happen before or after his punch?

"That was close," he says with a big smile. "I knew you two would be strong together. That may have been the best fight of the day." He extends his hand to lift us onto our feet. "There is such passion from the two of you when you fight together. I could feel it. Your fighting chemistry is on another level. With three more years of training, you two will be an unstoppable force for humanity."

"Chemistry?" That's not chemistry. I think Marcus is blind to her desire to destroy me. We both want one thing—to beat the other person.

"Good job, Lucas," Bianca says, shocking me to my core.

"Are you for real?" I ask.

She nods. "You did good."

79

I'm not sure what's happening. Five seconds ago, she wanted to kill me, and now she's singing my praises. It's stressful just hearing a compliment from her. What's next? Is she going to kiss me or something?

Never mind that craziness. I can't help but wonder how everyone will score. Marcus's words were nice, but a compliment isn't a high mark. Even though I didn't crack his plate before he broke mine, I did manage to last longer than Bianca.

After he receives all the cards from the judges and slides on another fresh shirt, he gets us in formation. "Here are your scores. Remember the categories: aura strength, field exercise, combat, and field potential. In each category, you can score up to one hundred points. And remember, a low score can still win fights, so don't beat yourself up if you didn't score the highest."

I wonder if that last comment was directed at me.

"Brock, you have great dedication and strength. Ninety in aura strength, eighty-six in field exercise, ninety-one in combat, and eighty-three in field potential. A total of three hundred and fifty. Well done. You have a strong sense of leadership, but you lack creativity."

Liam gives a shout and starts the applause. I think he looks up to Brock. Anytime there's an opportunity to support him, he does. And what's not to love about Brock, anyway? He's the shining example of a perfect soldier. He will make a great leader one day.

Brock has become the standard against which everyone compares their scores. Liam, Brooke, and Jean all score around three hundred and twenty. It seems everyone is doing well compared to their past scores.

"Now for Ryan—you showed impressive improvements and dedication to your craft. You scored a ninety-two in aura strength, seventy-three in fields, ninety-five in combat, and ninety in field potential, for a total of three hundred and fifty. Congratulations."

I'm stunned, along with everyone else. He tied Brock, and he's only a second year. Can anyone really do better than that? I mean, the guy went head-to-head with Marcus for a long time.

"Now for the last two. Bianca, I must say, for a first year you have a natural understanding of this. Your family would be proud."

"Thank you, sir."

"I know it's hard to have two blades of that size going at the same time, so keep at it. In aura strength, you scored eighty-five, field exercise an eighty-five, combat readiness an eighty-five, and field potential a ninety. That's three hundred and forty-five."

Her score places her right behind Ryan and Brock. It's no surprise to anyone that she did so well as a first year. Now I realize my dream of beating her was a bit ridiculous.

"That leaves Lucas. You still have a long way to go. You have yet to summon an edge on your blade, so despite setting a record time, in aura strength, you received a ninety."

I guess I can't say I'm surprised. I wish I could figure it out, I do. Nothing is more irritating that carrying around an oversized glow stick. At least when I take the lowest score, maybe I won't be too far from them.

"During the field exercise, you missed an enemy and dismembered a few others, giving you a seventy-three, but in the combat exercise you performed excellently with Bianca, showing great improvement as you complemented her very fast and aggressive fighting style. For that, you scored an eighty-seven."

Those scores aren't too bad—it's this last one that will kill me. Basically, what the leaders see in me, which would net me a zero. "You have a lot of potential, Lucas. You may not know it or see it, but I do. So, for potential ability, you received an impressive one hundred. That gives you a total score of three hundred and fifty."

"Three hundred fifty? But that's the high score Ryan and Brock got, the highest. And I . . ."

"Congratulations," Brooke says. "I've always known you were pretty good."

There must be mistake. The math doesn't add up, right? How could they see that much in me? They think I have the most potential, but it doesn't make sense. Just the other day I was a spy to them.

I look to the leaders for some sort of clue as to their ratings, but I don't get anything. The prime minister simply makes his exit as all of us are left in shock.

"Congrats," Brock and Liam say, patting me on the back.

"I did it," I say. I did what I said I would do. I finished this the way I wanted. The feeling is overwhelming—this kind of thing doesn't happen to me. My only hope is that it was enough to convince everyone here that I'm not worthless.

"Great job, everyone. The rest of the day is yours," Marcus says with a prompt salute.

And with that, everyone takes their leave. Bianca doesn't say anything more to me; she accepts her defeat gracefully. I almost wonder if I've made things worse between us. Does she feel threatened by me now? Does she hate me even more? Marcus said we have fighting chemistry, but I still don't agree with that. If we have any chemistry, surely it's the volatile kind.

Chapter 9

Uncontrollable. It's the only feeling I've ever had consistently in my life. Every time I feel like I've gained a hold on my life, it slips through my fingers. When I thought I had a family with Miss Caroline, they made me a Cogent. Just as things were going smoothly with Katelynn, I was almost killed. Now that I have everyone's respect, I can only wait for the day I inevitably let them all down.

It's been two weeks since the exam, and that respect has been hard to keep. I know I can't stay in their good graces. It's like the day I became a Cogent. I think I knew deep down things would get worse. It's almost as if my life is on a set track, and the most I can do is pause for a moment. I'm even not sure the Mover of Life loves me some days. Maybe I'm just tolerated?

"Hey, Lucas! Quit spacing out," Bianca says with a back kick to my chest.

I do my best to shake it off as I take her hand and rise to my feet. "Sorry. I was thinking of all the things I have to do today. The Military Ball is tonight, and I still haven't gone to the orphanage to get my suit."

"Well, you can daydream about it after we're done training. If we want to beat Marcus for the end-of-the-year exam, we're going to train like it's going to be here tomorrow. And you promised me you would train with me every day. That includes today."

A quick look around the empty training room fills me with regret. That promise I made to her after the fight was one of the dumbest things I've done. Honestly, I didn't know she would include the weekend. She's real persistent, though, and when she says every day, she doesn't just mean the weekdays. That's how I've ended up here, training, on the morning of the biggest day of my life.

"You're doing it again!" Bianca says, throwing a right hand across my cheek. The last time she slapped me was the first day we met. If she wants to relive that moment, I can make it happen. I slide in on her next strike and rotate her around my body until she slams into the ground. This time, I make sure to avoid groping her.

"Now who's not paying attention?" I say with a smirk.

She smiles, which throws me off. With a quick rotation, she quickly knocks me back, leaving us both defeated, lying on the ground. "I didn't know you could smile," I tell her.

"Don't get used to it—I've just been having a good morning."

"You're the only one that loves training that much."

My last comment must set her off, because she jumps back on top of me, ready to finish the job. Pinning me to the ground, she reminds me that she's the more skilled fighter. I laugh as if that's all that matters, and she does too. She smiles again.

"What?" she asks.

It's kind of cute, I guess. I've never thought of Bianca as cute, but I suppose she is. And maybe this is her starting to trust me. It's nice to not be attacked for breathing. I guess she's not so bad once she warms up to you.

"I like this side of you," I say.

My words seem to catch her off guard—the idea that someone can find her pleasant, I suppose. It's nice, though—I really do like this side of her. I could see her being a normal person, whatever that looks like for Cogents like us.

"So, Bianca, are you going to the Ball tonight?"

With a big sigh, she looks out the large glass windows. "Nah, I don't think I will. I'm not into all that kind of stuff."

"All that kind of stuff?" I ask. "You mean fun and dancing. And just when I was beginning to think your normal."

She laughs my comment off. "I've had my fun for today. I don't think going would make this day any better."

"Well, if you decide to, I'll save you a dance, okay? Under one condition, though—you let me lead."

She looks over at me and graces me with another rare smile. "As if I'd let you be in charge. If you were leading, you'd probably trip and pin me to the floor again."

The laughs we've shared this morning are refreshing after the ominous feelings I've had as of late. Maybe training these past few weeks wasn't so bad. The sessions were long and hard, but I feel a little fulfilled by completing this semester. This could be the start of a new future for Bianca and me.

After lunch, I muster up the courage to go back to the orphanage. Earlier this week, I sent a letter to Miss Caroline asking if she could get me a suit. While most people will probably be wearing their formal military suits, many of us have decided to wear our own. It's one of the few times we can dress however we want. I'm sure most of the girls will choose a dress over pants for the occasion. I can only hope that, in my suit, I look like I belong by Katelynn's side.

Back at the orphanage, I find myself less sad than I thought I would be. Most of my life was spent there, but for some reason that now seems like only a brief moment. The front door still seems to be jammed, so I improvise a little cutout to help it open. The building needs more love than I can give it, but at least it's one thing fixed.

Once inside, I expect someone to notice me, but I'm disappointed to find that no one is here. I take a step toward the kitchen table and pretend as if nothing has changed. The fruit and vegetables from the garden are still readily available for us to snack on. I take a big bite of apple; it really brings me back. I feel at home.

"Lucas?"

I don't recognize the voice, but I'm glad to finally be noticed.

"Lucas, is that you?"

Before my eyes is my friend, but he's grown somehow. He's different. "Justin—is that really you?"

"Whoa. Look at you. They really made you a Cogent? I can't believe it," he says, giving me a cross-examination.

"Me? Look at you—why are you so big? And your voice is so deep."

He gives me a very serious look. "After you left, everything changed. The boys all started being nice to each other, there was this sudden abundance of food, and I finally felt I was able to grow—because there wasn't someone eating everything."

I place the apple on the table, feeling like I've offended him. "Just kidding," he says with a quick air jab at me. "But don't think I can't kick your butt still just because you're a Cogent now. I told you. One year and I'll be there."

"Sure. I'll see you next year. Hey, is that a mustache?"

He grins. "Sure is. The ladies are gonna be all over me when I get to the Academy."

"Yeah, okay, but be serious for a minute. Where's Miss Caroline?"

"She's in her office. Is that really the end of our conversation? You haven't seen me in like six months—what's up? You got to tell me about this stuff, man. Like, what's this white sunlight stuff coming off you? You look freaking sweet."

I know he means well, and I do miss him. A conversation with him would be great, but I don't really have the time for that. I still have to get ready for this dance. "It's my aura."

"Does it hurt?"

I shake my head. "No, it doesn't, but it's strange from time to time. I don't remember what it's like to be cold. I'm hot all the time. Crazy thing is I have to drink constantly just so I don't explode from the inside out."

"For real? Maybe I don't want that."

"Yeah, it's not all great."

"I'm sorry. I know that's not what you wanted. I know how you felt about it, I was just trying to help you feel good."

His excitement and playfulness was all for me—he'd probably been thinking about what to say to me for so long. He even remembered how I felt about becoming a Cogent. "Thanks Justin. It's good to see you."

"So do they work you real hard?"

"My partner does, at least. The rest aren't too bad. I think you'll like them when you join next year and become a Cogent."

"Oh, I almost forgot. I should salute you." His hand jumps up to his head as he gives me a formal greeting. "What do you think?"

I laugh. "It's great, thanks. At ease."

Justin makes himself comfortable, leaning against the wall. "You know what, I was talking to the other boys here a couple days ago. We were talking about the barrier keeping us safe. I don't really think that's why we're safe here anymore. I like to think it's because of you."

"I don't protect anyone."

His words are incredibly nice. I know he's a really good friend, but I don't know how to tell him I'm probably the weakest Cogent ever made. No blade. No talent. I'm lucky to even be alive right now. I can still recall that Sinder Cogent, Hatcher, laughing at me.

I don't want to talk about any of this, though. "So, have you been keeping up with your training? You look stronger."

He pulls a confident flex to show me. "Every day. I decided if they could let a loser like you become a Cogent, I'll have a great shot at it."

There's no stopping him joining the Academy next year, but I hope they don't pick him. I don't really want this for him, even though I go back and forth about having him there with me.

"I'll see you next year, then. I expect you to be twice as big."

He smiles and nods. "All right, I'll quit harassing you and save some for when I can get you in a headlock again."

With a quick salute, he dismisses himself to the back of the house. I follow for a moment, pausing at Miss Caroline's door. I knock, interrupting a conversation she's having with someone.

Upon opening the door, I see it's the director of our city's food bank. In the past, he's helped the orphanage with extra food. A decent guy. I feel he doesn't get the recognition he deserves for his hard work.

"Lucas! Welcome," she says, standing up. "Have a seat."

The director takes his leave, and out of habit, I follow her command. Taking a seat, I feel like a little boy again, in trouble for something. But I've done nothing wrong. It's she who should be in trouble. I have to hold back, though—that's not why I'm here. Nothing has changed between us, but I still need this suit.

"Here you go," she says, draping the suit over her desk. "It's a suit from the old world, very classy. I recommend wearing your heat resistant base clothes underneath. I don't know how well it will hold together."

"Thanks."

"You know, I wasn't sure I'd hear from you for a while. The last time we spoke, you seemed upset."

I nod and smile through my closed mouth. I know what she wants, but I don't want to give it to her. An answer is too generous, given how few answers she's given me.

"Go on," she says.

"You owe me an explanation."

"For what, sweetie?"

"You know what! I saw you the day I became a Cogent. I know you were the nurse that injected me. I saw your face through the mirror. And you were there counseling Maxwell after my date with Katelynn."

She fixes her tight gray curls with a soft pat. "Lucas, I was invited. I'm your moth—"

"No, you're not. And you shouldn't have been there. There was no reason for you to be there. I want to know why I keep seeing you at the Academy when you're supposed to be here at the orphanage."

She holds firm. "I told you, I was invited. And I want to be there for you when I can."

I'm so upset I don't even notice my hand slice through her desk. "Like you were there for me the day they made me this monster? Some good that did."

"Lucas Andrew Conley! You will not talk to me like this. I've raised you better than that. I will not sit here and listen to you treat me as if I'm not the woman who raised you. There are some things in life that you have to let go of and move on from."

I let my fist drop to my side in defeat. I want to love her; I want this to be different, but it's not. She lied to me, and she's hiding something. I don't want to move on, but maybe I should. "You're right, I don't belong here anymore."

Without looking at her face, I grab my suit, thank her for it, and leave.

It takes me about two hours to calm myself back down. I'm exhausted coming up with excuses for her. More than anything, I want her to have a good explanation, but after seeing her with our prime minister, I'm inclined to believe she planned this all along. The orphanage is probably some sort of place they want to start taking kids from and turning them into this. That way, when they die, no one will care. And now there's no time for me to care. Katelynn will be here at any moment.

With a few gentle slaps across my face, I try to focus my attention on the bottom of the school stairs. Moments later, she arrives in a long black car with silver trim. It's probably the nicest personal vehicle in the city. With a loud click, the driver hops out and opens her door. Her slim leg extends as she emerges like a beautiful butterfly, her dress a magnificent yellow. About half the school stops in their tracks to witness her arrival.

"Wow. You look amazing," I say to her.

She gracefully lifts her dress to clear the last step. "Thank you. I love your suit," she says, flashing a big smile. "And you wore your necklace. I thought you lost it." She clasps her matching necklace, which she's worn every day since school started.

"I usually don't wear it, because I'm afraid to lose it. Or you know, melt it."

"Don't worry, I can get you another if it does," she assures me.

"Shall we?" I say, extending my hand before realizing what a stupid thing that is to do.

"Yea. Let's go have fun."

At the door, we're greeted by several active duty soldiers in uniform. They are holding up metal swords point to point, creating a tunnel.

Normally, these soldiers are stationed on the wall, but tonight they're here for us.

We follow the flow of people into the school until we make it to the event room. It is like nothing I've seen before. The main lights are off, but several smaller colored lights sweep rapidly across the floor to the sound of music.

After a few minutes of looking, I spot Brock and the others off in the corner. Their auras blend in well for once. I'll say hi to them soon, but for now I just want to be with Katelynn. Tonight is all about her, after all.

"So, what should we do first?" she asks. "How about pictures?"

"Of course," I say. I think a picture is a great idea. That way I can show all those snot-nosed kids back at the orphanage that I was serious when I said I was dating the hospital chief's daughter.

No one tells you how awkward pictures can feel, especially when you can't touch someone for more than a second. They put her in a chair in front of me. I hope she's smiling, or everyone might think I'm holding her hostage.

They tell us the pictures won't be ready for a few hours, but that's okay, because Katelynn's thirsty now. On our way to get drinks, she lets out a huge shriek of excitement. Her friends lock eyes with her and run into her arms. I remember Niki from the sparring test on our first day. She's wearing a similar yellow dress, but not of as nice a quality. It seems she still wants to be just like Katelynn.

After a few moments of them sharing stories, I decide to make my entrance. I give the girls a general compliment on their clothes and follow up by handing Katelynn the drink we walked over to get. A few more girls join, growing the group to an uncomfortable size. At this point, I think it's best to watch in silence.

I'm not sure if they're genuine or jealous, or if there's even a difference. Everyone loves Katelynn—her curls, her dress, her elegance. Some of them are even proud of her for dating me, like I'm some sort of charity case.

The bell chime echoes through the room, safely stopping the cackling laughs of young girls. Our anthem begins to play, and a line of soldiers march straight through the dance floor to the stage, proudly carrying our Rockcliff flag.

Commander Marcus walks up to the mic. I think some of the girls are disappointed he's wearing a shirt today. "Remember, soldiers—remember

89

why we are here tonight. Tonight is a reminder that we can celebrate our lives thanks to the soldiers that defend us each day. Soon, it will be your turn up on that wall, defending the students who will celebrate you. So be proud, have fun, and stay safe! For country and humanity!"

A round of applause breaks out as he walks off. Brock appears next and cites the Rockcliff pledge. "I pledge allegiance to the Flag of Humanity and to the Rock for which it stands, one nation under the Giver, indivisible and unwavering, with justice and hope for us all."

At the end of the pledge, it's customary for soldiers to take the salute hand angled over the heart and create a fist. Then we pound our hearts and let out a grunt of power. This always makes me feel uncomfortable, as if someone is watching me pretend.

Marcus steps up to the mic once more, and this time introduces Prime Minister Maxwell. The crowd cheers as the man enters the spotlight.

"Welcome, welcome," he says, raising his hands to quiet the cheers. "Ladies and gentlemen, welcome to our Military Ball. I hope that all of you are ready for a great time. I want to take a moment to thank all of you fine men and women who put your lives on the line to protect humanity from the evil beyond this barrier. And I especially want to thank the Cogents who gave up their own humanity to fight for our safety on the front lines, going toe to toe with evil. For humanity!"

His last words echo through the room. It's a nice sentiment, I suppose, but one that misrepresents my experience with the process. To this day, I've never wanted this, and yet no one cares.

"Let's go dancing," Katelynn says, rushing over to the dance floor as the music resumes.

I know she means well, but fast-paced dancing isn't going to work out for me. Everyone would move twenty feet back from me if I did, and she should too. I wouldn't dance even if I could, though—it's not my thing. She must understand this. I think that's why she doesn't continue asking. Instead, she has fun with her friends, like she should.

She makes sure to check on me after each song. This next one is different, though—it's slow, and the girls quickly break up their group and find their dates.

"Can I have this dance?" Katelynn is smiling up at me.

I shake my head, wondering why she would even ask, but then she surprises me. From under her dress, she pulls out two long white gloves.

Her hands meet mine as she pulls me out onto the dance floor. I'm left in shock as she continues to hold my hands without burning. She's done something, but how?

"Surprised?" she asks. "I had these made from the tough, heat resistant fibers they make your Cogent uniforms out of. I know it won't last forever, but they should last a dance or two tonight."

"I don't know what to say. I—I don't deserve you."

"Do you believe that?" she asks.

I joke, "Well, our prime minister can't believe you love me."

She smiles. "The prime minister doesn't see what I see."

"And what do you see?"

"Lucas."

Her words are simple and deep. To be seen as just me is overwhelming. For so much of my life, I've wanted to be seen as something different. Not the eldest in the orphanage, the son of a slain mother, a hopeless soldier. She sees me, the real me.

Gliding over the dance floor with her hands in mine, I can feel the Mover of Life's love for us. I pray to hold on to this moment for any amount of time. No matter how long it lasts, it will never be long enough. With the end of the song, she releases my hands and quickly hides the damage I've done to them.

"How about another break?" I propose.

"Yeah. That sounds great. I'll be right back—I want to go check on the pictures."

Katelynn is truly something special. I don't know where I would be without her. I just wish she wouldn't try to pretend like everything is okay all the time. She can hide the discomfort she feels in her hands from everyone else, but not me.

"Hey Lucas!" Brooke calls to me from the corner of the room. "Come join us."

She and the others continue their so-called dance moves, but it almost looks like sparring without blades. I wonder if Brooke has any ideas for me tonight. You never know what that girl has cooked up.

"You two are so cute," she says while giving me a hug. "You know you can dance over here with us."

Liam bumps into me, nudging me out of the way. "Sorry about that. Just need my dance partner back," he says, grabbing Brooke's hand and spinning her around.

Cameer fills the awkward space left in front of me. "Where's Bianca?"

"I don't know if she's coming. Where's Ryan?" I ask. She shrugs and says she was hoping to dance with him later but hasn't seen him all afternoon.

I know she has a fondness for him—I think everyone does. "I'm sure he'll turn up soon."

"Lucas," I hear from behind me.

I turn and find myself without words. Bianca came. She went all out, too. Her sleek red dress looks masterfully put together. Her purple hair swoops down her cheeks, framing her smile.

"Wow. You look nice. You're like a different person," I admit.

She smiles and looks down at herself. I can tell she's not sure how she feels. "Well, it's different. I guess you might be right—I'm allowed to have some fun from time to time too."

I nod. "Absolutely."

"Hello! You must be Bianca, Lucas's partner. It's so nice to meet you," Katelynn says, sliding in in front of me. "I love your dress, by the way—did you make it yourself?"

Bianca looks off to the side and nods. I'm not sure if that's true or not. If she'd made her dress, she would have had to work on it for a few weeks. With all the training we've been doing, when would she have had the time? Plus, that would mean she intended to go the whole time. Besides that, she only ever wears tank tops—she's not like Brooke, who's always wearing a skirt over her uniform.

"She looks nice, doesn't she?" I say to Katelynn, hoping Bianca can feel a little more self-assured about it. She never acts shy like this. She usually commands attention so much that she's hard to look away from.

I think my comment gives her confidence, though, as she looks me in the eye once more and talks directly to me. "Hey Lucas, thanks again for training with me so much recently. It means a lot to me that we get that extra one-on-one time."

Then the strangest thing happens—Bianca leaps into my arms and gives me a hug. I tell her it's no big deal, but she seems really overjoyed about it. I've never seen her so happy.

"Thank you," she says. "You're the best."

With Bianca tightly gripping my waist, Katelynn turns to me and, her voice filled with rage, says, "I'm really happy for you two!" Then she storms off.

Bianca and I are left confused as to what just happened. "What was that about?" she asks.

I rack my brain trying to understand. What did I do to make her mad at me? When I realize it, I can't believe I was so stupid. Bianca can hug me without a second thought, and Katelynn can't. I need to tell her it's nothing. Bianca and I are just friends.

"So, about that dance?" Bianca asks.

Across the room, I see Katelynn find her friends once more. "We can dance in a minute. I just have to take care of something," I tell her.

I make my way to Katelynn slowly, allowing myself time to practice my apology. There isn't a good way of saying sorry that some other girl can touch me freely because she's a Cogent. I honestly forget Bianca is a girl sometimes. She's so tough, I guess I feel like I'm back at the orphanage, fighting for my dominance.

Katelynn's still fifty feet away when the room's atmosphere shifts. Soldiers frantically rush in through the door. Katelynn makes eye contact with me, her face washed in fear. Time slows as I'm pushed farther and farther away from her, and then I can no longer see. I'm thrown into a dark abyss, my thoughts a fog and my ears ringing loud.

What is this?

I can't see my hands. I'm trapped. Trapped under piles of concrete, but how? An explosion. How is that even possible? From what? Was there an accident? My mind recalls the terror on Katelynn's face, prompting me to action. I summon my blade and begin hacking my way through the debris until I reach the top.

"Lucas!" Katelynn screams. "Are you okay?" Her panicked voice is a bit of relief—at least it means she's fine.

"Yeah, I'm okay," I say, climbing out.

"Something's wrong."

Something really is. The dance floor is now covered in debris from the collapsed roof. Screams of pain and fear blend together. I've been here before. I know what this is. It's exactly like the day I lost my parents. The war is here. We're under attack.

Part II

Chapter 10

For a moment, I can see two days at once: the day I lost my mother and today. The screams and fear-filled faces are interchangeable, indistinguishable from each other. The loud sirens pierce my ears as I try to orient myself once more. I can't help but see myself back in Sincliff, losing the person I loved most in this world. I'm afraid it will happen again.

Katelynn and I join the others, frantically digging to get everyone out of the rubble. We only stop when no more screams can be heard from below. I fear that if anyone else is still down there, they didn't make it.

Katelynn hastily shreds her once beautiful yellow dress to bits as she applies pressure to the wounds of those injured. She knows what she has to do in a time like this. I try to remind myself to move, to take action, but the thoughts of what's coming cripple me.

"Lucas! Get over here," Brock calls out as he gathers our class. "All right, everyone. The room should be secured now," he says, trying to catch his breath. "We have to join Marcus and the Cogent Guard—they're probably headed to the front line. Cameer was able to get some intel for us from a soldier's radio. It appears they're going toward the north gate. This is likely a Sinder attack. Please watch over your partners and protect them at all costs. Now, let's go."

I'm torn about my duties. I know I must protect and aid Bianca, but I'm not sure I can. Someone has to be here for Katelynn. She's working furiously to save these people. How can I go?

My indecisiveness doesn't matter to the rest of the group, as they quickly make their way out of the building. Bianca notices I'm not there and looks back at me, waving me on. Katelynn locks eyes with me. She seems worried.

"Don't leave me," she says. stopping me in place. "I know it's selfish . . ."

Her face says it all. She's afraid. I'm afraid too. I wish I could hug her right now, tell her it's okay, but I can't. And as much as I want to stay, I have to go. It would be best for me to keep them as far away from Katelynn as possible.

"I'm sorry, Katelynn. I have to . . ."

Adrenaline pumps through me at full force as I burst through the school doors and out into the city to join the others. I wasn't prepared for what I would find—Rockcliff is engulfed in flames. A city destroyed. I've seen this too many times in my life.

Brooke looks at me. "They took down the barrier. We're taking mortar fire."

They took down the barrier. But how? How is that possible? "The traitor!" I say aloud.

"What?" Brooke asks.

"The other day, when I got in trouble, the prime minister thought I was a traitor. He believed someone was meeting with the Sinder Army. Whoever disabled it knew how to—they could be there right now. We have to go stop them and get the barrier back up before it's too late."

"No," Brock says firmly. "It's already too late. That doesn't matter now. We must join the others on the front line. They will breach the city soon."

Everyone else agrees with Brock, and I'm inclined to follow his lead. I wish we could catch the traitor, but the damage is done. We have more important issues now. Our human soldiers can handle the recovery, but we have to be the defense that slows the Sinder Army's advance.

Even running as fast as we can, it takes about ten minutes to reach the north gate. As we get there, the aerial bombardment subsides. Marcus stands at the center of the gate with twenty Cogent Guards.

"Marcus," Brock shouts from several feet away, making sure he sees us. "We're here."

We watch as he radios several commands to our army before walking over. "Listen, there isn't a lot of time to explain. We are under attack. The Sinder Army is here, and this likely won't end well. I want you guys to stay out of this fight."

"But we're ready, sir," Brock says.

It's a strange moment to witness. Marcus wants to keep us safe, but he knows he will need all the help he can get. "All right. Brock, Liam, you're with us. Join the guard on the front line. Everyone else, I want you to hang back. If things go south, I'll need you to lead the evacuation. Get the civilians as far away from here as possible. Don't do anything stupid. These guys are here to kill you. Watch each other's backs."

Marcus looks at Cameer, and his eyes widen. "Where's Ryan?"

Cameer shakes her head and admits she hasn't seen him all day.

"All right, just stay together and you'll be fine," Marcus says, rejoining the front line.

Brooke becomes the active high-ranking officer in our group as Brock and Liam leave us. "Let's get to the wall," she says in a commanding voice. "It will be best if we have the high ground to see what's going on."

Everyone agrees and quickly falls in line as we scale up the steps leading to the top of the gate. Looking out, I can see several glowing soldiers off in the distance, along with what appears to be thousands of regular soldiers. Our troops meet them in combat, firing violently into each other before their Cogents quickly descend into the fight. The Sinder mortars begin to target their retreat, forcing them to face swift death at the hands of the Sinder Cogents.

I'm not sure what they plan on doing, but we're losing lives here. Finally, our Elite Cogents, the Palis Guard, step forward, led by Marcus. They give aid for our soldiers' retreat.

"Look, there's Brock and Liam," Jean says.

Brooke breaks from her commander role for a moment to shout to Liam. "Hey Liam! Don't do anything stupid. Come back to me!"

He looks back and nods. He'll take it seriously, I'm sure. One thing I've learned about him over these past few months is he knows how to shut it off if he really needs to. I feel bad that I didn't notice their relationship sooner. I always just talk about myself and Katelynn.

"Don't worry, Brooke—Brock has his back. He won't let anything happen to him."

I'm lying to her, of course. Nothing is guaranteed in war. I know that more than anyone. I wish it were different, but that's not what I've experienced. We must do our best to keep the people we love safe. I understand where she's coming from—I get it.

With all the intensity in the world, we watch as the hundred Sinder Cogents and five hundred human soldiers stop thirty feet from our insignificant twenty-two Cogent Palis Guards. After a minute, a man from the Sinder Army steps forward. He is much larger than most soldiers, and his ominous dark-purple aura rises and swirls a foot off his body.

Bianca whispers from somewhere in the group, "Is that Silas? Their leader?"

"I think so," Brooke responds.

"Don't worry, Marcus can handle him," I say, trying to bring down the tension. "He's beat him in combat before."

"Yeah, you're right. Marcus is the strongest Cogent that ever lived." Bianca pauses and takes a deep breath. "Thank you."

I force a smile and nod before turning my focus back to Marcus and Silas, who now stand only feet apart. We can do nothing but watch their two burning auras challenge each other. I imagine Silas is threatening his life. But Marcus is no coward. He will stand up for us. Our only hope is that he prevails here.

The two Cogent leaders seem to discuss their fight for a moment before drawing blades. Silas wields a two-handed weapon with a very sharp, triangular point. Marcus matches his intense aura and blade to meet him in battle. The fight we are about to witness will determine our futures—right here, right now.

It's fair to say Silas is skilled. After all, he holds his ground going head-to-head with Marcus. It's obvious that he will lose, though. Silas must realize this too, as he resorts to cheap tricks to gain any slim advantage that he can. When it becomes apparent these tricks won't be enough, he retreats behind his Feren Guards. It seems the terms of their duel have been nullified. Now it's ten on one.

"That's not fair!" Jean shouts. "We have to help him."

"We can't. He gave us a command," Brooke says. "Besides, the Palis Guard hasn't joined in yet. We have to trust him."

She doesn't believe herself though. I can see it in her face. Brook can't stand up here while the person she loves is down there, ready to fight. She would give anything to be by Liam's side, just like I would give anything to be by Katelynn right now.

"Look," I say, trying to draw attention to Marcus.

He's amazing. Even ten of Silas's Elite Feren Guards are nothing to him. Marcus's speed and proficiency is nothing short of legendary. I knew he was good, but I really had no idea how good he was. Seeing this makes me confident we can hold them off.

Even though Marcus hasn't killed anyone yet, it's obvious he will win. This must make Silas very unhappy, to see the Hero of Humanity so easily defending us against his Elite Feren Guards. As soon as the Palis join him, it will be over. He must be making a statement though, showing the enemy that our one is better than their Elite ten. It would strike fear in me.

"Marcus! Marcus!" The soldiers' chant spreads among all of Rockcliff.

His name has become power itself. As they chant it, I can feel the hope it brings us. He's the Hero of Humanity, and now I know why. No matter what tricks or overwhelming attacks they throw at him, he's ready with an answer for everything. He has become hope.

With the rallied support, everyone joins him in battle. They feel inspired by his abilities. Seeing this, Silas continues his retreat, waiting for the results of the battle. When everything settles down, we've lost three soldiers. That's harsh, but nothing compared to the fifty they just lost. Their confidence has diminished, and even though their Feren are mostly alive, they haven't hurt Marcus.

The game of numbers will soon flip in our favor, with Marcus counting for twenty men himself. It's Silas's move now, and all he can seem to do is retreat farther back.

This may not be over, but it seems Silas has recalled his Feren Guards. They haven't made any progress and only managed to hurt their numbers. They'll need a new plan if they want a chance at stepping foot in this city.

Liam screams with enthusiasm at Marcus's victory. Some soldiers come running out with a barrel of water to hydrate the man. It seems he needs a moment to recover, but that's to be expected after such a display. I feel better knowing their numbers don't mean anything against our strength.

Before the recovery can finish, a frantic scream for help comes from beneath us. The south gate has been breached. We finally locate the cry for help, and it's Ryan, running straight to Marcus. Stumbling before he makes it there, he manages to collect himself.

"They're at the south too?" Brooke asks.

Cameer steps forward, clenching her fist over her chest. I think she feared she had lost him. It's good to know he was out there helping—the dance probably seemed like a waste of time to him.

Marcus greets Ryan, who gives the details of the situation at the south gate. It seems their main force was here, so the ones that took the south were human only. I doubt they have more Cogents. He must have been fighting them the whole time, but couldn't keep up with their numbers. I have always been told their army is big, but I had no clue how vast they really are.

"We should get ready to help at the south gate," Brooke says.

We all agree, but then we hear Cameer gasp as if the life has been sucked out of her. Our eyes follow hers to the battlefield. The image that waits for us there is gruesome.

The air feels thin as our breaths leave our bodies in a collective gasp. Our hope is dying in front of us. Ryan's oversized blade is lodged in Marcus's back.

Marcus drops to his knees, searching for an explanation from his betrayer. His lips move, but only Ryan can hear him. We can do nothing, forced to watch as he slumps over, Dissent still jutting out from him, until he vanishes into a violent blue mist.

"Marcus . . ."

This has to be a dream. A nightmare. He was here a moment ago—he can't be gone. He's our hero. He was right here, but now . . . he's not. I pray the Giver of Life makes this make sense.

I want nothing more than for Brooke or Bianca to tell me I'm wrong. That I'm mistaken. But their faces have all confirmed it: our hope is gone. There is no hiding it. Cameer drops to her knees, ill. Brooke and Jean hold each other, and Bianca summons her blades, ready to fight.

While everyone is still in disbelief, Ryan runs to the Sinder Army. Hatred quickly fuels Brock and Liam as they lead the charge against him. Full-on war breaks out again while the five of us try to put ourselves back together.

"This isn't real. This isn't—" Brooke says.

Jean tries to comfort her for a moment before directing all her rage at Cameer. "What has he done? Why did he . . . How could he?"

Cameer sobs uncontrollably. She can't raise herself from her knees to accept what Ryan has done. It's obvious from her heaving that she had nothing to do with it.

Bianca is the only one who seems to still have herself under control. "She didn't know anything," she says, defending Cameer. "None of us could have seen this coming. Ryan betrayed us. We can't break down here. We must be strong, for Marcus and the others. Rockcliff needs us right now."

Brooke looks at Bianca and nods in agreement, signaling for her to continue.

"Now, this fight will probably not go our way. We need to follow his command and start the evacuation. We need to get everyone out of the city. They can take refuge in the towns to the west. Cameer, you can start here, on this side of town."

"I'll evacuate the school," I volunteer, hoping to influence her decision.

From her eyes, it's clear that she deciphers my intention, and yet she still allows it. "Lucas and I will take the school to the east; Brooke and Jean, you have the west."

"What about the south?" Cameer asks, still shaking.

Bianca acknowledges the possibility that Ryan may have been telling the truth, but says that it would be too risky to go there ourselves—we'll have to rely on the radio evacuation signal.

"You heard her," Brooke says, looking out over the fight.

It's chaos out there. Liam is getting overwhelmed. Brock manages to save him from a deadly blow that has Brooke biting her fingers. I hate to leave them; I know she does too. This is our job, our instructions. "Hang in there!" she calls to him.

"We have to go," Bianca says, trying to pull us away from our own self-defeat.

"She's right," I say, focusing on Katelynn. "We have to get as many as we can to safety."

Without further hesitation, I take off toward the Academy. Katelynn is surely waiting on me to come back. I'll have to get her to safety as soon as possible. Unfortunately, we seem to be too late. The school looks abandoned.

For a moment, I lose myself. What could have happened? Bianca has to talk some sense into me. "They've probably all gone to their posts. That's good. I wasn't sure if everyone would know to do that."

"Yes." If she's right, that means Katelynn is taking the injured to the hospital on the south side of town now. I recall the army Ryan spoke of. I hope he was lying. Either way, I have to get there now. Bianca calls out for me to wait, but I don't stop. I can't.

Moving at a full sprint, it's not long until I can see the towering hospital from the south. Fire blazes from the side of the building. I realize I can't be taking roundabout paths if I plan on getting there before the Sinder Cogents do, so I plow through walls and obstacles that would stop most normal people. I must get there faster. I can't hold back. I have to keep pushing through wall after wall, building after building.

As I slide to a stop in front of the hospital, I notice a long line of Rockcliff civilians. It appears I'm too late. The Sinder Army is taking them as prisoners, killing those who refuse to or can't go.

Instantly, our attackers notice me. They radio for support, and Ryan is the one to answer the call. I want to end him, to destroy him, like he did

Marcus. But then I see Katelynn escorted out of the building. If Ryan sees her, I know he will use her against me. I have to distract him, allowing her some distance.

"Ryan!" I yell, commanding his attention. "You traitor!"

Katelynn recognizes my voice. Our eyes meet, and I can tell she's figured it out. She shakes her head as if to tell me not to fight him. But I have to. If I don't kill him now, I will lose her forever. There has to be a way to save her.

Ryan steps forward, unresponsive to my taunt, his face expressionless, eyes empty of any light. I shout at him, reminding him what kind of vile garbage he is until I finally snap. My hatred for him propels me forward. I'm ready to kill him, to beat him to death in order to get to Katelynn. I don't care if my blade has no edge. I'm ready to do it.

"Ryan, I found you!" someone shouts from my side. It's Cameer, Pain and Purpose already drawn in her hands. "He's mine, Lucas!"

She steps between us with a look of vengeance. I can't blame her. I know she respected him, probably even adored him. Often she would speak for him in training, trying to help us see what we didn't. The blade he put through Marcus must have felt like it went through her as well.

"How could you, Ryan? Marcus was our leader. He trained us, he protected us, and you—you betrayed him." She looks at her hands holding her blades, no doubt contemplating what she's about to do.

Her voice shifts from anger to sadness. "You betrayed me—why?"

Nothing.

"Answer me!"

His face is like a stone wall, devoid of any emotion. He would have to be disconnected to kill our commander. Ryan can't explain his way out of this. He knows his sins. It's unforgivable.

"Draw your blade, or don't," she says. "Either way, you die here."

Then Cameer leaps forward, going straight for Ryan's neck. She darts around him in an orange flash, the kind that earned her the nickname "sunlight assassin." Somehow, Ryan manages to stay alive. Blow after blow, she whittles him down until she's landed so many small strikes that he stumbles backward, immobilized.

Ryan drops his blade, accepting his defeat. He can't counter her with words or a weapon anymore, and now it's time he gets what he deserves. I hate the feeling of gratification I feel as she places her blades on his shoulders like a large pair of scissors, ready to take off his head.

For a moment, I can see her struggling. She knows what she must do, but she can't bring herself to finish it.

"Cameer. Don't do it," I say. "I know he deserves it, but it just doesn't seem right."

She looks back at me as if she's crying, but because we are cursed, there are no tears. "Forgive me," she begs. "I have to set this right."

She closes her eyes, unable to look at him. I too look away until I can no longer hear the crackling of a Cogent blade as it goes through a body. When I look back, Cameer's body glows with an intense orange light, surging so bright I can only see her outline. Eventually, her glow collapses inward and bursts into a sparkling, gas-like substance.

The absence of her aura confuses me. She is supposed to be there, and Ryan isn't. Instead, Hatcher, the soldier from my previous attack, has taken her place, along with her life. He stands there looking gleeful as Ryan and I struggle to understand what just happened.

"Don't worry, Ryan, I got you. We almost lost you for a second. Wouldn't want our war hero losing his life after defeating the legendary Marcus, now would we?"

Hatcher lifts Ryan to his feet as his two companions, Hara and Bear, join him. It's at this moment I know I must run, but my legs won't move. I know they will kill me, but what do I do, where do I go?

"Ah, I see the anger in your eyes," Hatcher says. "Was that someone you cared about? A friend, perhaps? Good."

He drops his blade as if to taunt me into attacking, knowing it's four on one. "You know, I'm sure I've seen you before. No? Oh, that's right, you're the dumb rookie that can't even summon a proper weapon. I thought I told you to get stronger for the next time we meet. Didn't you know I was coming back?"

"I'm sorry, Cameer," I say, hoping the Mover of Life will carry the message to her. I should kill each one of them. Stop them right here. It's worth the attempt—until I remember Katelynn asking me to run.

"You'll regret this," I tell Hatcher. "You don't realize what you've done. You just guaranteed your death, and you don't even know it . . ."

Katelynn looks back at me for a moment before reaching up and squeezing her necklace, as if to tell me to trust the Mover and Giver to bring us back together in the end.

My lips move before I can even process my feelings. I will find a way. I will not give up. She has to know that I haven't abandoned her, that I will find her again.

I yell to her, "I'M COMING BACK FOR YOU!"

Chapter 11

Thirty seconds—that's all the time I'll get to make my escape. My legs pump with an unrivaled ferocity. I have no other choice, I tell myself. The only way to save Katelynn is if I run away right now. I have to go faster. If I'm too slow, they'll catch me and kill me, and no one will come for her. I'm all that's left, and she needs me.

Don't turn around. It will only slow you down. I can't help it though. I find myself ignoring my own advice. Upon looking back, I see the trio is out for blood. I'm sport to them, the prey running for dear life. My head will be mounted above their dinner table in the end.

I'm barely fast enough. A few steps too slow, and I'll be a goner. Obstacles mean nothing to them, so how will I create any distance? Maybe if I can hide somewhere, I can buy enough time to get away. My mind at once jumps to the place with the most buildings crammed together—the market.

As I head toward it, I summon Lucid, dragging the blade along the ground behind me as I run. I'm hoping to stir up a bit of a smoke screen, like Cameer did in her fight against Marcus. Nearing the center of the market, I slam myself into the ground and spin around as fast as possible, lifting the dirt and concrete into a haze. I bolt into the second-closest shop and lie down.

Thankfully, the three Sinder Cogents go rushing by. I can finally rest. For a moment, I can slow my breathing. Once I've done this, I realize how thirsty I've become. At the rear of the store there seems to be some water. Bottle after bottle, I drink until I'm full. The back door swings open, clanging loudly as it hits a shelf.

A terrified boy enters and slams the door shut, resting against it. When his eyes meet mine, he screams as loud as he can. He must think I'm the enemy. I assure him I'm not, but he cries anyway. I tell him I can keep him safe, but that's not true. He removes his hands from his chest to reveal the bullet hole through his stomach and then slumps to the ground.

What am I doing? What is happening? I can't seem to find the answers to any of my questions.

"There you are," Bear says, peering through the store window. They've come back.

I take off through the store wall, only to be met by an arm to the face. My head jerks back, and the world spins rapidly. I know I have to regain my focus; he won't hesitate to kill me. The bright light is all I see as I avoid its growing size. Strike after strike, I elude him with nothing more than instinct.

Bear's attacks grow more rapid, but I'm limited. It's only a matter of time until his blade connects. I've had some close calls in practice before, even some small cuts, but never an attack meant to kill me.

When his blade hits my shoulder, I can feel the inside of my body for the first time. I'm not supposed to feel this. My body wants to scream along with my voice. This can't be real. He grins. "Oh, bet that stings."

Bear removes his blade slowly, and an overwhelming smell of burned flesh overtakes me. I can't be done here. I know I have to get out of this. I believe the Mover of Life will get me out of here. It has to be true, but I fear it's not.

"I can't give up here!" I yell at him. It's not for him—it's for myself. It gets me thinking though, and that's all I need. My eyes settle on the gas tank outside the shop. With my blade in hand, I throw it, causing an instant explosion. It won't hurt him, but it should blind him for a moment.

Sweeping his legs out from under him, I rush out through the explosion as fast as I can. I know I don't have time, but I have to look at my wound while running. I remember Marcus's advice to apply pressure and increase my aura heat to seal it.

I'm slower this time, but I have more distance. I need to make the best of it. My shoulder throbs with pain, reminding me I'm not stable. Water is the only answer, but I need a lot of it. My ears catch the sound of rushing water and I realize I'm still near the river that runs through town. Here's my chance to gain the separation I need.

I make my way to the top of the wall with my three assailants still hot on my trail. This is my chance. I leap from the wall, gripping my shoulder tight. This should be enough—surely, they won't pursue me over the cliff.

During the fall, my body becomes relaxed. There's nothing to do but embrace this moment. I've given up slowly as I sink to the bottom. If they come, I'm dead. All I can do is wait anxiously underwater, watching for any sign of light. It never comes.

Eventually, the bubbles lift me to the surface and carry me downstream. I had hoped to make that jump again under better conditions, showing off for some new recruits possibly, maybe having a laugh after about how I got stuck in the barrier the first time.

Exiting the water, I see there isn't much left of my fancy suit. A few scraps of clothing still cling to me, but beyond that I'm naked. I should thank Brock if I ever see him again. The clothes under this tree have come in handy again. To be honest, I almost don't care, but later I hope this uniform will be the thing my enemies remember. Right before I end their lives.

I start walking out of the city. I know I have to rest, and that will mean getting far away and finding some cover. Being a glow stick at night has its disadvantages. Even though my wound is healed, and my aura is stable, I feel horrible. My legs feel like they're barely holding me up.

Maybe I've made it a mile, I don't know—I can barely keep my focus. At this point, my body has shut down. Every part of me is telling me to stop. There's a nice cluster of rocks and bushes next to me, and that becomes my home. Two more steps, and I fall like a tree, my face planted firmly in the ground.

Succumbing to my pain, I wiggle my body, digging a little foxhole. I can't even bring myself to lift my head. It's okay though, the pressure against my face feels relaxing. I need this right now; I need to feel the ground pushing back at me, reminding me not to slip deeper.

The morning comes quickly as I bounce from sleep to consciousness. Every rustle of a bush in the wind makes me think I'll be discovered. If it weren't for the lull of the morning birds, I might not ever relax. At daybreak, the sky beams with blues and yellows I haven't seen for some time. It's been a while since I've been beyond the walls. For a moment, I imagine I'm a kid again and my mother is waiting inside for me.

I'm torn away from this fantasy by a sharp pain in my stomach followed by a loud grumble. Suddenly, I recall Marcus warning of self-destruction and take off for the nearby river.

After recovering, I sit beside the water and try to come up with a plan to get Katelynn back. I know I've gone east, closer to Sinder territory, and she went south. They'll likely move her along the southern road until they can go back east, which means I have a little bit of time. I doubt they had enough transports to move everyone in vehicles.

It takes me twelve minutes of nonstop running to reach the southern road, and another five until I hear soldiers and gunshots. I situate myself at a high point that looks over a large section of the road. There must be a couple hundred people in this group, but no one seems to be in a bright yellow dress, which makes me think she's either not here, or she ripped it up into a million pieces trying to save people.

With each shot, I fear I will find Katelynn's body lying on the ground. I want to rush down there and free them all, but I know I can't. My edgeless blade won't be enough against them. If I'm going to get her out when I find her, it will have to be by stealth.

Once they've moved on down the road, I follow them, examining the bodies of the dead left behind. While I'm relieved to not find Katelynn, I'm saddened at the loss of life. I feel responsible for this in a way. These people were sons and daughters, friends and siblings—they didn't deserve this.

I kneel beside a young girl and beg for her forgiveness. "I'm sorry. I'm sorry we weren't strong enough to stop this."

It's hard for me to do, but I squeeze her hand and increase my aura until her body vanishes into nothingness. "Rest now—become one with the Mover of Life."

I return to seek cover among the trees, following close behind the Sinder caravan. They keep everyone moving and crowded together for better control, like cattle being led to their slaughter. The Sinder soldiers poke and prod them with their rifles and occasionally fire into the crowd for fun, randomly killing to ensure everyone stays on pace.

For some reason, though, they stop moving. I see them check their radios multiple times as they lock down a perimeter. Did they spot me? The Cogents in their army summon their blades and enter the cluster of trees where I'm hiding. I do my best to stay hidden among a series of thick bushes, hoping the intense daylight will drown out my glow.

Two soldiers come right up next to me as they relieve themselves. "Why is this taking so long? We should have just killed all of them," one says.

"This is the doc's orders—I guess he's doing some new experiments again."

"Does he really need so many?"

"I don't know. Just follow the orders."

"Well, if I kill a few more before they make it to him, then I'd probably be doing them a favor. No telling what kind of twisted experiments that guy has cooked up."

I should kill these monsters right here and right now, but then I see her as her hood slips down for a second. I'd recognize Katelynn's golden-blond curls anywhere. She's concealing herself.

My hopes are quickly crushed as I hear an unfriendly voice once again. "Lucas."

I don't need to turn around to confirm it, but I do anyway. "Ryan," I say, scanning behind him for Hatcher, Bear, and Hara. "Where are your real friends?"

With his blade in hand, he shakes his head. "Lucas, I—"

"You know you deserve to die for what you did to Marcus and Cameer."

"I—"

"You betrayed us."

His head shakes as if that will somehow make it not true.

"Cameer trusted you."

To my surprise, he drops his blade to the ground and surrenders to me, hands in the air. "You're right. Cameer is dead because of me. I-I deserve to die."

A trick for sure, a ruse to make me drop my guard. He doesn't have a heart. But regardless of his real intensions, his lack of a weapon allows me to move a little more freely. I should make quick work of my escape and find Katelynn before he notifies anyone of my arrival.

I only make it a few steps before four Sinder Cogents appear over the adjacent hill, looking down upon us, Ryan's hands still held high. They take off in quick pursuit of me, ripping through the trees with a crackle of their auras.

In midrun, I realize I don't have a cliff to jump from like last time. There has to be another way to get out of this, but how? For now, I'll just have to keep my pace. I can't believe I'm grateful for running that wall every morning.

Out of nowhere, the trees become familiar, and I feel as though I can hear my name being called from an unknown distance. I decide to pursue this feeling until I come upon the church I took Katelynn to a few weeks back. For some reason, I feel that, if I can just make it to the door, I'll be safe, but I know that's not true.

I'm too late, though. One of the Cogents swings for my head, removing some of my wild hairs. I counter as quickly as possible only to lose every

111

inch of ground to their next attack. Strike after strike, they overwhelm me, until I'm backed up against the church door.

A knee connects with my stomach as I dodge a deadly blow from a swinging blade. The air leaves my lungs, forcing me to release my weapon. I scurry along the ground, trying to encourage myself to get up.

I shift all my weight onto my only sturdy leg and summon Lucid once more. The Sinder Cogents have won, and they know it. No church can save me from what happens next. They take the time to argue over who gets to end me. Seems these soldiers really enjoy killing Rockcliff Cogents—they treat it as a badge of honor.

Maybe I should accept my fate. Maybe the Mover of Life brought me here because it's a fitting place to die. Maybe this is to remind me to pray more often, to give me a last chance for my soul to be brought to the other side.

I decide to pray out loud, that I am not ashamed. If I am to die here, I hope to bring glory to the Giver of Life one final time. My words are true and clear, and they resemble the meaning of life as I embrace death, but before I can finish, the old wooden door creaks open, pausing my confession.

An old foreign man emerges, with long, dirty black hair and a beard that reaches to his waist. He looks homeless, yet he wears the clothes of a father, a red robe with a black rope tied around the waist. They're tattered and look to be from the previous generation, but they're undoubtedly holy garments of the church.

"Who the heck are you?" the soldiers ask him.

He ignores them. "Are you hurt, son?"

"He's about to be, old man. And you will be too if you don't turn around and walk right back into that church."

The father moves slowly, only pausing to examine my face for a moment. He then explains to us that he believes the Giver of Life has made a request of him to end this fight. While I do believe, I don't think the Giver would send an old man to save me. I don't truly believe a prayer will make these men turn away.

"Please go, sir. Father," I beg him, "the last thing I need is to watch a priest get killed alongside me."

He doesn't heed my warning or the soldiers. Instead, he kneels to kiss the ground and give praise right in front of us. He is devout, but crazy all the same. "Please," I ask once more.

112

"The Giver of Life has written what is to come in the book of life. I am charged with protecting that which the Giver desires to protect. Every action you take against me will be met with condemnation. While you will probably continue, I must say before we get started, I will not kill you. However, defense of oneself is a commandment by the Giver of Life. So should we continue, my defense will scale in violence. I am bound by what is written by the Giver."

The father's speech has no effect on the soldiers—if anything, they seem more annoyed and ready to kill us both. I wish I could save him, but he won't listen. It's already overwhelming to know I can't save Katelynn, but now I have to get a priest killed alongside me. I can't handle it, even if he is senile.

"I think you've been living under a rock, old man. You don't even know what you're opposing right now. We're from the Sinder Liberation Army. This boy you're protecting is a risk to our freedom. He will be brought to justice now, and you will too if you defy us. This is your last chance to go inside before you meet the Giver of Life in person."

That's the first time I've ever heard anyone call themselves the Liberation Army. What's liberating about killing thousands and enslaving thousands? The Sinder Army doesn't liberate, they murder innocents.

The man's response is unwavering. "I've said the will of the Giver of Life. Now make your choice. Continue and face defeat, or leave and spare yourselves certain pain."

It's ever so sudden and could easily be missed, but if I'm right, this priest knows how to fight. I can see him widen his stance, ready to counter. His holy garments seem to mask his intentions, and a soldier approaches, blade in hand.

He swings at the father with the intention of removing his head, but the priest erupts with a red aura and catches his blade with one hand, pinching it between his fingers. The blade shatters at the point of contact, and his fist comes shooting out from his robe into the chest of the soldier. The man rolls over in agony. I think I hear his ribs break.

"He's a Cogent!" one of the others shouts, now on high alert. They check on their comrade, but I don't think he'll be getting up anytime soon. It looks like he's passed out from the pain and his aura overwhelming him.

"You messed up, old man," another says as they all prepare to take him on at once.

With no more talking, they attack together with every intention of killing him, but that's not what happens. The priest bounces from block to block without even summoning his blade. His hands catch, strike, and counter each blow. The Sinder Cogents couldn't be more outmatched as he immobilizes them with the sheer force of his fists.

When it's over, he turns to me and extends his hand. "You still okay?"

I nod, stunned by what I've seen. "You beat them, all of them. You're a Cogent?"

He lifts me up and resets his clothes to a suitable position on his body. His once bright red aura vanishes back to nothing.

"Are you here to help me?"

I never thought it possible, but maybe he was sent by the Giver of Life to aid me in returning Katelynn. Maybe he is an answer to my prayers.

"I only go where the Mover takes me and the Giver commands me," he says.

"Are you some sort of soldier?"

He shakes his head.

"Well, thank you . . ."

"You may call me Father Jin."

Chapter 12

I wish I'd had the foresight to never leave her side. I wish I'd done so many things, but now I'm standing here, where she was a little while ago. How could I let this happen to her? I'm supposed to protect her. I'm supposed to keep her safe from all of this.

"Are you going to send them off?" Father Jin asks, kneeling beside the bodies on the ground before me.

I say nothing, hoping to avoid it. Not because I don't think it's necessary, but because it's hard. Every time I kneel next to someone, I envision Katelynn. It pulls me apart. These people didn't deserve this. If I could have done something, maybe they would be alive right now.

Five minutes. Five minutes of prayers for the dead. It's a painful thing to hear when my action could have potentially prevented this. Now it's as if they never existed at all, and no one can hold me accountable either.

"It is done," Father Jin says.

"Thank you, Father."

"They will live on with the Mover of Life now."

I nod, hoping what he says is true. I have trouble imagining it, though. What does living with the Mover of Life even look like? "Do you think I will see them again?"

He looks at me without expression as if to say, *What for?*

"I want to apologies to them. To beg for their forgiveness."

"They only live with the Mover now. There is no need for forgiveness. The Giver of Life has closed their purpose."

Their purpose. Is that all we are? Do we exist for nothing else but the purpose of our creator? If what he says is true, I don't know if I should be happy or angry. To feel pain because the Giver of Life designed it that way seems evil, yet to feel at all seems like life itself.

"I don't understand."

"We all serve a purpose. Love or hate our role, we are simply tools for that higher purpose."

He places his hand on my shoulder and allows his aura to fade into nothingness with a relaxing sigh. His beliefs are different from what I was taught about the Mover, Giver, and Life. I'm beginning to question his understanding of the church.

"May the Mover of Life guide you on your path, Lucas."

Without another word, he walks off to the south, into the trees. My mind is telling me to continue pursing Katelynn on the road leading east, but my heart challenges this, telling me to follow the priest. I have a feeling I'm not done yet.

My feet carry me into the trees behind Father Jin. I guess I've listened to my heart on this one. Hopefully I'm right, and he can help me in some way. He's already shown himself to be incredibly strong.

As I catch up to him, he doesn't slow his progress at all. I would say he completely ignores me, but I'm not sure. He could also be praying and walking. I try not to interrupt him, but I can't take it after a while.

"Father Jin?" I say, hoping to address him correctly. "I, um—I don't know where to go or what to do right now. I was wondering if the Mover of Life may have told you?"

He pauses, and with a very snarky tone, tells me, "The Mover does not tell you what to do. The Mover brings you through life. Do they teach you nothing in that big city of yours?"

I admit I paid little attention during church growing up, and I've never really given much thought to my faith. The Mover moves life, and the Giver gives life, and then there's Life itself. But I'm not sure I understand what all that really means sometimes.

"I'm sorry, is that a no?"

He pauses once more and promptly swings his cloak around toward me. His foreign eyes are dark and empty. I keep hoping for an answer, but I'm only met with his glare. I'm beginning to question his fatherhood at this point. Maybe this guy was kicked out or something. He seems a bit off.

Jin is about as grumpy as they come. Letting out a huff doesn't count as an answer or excuse him from talking to me, educating me. It's not like this guy has anything else important to do. He's literally homeless and filthy, walking around like he knows everything.

I contemplate returning to the road in pursuit of Katelynn once more before it's too late. I could do it, but then how would I get her out? This father seems a little less than helpful right now, and I was really hoping the Giver of Life had a plan for me. That's it. Maybe I just need to learn more about the Giver. I'll force it out of this old bag if I have to.

Back at his side, I pay no attention to his grumpy demeanor. He won't strike me down, so I'll just keep asking him what I want to know. "You said the Mover of Life brought you to me or something like that. What did you mean by that? Is that like a real voice?"

I guess my question really strikes a nerve, because he pauses to answer for once. "Listen, kid. I am not your savior. I am not your mentor. I am not your father, in any sense. You can only go where the Mover of Life carries you, and I was taken out that door and to your side. Not because I wanted to, but because I was moved to."

I'm not sure how to decipher these riddles that he speaks. There's probably a meaning in there somewhere, but I only heard one thing that made sense to me. "So, if I follow you, it's not because I want to, it's because I was moved to."

For a moment, I think he might swing at me—he doesn't, though. I can see that there's a rageful side to this guy. I suppose that's why he was able to take out all those Sinder Cogents. He's probably been through some stuff given how old he is. I get the sense he's still good, though.

"I'm not good to be around, kid."

"Doesn't bother me. I'm still coming. Consider me Moved."

He clearly doesn't like my response, returning to his silent treatment. We walk for another thirty minutes before I decide to bug him again. I start by asking him about our current destination, which he has kept unknown. I'm forced to assume it's some sort of secret place or another church further south.

"You know, for someone who's a priest, you're not very talkative," I say, hoping to get any type of response.

His social skills are so weak I'm beginning to think the last person he talked to was his barber a century ago. Even then, I doubt he could hold a conversation. It's obvious he doesn't like people, so I wonder why he became the father of a church.

"So, do you take care of that church?" I ask.

No response.

"I took my girlfriend there on a date not too long ago. The Sinder Army took her. I'm going to find a way to get her back."

No response.

"Hey, aren't you supposed to be supportive or offer advice as a father?" I ask aggressively. "I'm over here trying to figure out what I need to do next and . . ." I pause to see if he'll respond, but still he says nothing.

"See, this is what I'm talking about, you're—"

117

Father Jin halts again, but this time it's different. The rest of his body is still as he slowly raises a clenched fist. A military sign to hold position. I drop to a knee to avoid detection. Maybe they don't know we're here? Maybe we've been heading toward the enemy this whole time? I really wish I knew right now, but this guy has been a closed book.

"Are they here?" I whisper. "Have they been following us?"

The only thing making any noise is the tall grass as it bends in the slow breeze. Then I hear it, off in the distance. A groan for life. Something is dying over there. With my worst fears in my head, I take off to the source, pushing through the thick grass until I finally come upon it.

It's like something I've never seen, a large beast covered in golden fur. I should be afraid of it, and I still am slightly, despite the blood rushing from its side. "What is it?"

"A lion."

I recall the fountain statues and the stories of wild animals like this, but they said they all died off, and yet here he is. A mighty animal once feared by everyone, now dying in the grass alone. He lets out a deep moan, seemingly embracing death. We probably look as strange to him as he looks to us. Yet he knows that we are the cause of this.

With my belief that the Mover only brings me places I was designed to go, I must be here for a reason. I must have been sent to finish the job and send this great beast beyond. I drop to his side and run my fingers along his great fur, wishing I could feel its softness.

Summoning my blade, I feel a sense of pity for him. I wonder what led him here, to death's door. Such a powerful being, yet powerless against a new weapon created to kill him without effort.

As I move my blade into position, the father gently grabs my wrist. "He should not die today," he says.

Then he proceeds to place his hand over the lion's wound. A prayer spills forth, and Jin's aura gradually intensifies. The lion yelps in pain, but the father removes himself, claiming his work done.

"Get up," he says, as if the animal will understand the command.

Jin stands and says it once more.

I'm not sure how to process this. It appears the lion has died, and now he's yelling at it to get up. I'm not sure lions have are given a purpose by the Giver of Life, but knowing this man's crazy beliefs, he seems to think so.

"Hey, Mr. Priest, sir. I think the lion is dead. We should send him beyond."

"No. The Mover of Life brought me here. He will live for now."

I'm not sure what to make of this, but we leave anyway. A few feet from the site, I hear another groan, followed by a shuffling of grass. I look back to try to see the golden fur once more, but I can't pick it out.

The father was right again. I keep doubting what he tells me, but each time he ends up exactly right. So why do I keep holding back? He is blessed by the Giver of Life with a deep understanding, no doubt. Why do I feel such unease around him?

The night approaches, and the fatigue from walking all day sets in. I've followed the father for so long, the forest has disappeared. The sky is a dark red, and the air is thin over the now sandy landscape. Without hesitation, Jin walks through a cluster of warning signs.

I know where we are—we're in a red zone. Panic sets in as I look at the dead ground. I cup my hands around my mouth and yell at the father to warn him. He doesn't look back. I can't help but retreat into the trees as I recall the bloated corpse of a man who entered this place once and died a few days later. The radioactive poison somehow seeps into your body and destroys it.

What's wrong with him? How could he not know where he's walking into? He's going to die. No one just walks into a red zone. I find myself pacing back and forth, torn about what to do. On one hand, I think I should save him before it's too late; on the other hand, I feel like I should run far away. Maybe this guy is the way he is because he's been in there before. He is a Cogent, after all.

My mind plays out every possibility before I eventually give in. My only hope is that, since those L3 bombs didn't kill the Cogents, maybe were immune to it. If I want to save Katelynn, I'm going to have to trust the Mover of Life to carry me through this place. It's the best option I've got right now.

The red zone is as awful as they say. Life is truly dead here, with not a plant or bug in sight. Dry sand covers the ground and fills the air, forcing me to hold my military shirt over my face for protection. I'm not sure if it really does anything, but it makes me feel better. I keep checking myself the farther I go in.

I continue pursuit of the faint footprints left behind by the father. They lead me to a large crater in the ground with a patch of flourishing life. This must be the site of the original blast. Tall green plants surround a wooden house at the base of the hole. These crops must have strong resilience growing in this harsh climate. Some are even sprouting beautiful, vibrant red and blue fruits.

"I see the Mover has brought you here after all," Father Jin says from his front door. "Come in if you must."

His home resembles a different time. Strange patterns on fabrics and uncommon colors fill the pre-war looking room. I wouldn't take this for a father's home, but for him I suppose it makes sense.

"Did you make all these yourself?" I ask, cautiously examining a wall covered from top to bottom in the three-line symbols of the church, each one meticulously crafted from metal, wood, and stone.

He only grunts.

"I'll take that as a yes."

I would never tell him this, but if I'm being honest, even the orphanage looked better than this place. Miss Caroline would freak out if she saw the state of his common room. Papers and junk cover the floor. The windows are boarded up, but that makes sense given the undesirable location.

"Have a seat," he says.

I scan the room, and he leans something forward. Stacks of paper and holy garments fall to the floor, revealing a small chair. I accept his welcoming offering and sit in silence with him.

"So, Father. This is your place? It looks—cozy."

He grunts again, then stands up and walks to his table. He slides several papers off with no regard before pulling out a single piece, as if he knew exactly where it was in the chaos.

Jin reveals a photograph of him standing with his wife in front of this house. "I had to rebuild it."

I hold the picture carefully, knowing it cannot be replaced. He returns to his chair, somber. "This used to be a thriving city of the old world, you know. Millions lived here. They were . . ."

He pauses, seeming unsure if he wants to relive the past. I experience that feeling firsthand every time I think of my childhood. This man lived in two worlds, though. If the stories are really true, millions of people lived here in America before the war. I'm not sure if he is blessed or cursed to have known that life.

"You were a soldier for America?" I ask, noticing the flag on his jacket. "The moves you used back there to disarm those men—they're from before the war, aren't they?"

He grunts, grabbing the pitcher of water on the table and pouring a cup for each of us. "Drink."

The water feels clean and pure despite where we are. The jolt of life-giving liquid surges through my body. I had almost forgotten how thirsty I'd become since earlier. My mind has been so focused finding Katelynn.

With a quick gulp, I finish my drink. "Thank you, Father."

He looks at me and raises his glass for some reason, then proceeds to finish his cup.

"So, how did we get here?" I ask, curious if his story deviates from what I've been taught, much like his religious teachings.

"Humanity has always struggled—even if we tried to choose the right thing, we always fell short. We are flawed beings, chasing after righteousness. It took me too long to realize what real evil is."

"And what's that?" I ask.

"False righteousness. Good men doing evil acts in the name of our Giver. 'Slay your Giver's enemies,' they would say. These men worship death. They are beasts that need to be tamed by our hands. For too long, I never questioned this. I was a lost soul, one without the Mover working in my life." He leans forward. "Let me ask you this, boy. Do you believe the Giver of Life has the ability to command acts of violence?"

I pause to consider his question. "I have to admit, I've never really thought about what the Giver of Life is able to do."

Father Jin clasps his hands and leans back in his chair. "Of course, the answer is yes. The Giver is the creator of our world and has the ability to do anything. The Giver has dominion over life itself. So now I'm left with another question: Why? I hope to ask the Giver of Life that question someday."

I do my best to answer it for him. "I don't know if this is an answer, or where I remember it from, but maybe the evil we see is a reflection of something the Giver and Mover know about life."

These questions he has for our creator must swirl in his mind a lot. I can see why he joined the church. I suppose I need to believe that answer more than him right now. I need to believe that there is more to this life than the suffering I know.

"My mother had this saying," I tell him. "'When death stares you in the face and all hope seems lost, the least you can do is turn the page. Don't give up before the story is actually over.' I think it's what's kept me going all these years without her. The hope that, by turning the page, no matter how difficult life got, I would keep going—to see the end."

He grunts. "Sounds like a smart lady."

The thought of her words brings a smile to my face. "She was. And that's what I'll do. I'll keep turning until I reach the end."

"Then may the Mover guide you there."

I want to hang on to this happy memory of her before it gets dark, so I stand up and examine the pictures around the room to distract myself. Each one is a snapshot from Father Jin's life. I find myself consumed by trying to understand his story through them. I pause on one that must be him as a child. He's a little boy in a brown uniform with colored patches. It looks like a little military uniform. It seems he has devoted his whole life to seeking justice.

"Father, can I ask you something?" He doesn't respond, so I push on. "I know you've given up the life of the soldier. And I agree with you that fighting seems unjustified, but right now, I need to fight. I need to get someone back, and the only way to do that is if I fight them."

He huffs, "If you go down that road, you will not live. I've fought the Sinder Army before, and now I'm here. Your chances don't even exist on a scale to what they are capable of. If you fight Silas, you will die. The Giver of Life has told me so."

"Aren't you supposed to protect life? Did the Giver of Life tell you I couldn't get her back? No? Then there's still a way. The person I love is out there waiting for me, right now. She needs me to find her."

"The life I'm trying to protect right now is still yours. If you continue, I cannot protect you."

"Don't you know what it's like to lose someone you love?" I scold him.

"I do," he says, looking at his picture. "I was married once. I was even blessed with a daughter. But I've also taken the lives of many loved ones. Being a soldier means you kill others too. Are you prepared to do that? To step down that thin line?"

"I am. Or at least I want to be. This person is the last person in the world that loves me. I don't want to lose her. I can't lose her."

Not a muscle moves in the father's face. "I can't help you."

Father Jin knows he can't win this argument, so he's removing himself like the coward he is. He jumps up so fast he knocks over his own furniture, sending papers and statues skittering over the ground. "I am tired. It's been a long day, and we both should get some rest. We can discuss it more tomorrow."

His refusal to help me feels like a blade piercing my side. I grit my teeth in anger, ready to beat down his door as it slams shut. More than anything, I want to demand we finish talking, demand he stay until he gives me what I want—a way to find Katelynn.

That's when I see it, among the scattered papers. A Sinder Army crest. I pick it up to examine it further. The guided hand of the Mover has brought me a map. All the Sinder strongholds, bases, and cities lie waiting for me to find them. He must keep it to know how to avoid them.

Quietly, I slide the map into my military jacket and sit back down. I know what I'm supposed to do right now. I'm supposed to stop, to rest, but how can I when Katelynn is out there fighting for her life? I'll never change this stubborn old man's mind. Every minute I wait is a minute I could lose her. I have to turn the page.

Chapter 13

My first impulse is to run to the closest camp, and I do. They can't have taken her too far since yesterday, so there's a good chance she'll be there. It's not the best idea, but it's all I have. I only stop at daybreak as my body begins to burn in agony. I fear I've overdone it. The pain in my muscles reminds me of Marcus's warning to drink my body weight or more every day.

There's no time for rest, but if I can barely walk, I'll be dead before I step foot in that camp. Recovery doesn't go as I planned. I was hopeful that catching my breath would be enough, but my flickering aura says otherwise.

The fresh, crisp scent of water hits my nose, driving my senses wild. I can barely hold myself back from tumbling down the hill toward the stream. With each gulp, I gasp in relief as my pulsing aura stabilizes. This stream is a lifesaver, and I should note it on the map. Who knows how hard it will be to find water again?

My relief is short-lived as the thunderous clap of a gun echoes off the trees, scattering a nearby flock of birds. I know I must be close. Now is the time to come up with my strategy to save her. Peering over the hill, I see the Sinder Camp with its long metal fences wrapped in barbed wire.

Guards patrol the perimeter in pairs of two. Humans, of course, but there are no doubt Cogents inside. That fence wouldn't stop them without a Cogent or two. As I make my scan, my eyes fall on the man lying motionless just outside the front gate. It looks like he tried to flee and was gunned down. The soldiers kick him to make sure he's done in. A bunch of slimy cowards, shooting him in the back.

It looks like this camp is more permanent than I thought. There are a few old concrete buildings near the center. I suppose this is where they take the people they've captured until they can get them to the Sinder territory, to be sold as slaves or whatever they do with us.

Another shot rings out, this time from inside the camp. The crowd of captives scatters against the fence in a panic, making it easier to see everyone. For a moment, I think I spot Katelynn in the chaos, but I can't be sure. I do, however, notice the five Sinder Cogents that emerge from one of the concrete buildings. It looks like their regular soldiers can't handle it.

I know my next move is to infiltrate their camp and search for Katelynn. It will be easier to search through the hundreds of people if I'm up close. The only problem is I won't blend in. Not because of the uniform, but because I look like a glow bug.

I recall Father Jin the other day, how he'd somehow found a way to mask his aura from everyone. I wonder if I could hide mine. It would surely make this rescue easier if I could look like everyone else.

Even though I'm not sure how he does it, I have to guess it's something like when we amplify our aura to be more violent. I wonder if by focusing on my aura, I can make it fade too. But if that was the case, I would have been able to do this a long time ago.

My attempt is an instant failure, as my aura grows in intensity. Seems this isn't as easy as I'd hoped. I need to focus, but it's hard with the occasional gunshot going off in the background. Every shot I hear, I imagine it was Katelynn that was killed, which only makes me more frustrated.

This goes on for about an hour before I give up. It's obvious this isn't working the way I wanted it to. It's time to accept defeat here. I don't know why I ever thought I could do it, anyway. I'm sure this is some advanced technique that takes years of practice or something. I wish I knew what Father Jin did—that would make this so much easier.

When I think back to it, he was praying before he left the church. I wonder if it has anything to do with the Giver of Life. Maybe the power to mask one's aura comes from the divine. I know that when he opened that door, he looked so carefree and happy, as if he had just been created. Not a concern in the world.

I wish I could be like that. I wish I could forget the problems the world has shown me exist. Lying here among the trees kind of reminds me of being a kid. Back then, things were simpler, before I lost my mom. I never really worried about anything. I was innocent, and so was the world.

To go back is a fantasy, a lie I wish I could tell myself. That place only lives in my memory now as a time simpler than this. It's a nice thought, though, and one that I have to smack myself out of so I can go save Katelynn. As I do, I notice the most bizarre thing—my hand looks like my hand, and not a Cogent's. A smile comes over me, and I jump up only to be met with the return of my glowing aura. Then it hits me. It's not focus, it's relaxation.

I can do it. All I need to do is put myself in a state of pure relaxation. I need to allow my aura to recede from the forefront of my body. I start by closing my eyes, and from head to toe I release all the tension in my body. Upon opening them again, it's as if I'm human once more. It's an overwhelming sight to see, one that makes me believe their still might be a way to get back here someday.

Before I go rushing in there, I should make sure I can hold my aura at this level. The first thing I do is walk back and forth with my aura still repressed. Success. Next, I pick up a rock and squeeze it in my hand. My aura springs up as the rock dissolves. Not a surprise, but I wonder how good I could get at this. If I can make it out of here, I'll have to try to improve.

Now to get into this place. I can't run and keep my aura hidden. So, I'll likely have to sneak in. There appears to be a waste zone near the back corner of the camp. My best opportunity will be to come in through there.

I get started, moving from cover to cover until I make it to the large pile of junk. It's an easy entrance once I raise my aura to walk through the fence. Inside, I move rapidly around the large piles of trash until I come to the first concrete building.

A voice startles me, and I shuffle backward, tripping over my own feet and stumbling into the large pile of trash. My aura flares up, and the trash starts to catch fire. Quickly I focus on relaxing, halting the disintegration of the garbage. Once calm, I slowly move farther into the trash. I may be relaxed, but the rotten smells and unknown liquids that steam up around me send me into a dry heave. By the look of it, it's some sort of medical waste.

The voices get a bit louder as they dump a large pile of garbage on top of the heap. Just as they're about to leave, my aura disintegrates a large chunk of debris. The men stop, concerned.

"Who's there?" the first one calls out.

"Rats probably," the other soldier says.

Staying as still as possible, I repress my aura, hoping to slow the decay of garbage around me and avoid being found.

It's no good, though. Several gunshots ring out as the first man fires recklessly into the trash pile, striking me.

"Well it's dead now."

I wait until they're gone before carefully digging myself out. As I emerge, I see the man they shot earlier now lying motionless on top of the garbage. I know I can't leave him here like this, so I do the only thing that's right and give him a battlefield send-off.

"I release you to the Giver and Mover of Life. May you be remembered."

These soldiers of Sinder are the worst. If there weren't so many Cogents here, I think I would take them all down right now. It's going to be hard to stay calm, but that's exactly what I have to do.

Inside the main part of the camp, I navigate through the ever-moving maze of Rockcliff soldiers and captured citizens. The guards even yell at me once to stay away from the edge, which makes me feel confident they don't know.

However, my confidence is quickly shaken as someone bumps into me and lets off a terrible scream. I turn back to see a man gripping his elbow and screaming in agony. In a weird ironic misfortune, a lady screams at the same time, and everyone flocks to her instead of the man.

I don't know when it happened—I don't remember hearing the gunshot—but blood spills from her side as one of the Sinder soldiers kicks her to the ground. I should defend her, but I don't. Instead, I carefully observe the altercation, thinking that Katelynn could show up at any time to treat the wounded. I know if she's here, and she's able, she'll be helping people still. That's simply who she is.

Everything escalates rather quickly as several men jump the guard who beat and shot the woman. The Sinder soldier only gets one more shot in before they stomp him into the ground. The cheers of triumph are quickly snuffed out, though, as this assault brings two Cogents to subdue the attackers. They do their best to slip into the crowd, but two of them are quickly caught and turned into ashes instantly. The Cogents search furiously for the others involved, walking back and forth among us.

One of the Cogent soldiers starts pointing people out and has them step forward. My heart sinks when he nod at me. I can only assume it's because I'm still in my uniform. With about six of us selected, he goes down the line, asking for someone to point out who was involved.

The first man says he doesn't know, but the second rats him out almost immediately. In an instant, a blade goes through his neck, and the man is no more. Everyone calls the man who told on him a coward for getting him killed, but I don't think he cares, and I'm not inclined to blame him. The soldier questions him again, but he has no one else to offer up.

Moving down the line, the third soldier shakes his head when asked if he saw anyone else involved. The Cogent doesn't even give him a chance, killing him instantly, which causes me to flinch and almost draw my blade. I hold myself back, trying to maintain my aura level.

The Sinder Cogent notices me, probably because I look unafraid, as I refuse to cower. His face comes inches from mine, and I do my best to hold my aura back, but for a moment there I swear he can see it.

If he tries to kill me, I'll have to defend myself. I focus on the attack that he used to kill the other two guys and imagine defending against it. It's straight for the head, so it's easily countered if I know it's coming. The only problem is, once I do, I'll have to kill him quickly and then kill the one behind him. What's worse is there are three more in this camp, and I still haven't found Katelynn.

Fortunately, my interrogation ends abruptly at the sound of a convoy. Sinder trucks come barreling through the front gate, sending the crowd into a panic as they try to avoid getting run over. I slide back into the mix, hoping I won't be pulled out again and can continue my search.

The convoy stops, revealing several Sinder Cogents, about ten in all, who exit the vehicles and form two rows. Many of them are recognizable as the Feren Guard with their red military jackets. Then, from between the two rows, the large purple Cogent, Silas, appears. This is my first time seeing him up close, but the square face and intense aura give me no doubt that it's the leader, even if he looks a bit younger than I imagined him. I can't forget his fight with Marcus.

His presence sends the camp into a panic as guards and the captured all stand at attention. It seems everyone knows their life can be taken in an instant when he's around. They all watch with anticipation as Silas walks back and forth, surveying the prisoners. I stay focused on him until I notice a familiar face among the guards he arrived with. Ryan.

I wish I could plunge my blade right through that guy's chest this moment. I can't help but imagine killing him in the worst way possible as he gasps for life. He's lucky right now.

He must be able to hear my thoughts, because he looks directly at me. I assume he knows I've just murdered him in my mind a hundred different ways. It takes me a moment to regret staring at him, because I've completely forgotten that he knows who I am and will call me out. I'm dead, and there's nothing I can do about it.

This terrible realization is really coming too late. I see him shake his head as if trying to understand why I'm not glowing. It looks as though he's about to step forward to identify me, but Silas begins a speech, and he falls back in line.

"Citizens of Rockcliff. Welcome. I have freed you from a life of servitude. You no longer need to serve the inferior human race. You have the opportunity to serve the superior Cogents before you. Many of you may see our methods as evil, but that is not the truth. You have been fed lies by your rulers. The Sinder Nation is the future, selected by the creator to inherit this world. Not as humans, but as the superior Cogents we are set out to be."

"Cogents are abominations of mankind's sins!" someone shouts.

For a second, I think that person will be ripped out of the crowd and executed, but Silas calls off his guards and answers the challenge.

"It's true. We are the chosen, selected by the Giver of Life to inherit the earth. That's why I've come to offer you peace. Now separated from your meaningless struggle, you can devote yourselves to us. You don't have to remain prisoners. If you desire, you can accept our way of life. Join us and serve under a Cogent house. Each person who joins will be granted protection, and someday, if you work hard enough, you can join the ranks of the Elites yourself and help us shape this world into a better new society. One that transcends humanity, allowing us to move past the petty weakness of human life."

Move beyond human life? What does that even mean? There is no way this is what the Giver of Life wants. Cogents aren't natural—they were genetic experiments gone wrong. I don't understand how they can come up with these wild claims. How can we all have such drastically different understandings of the Giver of Life?

"Join us."

To everyone's surprise, a young man steps forward and drops to his knees before Silas. Grace and mercy are what he asks for, and Silas grants it to him. This doesn't sway anyone else, though. Someone calls the man a fake, and the crowd erupts in mockery of him.

I admit he's a coward, but I can't help but wonder if he's trying to stay alive, too. He knows nothing good will come from opposing them. Much like the guy who ratted the other one out earlier, he has saved himself. I don't agree with what they've done, but no one can argue that they didn't save themselves.

Is that where we are, though? Should I be trying to save myself? If I accepted their offer like Ryan likely did, would I be safe? Could I save Katelynn this way?

Another man comes forward asking for mercy, and Silas accepts him. It's clear that some believe him. They want to believe that the Sinder Army will treat them right. But I know better. At least for my mother's memory, I cannot join them.

"You have until I leave this place to accept this gracious offer."

Silas then makes his way through the crowd and into the concrete building. Everyone becomes restless as a few others step forward. Instantly, the crowd become an uncontrollable mob, attacking the traitors as they try to accept the offer. It seems not even the Feren can control the emotions of these people. They've had enough, and not even death scares them now. They'd gladly die for their country, for humanity.

As the chaos continues, Ryan locks eyes with me again and slowly begins moving toward me. I retreat behind the unruly crowd at a similar pace, hoping to keep a good distance from him.

If Katelynn is here, I need to find her quickly. I know that. But the only place I haven't checked is the building Silas just entered. Keeping with my slow backpedaling, I ask a lady near me what's in there. She shakes her head in fear.

Katelynn is inside, I know it. The love of my life is feet from me, and I can't get to her again. Ryan notices me—or my aura, I'm not sure—but he finally starts to yell and make his way through the crowd faster.

"Hey you," he shouts.

I keep moving, but a familiar whistle stops me dead in my tracks. The ground shakes as a vehicle erupts in a ball of fire. Strike after strike, the edge of camp gets meticulously hit by mortar fire until all the guard shacks are destroyed. Inside, the walls become a chaotic stampede as everyone rushes to escape.

The Feren Guards and Ryan rush to Silas, who darts out of the building. Many of them jump in the remaining vehicles and drive off to find the attackers, who are nowhere to be seen. With them out of the way, I do my best to keep the chaos going, and set fire to some of their surroundings before entering the building that Silas left.

Inside, I can barely hear the warning sirens. The building looks much like a small hospital of sorts, but I doubt they treated the injured. I'm afraid what I might find here, or what I might not find, but I continue anyway.

As I walk through the long hallway, I peer into each window, only to be met with painful sights. A man lying strangled in a chair, a woman missing her arms, a boy who looks like he erupted from the inside. It doesn't look like they came here to be treated—they were likely brought here and subjected to this.

This must be the work of the Dr. Finch I heard the soldiers talking about earlier. He must have experimented on these people. Disgusting. I swear if I find Katelynn here, I will kill every Sinder piece of scum.

I've almost reached the last few rooms when the door at the end of the hall opens. I dart into the room closest to me, hoping there's no Cogent still lingering around. The doctor, a weaselly looking man, rushes along the hall and out of sight.

No Cogents, I say to myself.

My relief is short-lived, however. The sound of a breath escaping someone's body sends chills down my spine, prompting me to turn around.

"Bianca!"

Chapter 14

I don't understand—she's a Cogent. Why does her body look like this? Her lips are cracked and shriveled beyond recognition. Her aura is barely stable, pulsing in and out, as if at any minute it could consume her. I watch her chest shift immeasurably as she gasps for air.

"What's happened to you . . . ?"

As I approach her, I notice her hand has several tubes coming from it. Somehow, they've managed to insert something in her. "Be okay, Bianca. Stay strong."

If I'm not careful, I could send her body into a complete shutdown. I gently grip the tubes and pull them from her skin. A strange liquid drips onto the floor. I comfort her as her aura shimmers with instability. She gasps a breath of relief and then winces in pain without opening her eyes.

She's not quite conscious yet, but she tries to speak. "Wwwaa . . . waa . . ."

"Water. I know," I tell her, frantically looking around the room. She screams in agony. Shelf after shelf is nothing but lab equipment. "Stay with me," I remind her. "I'll get you out of here."

With nothing but electronics and deadly chemicals in the room, I know what I must do. I have to get her to the stream I drank at before I came here. "Listen, I'm going to take you to some water. Do you understand? It's me, Lucas."

"L . . . u . . ." she tries.

This time her eyes open, but she can't hold them still for very long. I try to calm her and make her focus by placing my hand on her cheek before sitting her up. "Okay, here we go."

I lift her over my shoulder, kicking open the door. Our ambitious escape is met instantly by a hail of bullets raining down the hall at us. Bianca screams in pain, causing me to drop to the ground and cover her. I'm unsure if her aura is protecting her. "I got you. You're okay."

Once I've seen she's all right, I turn toward the soldiers, now overcome with fear as they throw their useless rifles to the ground. They take off running as they see I have every intention of ending them right now. I let them go, against that burning desire. I know it won't be long until they send the Sinder Cogents after us.

"Let's go, Bianca."

I plow through the building, finding myself near the garbage once more. It seems the explosions have turned into smoke bombs in order to mask the escape of the captured. Their tactics make me believe they are humans. Only humans knowing they can't win would fight like this. I give them credit for a masterfully crafted plan, and I wish them luck as they, too, flee the wrath of the Sinder Army.

It will be hard to track us through the thick cloud of smoke. Bianca moans again and then coughs up what looks like blood. She doesn't have much time left. "The water is just beyond the hill over there. Stay with me."

My legs propel us forward, out of the camp and over the hill. Once I see the stream, I tell her to get ready. With little time left, I run down the hill as fast as I can, only to find myself unable to stop with the added weight of another person. At the bottom, my feet begin striking through several layers of ground until I fall over and fling Bianca into the water. She comes skidding to a stop, her body lying motionless in the water.

"Drink, Bianca! Drink!"

I drop down next to her and begin tilting her head sideways to face the water, reminding her to drink. For a moment, her mouth hangs open as water flows against her lips. Her tongue springs to life as she tries to use it like a spoon. "That's it! You're okay. Drink. Just Drink."

My hands grip her firmly as I hold her in position, but this is the first time I feel like I can take a real breath since I've seen her. I want to collapse in this water with her, but I know she needs me now.

Once she's had her fill, her eyes come back to life, and she rolls onto her back and rests in the water with her hands outstretched. "It's okay, Bianca. Rest."

She doesn't respond, and that's all right, she doesn't need to. I focus on being near her in case she needs me, tensing up as I anticipate her swinging at me for abandoning her in Rockcliff. There is no excuse, and she's going to hate me, I'm sure of it. I hate me. We were supposed to be partners, and I left her so I could save Katelynn—and then I didn't even do that.

I try to think of a response for when I inevitably have to defend of my actions, but then I don't want to come up with one. She's hurting, and it's my fault. For now, I should just make sure she's safe.

"I know you're exhausted, Bianca, but we should get somewhere safe."

Without responding, she struggles to sit up, only allowing me to help slightly before she has to prove to herself that she can do it. Clearly, she has a lot of feelings and thoughts going through her head. "It's okay," I remind her. "Let me help."

She nods, allowing me to lift her arm over my shoulder. I pull her along with me as far as my legs will take us. After a few hours of walking, I have put enough distance between us and the explosions and gunshots to relax. They likely won't come after us—they've got bigger problems right now.

I've decided to take shelter inside a large cliff up ahead. Back at the Cogent training program, Marcus called this improvised refuge. With an amplification of my aura, I walk into the cliff, slowly carving out a cave. Once complete, I bring Bianca in to rest.

While she recovers, the next step is to gather food and water nearby. Before I run off, I chop a tree down for some wood and start a small fire inside. I hate the dark, and I imagine she would too if she were awake.

This whole time, I've made sure to stay somewhat near the stream I found earlier. It's completely critical to our survival right now. Who knows how long it will take Bianca to recover from what they did to her?

I fashion jugs to hold water out of the large stones around the stream. That's the easy part. It's the food that becomes a bit more difficult. Rabbits and deer don't come running the moment you need to eat them. I suppose I could find some edible fruit or plants nearby, but it doesn't look promising.

I should be happy with what I do have. That's when it hits me, and I realize I should give thanks.

"Mover of Life, thank you for bringing me to Bianca. Thank you for protecting her until I could be there. I thank you for this water. I selfishly ask that you bring me to Katelynn now. Thank you for your guidance."

A feeling of peace and calm flows through me. Sometimes I have to remind myself that my actions are guided by the Mover's hands. To remind myself that this is the Giver's plan for me. I need to trust in the Giver of Life, but that shouldn't stop me from trying.

So that's what I do. I try. I try really hard to come up with the right words to somehow make Bianca feel better. If I can figure out just what to say, then maybe she will forgive me.

Back at the cave, I place the water outside and pace back and forth, refining my speech. My thoughts are soon interrupted by the sound of a struggling animal. I look around the remaining parts of the fallen tree and see I've pinned a rather large squirrel against the branches. I finish the job the branches started and graciously take the nourishment sent from above.

I think this is a sign that things will be all right. My words will be accepted, and Bianca will help me on my journey to find Katelynn. "Thank you, oh Mover of Life."

Inside, it's so dark. It seems I was gone longer than I thought, because the fire is only embers now, and the sun has dipped below the horizon. "Bianca, are you in here?" I know the answer, or at least I should. There is no blue aura to be found.

My mind turns to every scenario possible. Was I too late? Did her aura consume her? Did they find her while I was gone? Where could she be?

There's no time to think about it. If she's been taken, she can't be far. I rush out of the cave, my blade in hand, searching for any sign of a struggle—a burned rock or cleared brush, anything. It's become so dark so quickly that I can barely see anything beyond my aura.

Then I notice something that calms my soul—blue light mixing with the yellow moonlight above the cliff. I dash to the top without hesitation and wrap my arms around Bianca without a second thought.

I'm overcome with everything—fear and joy swirl within me uncontrollably. I squeeze her tight, thankful that she's not gone. I wait for her to push me away and give me the vengeful attack I deserve, but it never comes. Instead, her hands slowly reach up and rest on my back.

"Bianca, I . . ."

My confession starts to slip out of my mouth, but then I pull it back in. My planned apology doesn't feel right anymore. She should have never been left alone and I—I feel horrible. I don't know how to explain to her that my head was in a different place then. How do I tell her I was only thinking about Katelynn and myself?

I can see the disappointment in her eyes as she pulls away. She's lost all respect she had for me. I'll never be able to recover our relationship.

"I knew you would come for me," she says softly.

Her words stun me.

"I knew that once you heard I was taken, you would find me."

"Bianca, I—"

I want to come clean, to tell her that her rescue was just an accident. But I couldn't.

"And you did . . . you came."

I'm not sure what to say. This isn't the Bianca I was expecting. She's changed. The girl I knew back in school was tough and had so much fight in her. Whatever they did to her, they took a piece of her.

"Bianca . . ."

My confession stops once more, this time interrupted by a strand of her beautiful purple hair as it falls from behind her ear. I want her to punch me, to yell at me for being selfish. I want her to be Bianca again. I want to spar, and argue, and insult each other—I want to go back.

All I say is, "I'm glad you're okay."

Her eyes meet mine again, and I see that it's not disdain she has for me. I'm her hero.

She flashes a gentle smile, as if succumbing to the emotions of being rescued all at once. Even though there will be no tears, I know she will be crying, and I will be too. I decide to save her from the embarrassment and embrace her in a hug so we can both save face.

"We should get back," I say, giving her an out.

She pulls away slowly, nods, and rubs her eyes. "Yeah."

Returning to the cave, I do my best to distract her. "You're probably hungry," I say, showing her the squirrel. "Grab some of that wood over there."

"Since when did you become a hunter?" she asks, a bit of her old spunk back.

At first I wonder if I should play up my hunting abilities, but then I figure this could get me into more trouble down the road if she asks me to do it again. "It was a bit of dumb luck. This guy was pinned by the tree I chopped down for firewood. A gift from the Giver of Life."

Piercing the squirrel with a stick, I try to place him over the fire. Marcus also told us we could cook food with our aura in our hands, but I don't trust myself not to burn it to ash. I don't think the Giver of Life would provide us with two.

"Here, let me do it," she says, taking control.

I slide out of the way and hand her the squirrel. She cooks it right up with ease and breaks it in half. The two of us eat in silence. Somehow, this is almost worse than the first time we met. That awkward tension seems to grow and grow.

"So, what happened to you after the attack?" she asks.

I look at the ground, wondering how much I should tell her. If this is the moment I will come clean. I remind myself that I don't want to put her through any more pain today.

"So, after the Sinder Army attacked, I tried to save as many people as I could, but they were too strong. I watched Rockcliff fall. I fled, hoping to save everyone later. The next day, I spotted them on their way back to Sinder territory. I noticed they were doing something with the people they've captured. Taking them somewhere."

Bianca grabs her arms and clenches her biceps. Of course—she has experienced what I only feared. I wait until she's okay to continue.

"I got overwhelmed again, outnumbered in a fight. They were going to kill me. But I was saved at the last minute, by a strange Cogent priest of all things. He never summoned a blade. He took on all of them at the same time. It was impressive. His fighting style reminded me of Marcus's."

Her eyes seem still and unemotional as she tries not to relive the moment again. I don't blame her, either. I understand avoiding painful memories, and I still can't do it enough. It's a pain to sometimes be in my own head. I'm never able to escape the thoughts that come. Sometimes I feel I am victim to wherever they want to go.

"After that, I followed the father, hoping to find where I should go next. That's what led me to you. And then—"

"I see," she says, ready to speak. "After the attack, I fought and fought until I couldn't anymore. I saved as many people as I could, but I too became outnumbered. We lost so many people—I couldn't get to them. I couldn't defend Rockcliff."

I can tell she believes she should have been able to do it somehow. All by herself.

"Eventually, they took me, exhausted and on the verge of destabilization. They brought me to that camp. A doctor . . ." She pauses, struggling to say the words.

"You don't have to," I tell her.

"They took my blood. They beat me. They kept me at the edge of death for so long my body was in a constant state of—"

Her cheeks tighten as her teeth press together. Had it been me or anyone else, we wouldn't have made it. The amount of pain she's had to endure must have been unbearable. To exist in that thin range of your aura, it eating away at your body for so long . . .

"Why would they do this?" I ask. "I just don't get it. What have we ever done to them?"

"I don't know. They're monsters," she says. "Do they really need a reason? You can't reason with beasts like them. They torture people and enslave them. They would kill their own people if it gave them more power somehow. They experimented on me, and for what?"

Her words turn my stomach. All of this, all this suffering, is caused by this curse. The world is almost gone from what it once was, and it still hasn't learned its lesson.

"But I saw humans in the other rooms," I say, remembering.

Bianca looks at me with more concern. "I could hear their pleas the whole time. They cried out for me to save them, but I couldn't do it."

She was on the edge of death for so long, and all she focuses on now is the pain she felt from not being able to save the others. Rockcliff doesn't deserve her, doesn't deserve her resilience. I know if Katelynn had been there, Bianca would have tried to save her too. I only fear she's still out there in one of these in-between camps on the way back to Sinder territory. I have to find her before it's too late.

"Look at this," I say, pulling the map out of my pocket. "These are the camps where they're holding these people on their way to Sinder territory. If we leave now, we might be able to get there by morning—if you're up for it."

She looks at me with no expression. I thought she'd be ecstatic to go get some revenge, but that's not it. There is more to her decision now.

"I have to go," I tell her, jumping to my feet.

She places her hand over my chest. "No! You can't go now. It's not safe—I haven't recovered fully."

I don't know how we reversed roles in our relationship, but Katelynn's still out there. "I have to go. People need me."

"You know, the first day I met you, Lucas, I thought you didn't care about anyone but yourself. I thought, how could they pick this boy to defend the people of Rockcliff? But now I see you ready to throw it all on the line. I admit, I was wrong about you. And I'm sorry. But please, please don't go now."

"Bianca," I say, stepping to the side.

"Don't," she says, positioning herself in front of me again.

"Tomorrow, I'll be better, and then I won't ever leave your side. I'll fight with you till the end."

There's an unmatched sincerity in her words. She believes in me too much. I want to tell her I'm not the man she thinks I am. I'm still the same selfish boy. My motives are purely for me and what I want. But for some reason, I can't.

"Okay," I say. "I'll stay."

Chapter 15

In the morning, we exit the cave to find that the world has somehow moved on. There's no sign of yesterday's struggles, no sign of pain in the air, no sadness in the clouds. I do feel better today, with Bianca by my side, and I thank the Mover I am here. Today will be different for me—I can feel it.

She doesn't speak. She's not mad at me, but I've come to learn neither of us is a morning person. All she has to do is nod and we start our walk to the next camp, only pausing occasionally to drink from the stream, which we try to stay nearby.

Hours of walking feel like only minutes as we make our way to the edge of our target camp. We've both decided that we'll assess it before entering. Our goal is to free as many people as possible, and Bianca's requested that she kill the doctor if we find him.

"So, what do you think?" she asks, gazing at our target.

My thoughts aren't on this assault—Katelynn is on my mind again. I feel guilty about it, too. Bianca thinks I'm in one place, but I'm not. I'm trying to remember what I said to Katelynn last before I promised I would come back. What was the last thing I talked to her about?

The memory of holding her hands at the dance comes to mind, and that seems like so long ago. I remember she was mad at me for a moment, upset that she couldn't be like me and Bianca. I need to find her, to be her hero. When I do, I'll tell her what's going on in my heart.

"I don't know. I'm not good at this."

"How did you get into the outpost I was being held at?" she asks.

"The other day, when I saved you, I slipped into the camp undetected."

Her eyebrow rises with every bit of doubt. "They didn't notice a glowing soldier walk in?"

Better to show her than to tell her. Closing my eyes, I focus on relaxing each muscle group in my body again, head to toe, until my aura fades. When I open my eyes, her head is cocked to the side.

"Uh, what are you doing? I can still see you. You didn't turn into the invisible man or anything."

She thinks this is a joke, but I assure her I can do it. This time, I rest my body against a tree so I can completely focus. Once you get the feeling, you can hang on to it, but it takes some practice to get used to it.

"What? That's amazing," she says, reassuring me it worked this time. "You almost look human, if not for the slight haze around your hair. But most people wouldn't look twice at that. Your hair's already a bright golden color."

"I'm still getting the hang of it. But I call it aura suppression. I picked it up from the priest I told you about."

"Show me how to do it," she demands.

Bianca tries to sit in the exact same position as me, mimicking my every gesture. She closes her eyes and focuses hard, causing me to laugh as I'm reminded of myself the other day. "Not like that," I say.

She opens her eyes and slugs me in the arm to remind me she's learning. "I can kick your butt today if you'd like. I feel well enough," she taunts me. "No laughing."

Her words bring a smile to my face. This feels like I'm back at the barracks, sparring with her again. I forgot how much I enjoyed the hours of fighting with her like this. The past few days have been rather painful, but this, this makes it feel all right.

"Okay, let me try again," she says.

"You got this. Just remember, it isn't about focus, it's about relaxing and then holding that relaxed feeling with you."

She gets a little too relaxed, slumping backward and spiking her aura back up as she tries to stay upright. "Here," I say, positioning myself behind her, "let me hold you, and you focus on relaxing. One by one, release all the tension. I find it best to start from the top. Your forehead, eyebrows, nose, cheeks, mouth."

I place my hands on her shoulders as I tell her to fall into them. "There you go. You're doing it."

Her aura begins to fade until it's barely visible. Only the slight blue tint of her purple hair remains. She opens her eyes and looks back at me, with no words for how impressed she is. I suppose she doesn't want to mess the moment up. "You did it," I praise her.

"Thanks," she says.

Bianca looks happy here with me. I feel happy too. The wind picks up, and her purple strands bounce wildly, whipping her in the face. She laughs, trying to keep her focus on me. I slide her hair behind her ear for her. "I taught you something."

She pushes me away, mocking me. "You better enjoy it—that might be the only thing you can teach. How not to look like a baddy Cogent, by Lucas Conley. Ha. Sounds like a horrible class."

I know she thinks being a Cogent is a privilege, and I respect that. But I think she's deflecting. We've all wanted to feel human again at one point or another.

"Okay, now back to the plan," I say, spinning around and peering over the camp.

The camp is roughly the same size as the one from yesterday. Similar shape and design as well. We're lucky. Today, fewer guards are at the outpost, but there are also fewer people. No trash area like the other to sneak in from.

"Lucas, I haven't seen any Cogents, have you?"

"None," I confirm.

"Good. It's time I get some payback, then," she says, jumping to her feet.

"But what about our plan!?" I ask as she sprints away furiously. I can only watch as she throws my plan out the window. She's not hiding anything, barreling straight up to the front entrance with her blue aura on full display.

That's why it's no surprise the alarm sounds. The guard at the lookout unloads a whole rifle magazine into her as she comes rushing up. Without hesitation, she runs through the bottom of his guard tower.

I scan the area once more from my vantage point to see if any Cogents have emerged from within the camp, then I hastily make my way through the front gate. I'm about a minute behind the chaos Bianca has created inside. People bounce from one direction to the next like someone has dropped a jar of marbles with nowhere to go.

"Bianca!" I shout, making my way to her side. "There's nowhere for them to escape. The soldiers are gunning them down at the gate."

"Then let's give them somewhere else to go!" she says.

Bianca and I burst through the walls, sending a surge of people rushing through. Our presence isn't enough to discourage these heathens from gunning down our citizens. Even with my imminent pursuit, they fire on them.

My eyes settle on a soldier, and before I know it, I've removed his ability to hold a gun, hitting his hand so hard it disappears. The soldier screams in agony and drops to the ground, writhing in pain.

"Don't kill me," he begs.

The audacity of this man—to beg for his life after he continued to shoot. I place my blade next to his face and remind him that I can if I want to. He won't be killing anyone else, though.

"Lucas!" Bianca shouts. "Over there." She points to what looks like the building I found her in.

I fear I will find Katelynn like I found her. I don't think she could handle it. I know I should stay with Bianca a little longer to make sure all these guards abandon their post, but I just have to know.

Opening the door, I pray once more to the Giver of Life, to spare her. Keep her from harm. Door after door shows the same horrid nightmare of men and women tortured through experimentation. My heart sinks as I recognize one of the boys from the dance.

A feeling of immense pain comes over me as I reach the last door. No one I've seen yet has been alive, and this is no exception. Anxiety fills my body as I push the lab room open and observe the slender figure that lies there covered. Her hand dangles from the table, lifeless. Blood pools below her hand, and in the center is the green gem necklace of the Giver that Katelynn wore.

My knees give way as I drop to her bedside. Pain surges through my body as I dry heave in pain. I slam the ground next to me, angry because I couldn't save her—angry because the Giver of Life didn't save her.

"Katelynn . . . I'm sorry . . ."

I recall my promise, that I would come back for her. But I wasn't fast enough. I should have never stopped, never rested. I worry her last thoughts of me were that I was a liar. That she felt let down by me because I hadn't been able to save her. I'm a weapon, but I couldn't use myself to get to her.

"No. No."

My body begins to shut down and I curl into a ball, focusing on her outstretched hand. The blood drips from her fingers, mocking me. "This can't be. Mover of Life, bring her back to me. Answer me! Bring her back!"

The silence feels like a death sentence. The Mover has made an effort to bring me here but hasn't brought her back. Why? Did I do something wrong? Am I wrong?

Darkness comes over me, and I stay there, held by its vast emptiness. I don't want to leave to move forward. I want to stay in this pain, to feel it just a bit longer, as if to let it go would be to not accept what's real. She's not here anymore.

"I'm sorry . . . I can't bear to look at you. I'm afraid. Afraid to see the pain you felt as you were dying—knowing I could have stopped that."

I don't know why I return, but I feel I must give her the send-off she deserves. I place the necklace she held on to so tightly back into her hand and gasp. Then, with the prayer she would have wanted, I kiss her hand one last time before releasing her to the Giver of Life.

"I'll meet you in the afterlife."

Her body flickers and vanishes in an instant. Not a trace stays behind, but all the traces of her life remain. "I knew you, Katelynn. You were sweet and kind and beautiful and compassionate. Smart and fun. I hope you can forgive me for my failure."

I don't know what to do now. Everything I've lived for is over. If she's gone, I surely don't want to be here. I wonder if I could even do it without an edge. Surely if I pressed hard enough, I could take my own life.

I practice once more making an edge, but with resilience, it snaps back into place. It seems like even if I wanted to, I couldn't. There's nothing lower than this for me. I can't even kill myself. I'm a joke. Pathetic in everything I try to do.

The room becomes filled with my thoughts as they grow louder and louder inside me. I can't seem to escape them, can't run from them, can't deny them. The screams of the people I love haunt me. I have nothing. I am nothing.

For a moment, I can see my mother again: straight golden hair hanging down to her shoulders, her cleanly pressed military uniform, her dimpled cheeks that frame her constant smile. "Turn the page," she says. "Find out what happens next."

I want to cry at the sight of her. I want to tell her it's too much and that I can't. But she can't hear me, and I know it. Wherever these words and feelings are coming from, they aren't from where I am. They are from above.

Now is the time to dig deep, to tell her up high that I haven't forgotten about her. "Okay, Mother. I will."

The Mover of Life must be working in me, because I find myself lifted to my feet. It's as if bright rays of sun peer down on me as I walk through the building. I want to find Bianca and return to the cave, to sleep for several days.

It's been a few minutes, and it seems the rescue was a success for everyone else, at least. I know I should be happy about that, but I'm not. "Bianca, we need to go," I say, noticing her blue aura from the corner of my eye.

"Where'd you go, pacifist?" a man says.

His voice is deep and slow. It's Bear, the grizzly-looking Cogent from Sinder. He presses his red blade firmly against Bianca's neck, halting my movement.

"What took you so long? Wasn't sure if you'd ever come out," he says with a grin.

I have a feeling he knows exactly why I was in there, but he taunts me nonetheless. If it weren't for Bianca, I'd graciously let him kill me right now. But I can't do that to her. Not after everything she's been through.

"I see you brought your beast master, Hara, with you. Where's the psycho, Hatcher?"

"Lucas, you can go. Run away. Leave me," Bianca begs.

She's worried about me, which I appreciate. I could run, I'm sure. But I don't want to. I want them to feel the emptiness that I feel—the pain I feel, the sorrow.

"That's right, run away. I don't think you'll get very far, though." Bear says, taunting me.

I would ask the Giver of Life to give me a blade that could kill them, but I doubt it would happen. The Giver didn't spare Katelynn. Why would I be helped now? All I ask is that he stay out of my way while I destroy them.

"Bear, didn't you, Hatcher, and Hara, want to fight me in the field? Well, this isn't fighting—holding my partner as a hostage."

His face perks up, and he bares his beastlike fangs as he speaks. "Who said we had to be fair?"

"It's pretty cowardly to hold a hostage just so you can kill a boy like me, who doesn't even have an edge on his blade. Don't tell me they only train cowards over there in Sinder, stabbing warriors in the back, attacking during celebrations, holding prisoners because they're afraid of a fight."

He huffs. "Cowards! Please, we have a job to do. We will not let you run around and destroy our outpost. We're in charge here, and we decide what happens."

"Then decide to fight me like a soldier and not a coward."

His rabid smile lets me know I have him exactly where I want him. He's overconfident and doesn't allow the reason spoken by Hara to affect his judgment. Bianca and I are both at our ends—we won't show mercy. This is a fight I know we both want.

Bear tosses Bianca toward me. "All right. I fight."

"Thank you, big guy—I'll make sure to end you quick," I say.

Bianca dusts herself off and takes position. She doesn't have to say anything. I already know. "Let's make them regret it," she says.

I leap behind her as her heel leaves the ground. Just before we reach Bear, she moves to the side, allowing me to lunge forward. My blade comes close to his face, cutting through his wild beard. Bianca follows up with a series of attacks at his legs. Blow by blow, she forces him to stumble backward.

Bear grins. "You improve. But not enough."

"Again," Bianca calls, trying to seize the moment.

I follow her aggression, bouncing from attack to attack as we trade blows with Bear. Each of our strikes is designed to take advantage of his sluggish movement. We want to win with speed, and attacking together is doubling our efforts.

It works for some time. We're able to land a few minor blows against him, but nothing that would end his life. At some point, Bear realizes he doesn't necessarily have to defend himself against me. Lucid will hurt, but it won't kill him. We all know this now, so I have to change my purpose. If he's going to accept I'm not a risk, I need to set up Bianca.

We go again quickly, before Hara decides to step in. We even make it look as though Bear is doing all right, his attack focused on defending against Bianca.

"Now, Lucas!" she shouts.

She creates an opening for me to hit Bear as hard as I can, and I don't hold back. With all my power, I slam my blade into his right bicep, letting out a thunderous clap as my aura connects with his. I'm almost certain I broke his arm.

Hara calls for an end. "That's enough, Bear, you dumb oaf. You should have listened to me. You're being played."

He grips his arm in pain. "It was a lucky hit."

"Sure. Just stand back and watch."

Hara springs forward, going straight for Bianca. I jump to her defense, but she twirls and kicks me away. I keep trying to rejoin, but somehow, she keeps redirecting me away from the fight.

Hara seems to have the upper hand, keeping Bianca on the defensive. Their blue auras meld together, making it hard to see which blade is which. The only reason I can keep track of Hara's at all is because it's spiral-shaped.

Bianca asks me to not come to her aid, clearly afraid for my life. She knows injecting me into this fight isn't possible. I've tried enough, but it's hard to sit back. "I trust you."

Bianca separates herself from Hara once more. This time, I think she has a new plan. She knows Hara is as fast as her, so I wonder what she's thinking. "I thought you were going to show Bear how it's done?" Bianca taunts her.

Hara removes her black uniform jacket, already shredded to pieces, and smirks with confidence. "Let's go, pixie."

Bianca braces for Hara's onslaught of attacks, just as before. It's not the same, though. Bianca accepts each swing with the direction of her attack and spins to cut her over and over with her second blade. She's identified her fighting style and is now fluidly countering every strike.

Frustrated, Hara tries to change styles, but this creates an opening, and Bianca quickly takes advantage of it. She strikes Hara's wrist with her blade, and then in a flash lands seven rapid hits to her chest. The strikes are so fast, Hara immediately bursts into the shiny Cogent gas.

Bianca's eyes quickly lock on to Bear as he grips his hand and inches backward.

"Please no," he says, begging for his life.

Bianca doesn't hesitate. She rushes to him and plants her blade in his neck before he's able to utter another word.

She killed them, and rightly so, but the air is still heavy with the weight of lives lost. Katelynn is still gone, and their deaths won't bring her back. I should be able to breathe a sigh of relief right now, but I can't.

"Lucas. Are you okay?"

I shake my head, unable to express what's on my mind. She doesn't need an answer from me. I slump to the ground, and she holds me, quiet for a minute. We only have each other now.

"I know. I shouldn't have rushed in," she says, breaking the silence. "I couldn't take it, though. The thought that they might do what they did to me to someone else just sent me over."

I get it. I understand. I'm not mad at her. I feel like if I acted more like her, Katelynn might be here. She stayed and fought when I ran.

"What is it?" she asks, searching my face for clues.

"Katelynn is . . . gone."

Her lips tighten, and her eyes move over me. "I'm sorry," she says with genuine sincerity.

She hugs me tightly, forcing me to feel her arms around me as if to say, *Don't give up*. And I know I can't. She needs me by her side. Whatever may come now, I'll do it, in the name of keeping Bianca safe.

"Lucas, I think it's time we make them pay. It's time we punish them for these crimes against Rockcliff and humanity. It won't bring back the people we lost, but it's the right thing to do. We are the justice of humanity now. Katelynn would want this."

I look at her face, disheveled from battle, exhausted from days of torture. She speaks the truth. Katelynn would want me to save as many people as possible. If there's one thing I can do now, it's honor her wishes.

"What did you have in mind?"

Chapter 16

Bianca has put a lot of faith in me. I know because she hasn't hesitated about anything I've said or done lately. She really believes in me, despite all my failures. Right now, we both want the same thing: to get revenge on the Sinder Army. Even knowing we can't stop them, we want to hurt them. And we will.

Our plans have me going to the one place I thought I'd never return to—Sincliff. The town is not too far from these camps, and likely their last stop before making it back to Sinder territory. I know I told myself it wouldn't happen, but I agree it's the best strategy. A lot of information can be gained there.

A half day's walk is all it takes. When we arrive, we intend to gather as many resources and as much information as possible about the Sinder Army and the status of their return to the Sinder territory. If we know where most of their Cogents are stationed, we can liberate their weaker convoys.

Upon arrival, we mask our auras and remove our military jackets to keep a low profile. The last thing we need is for rumors to get out that two Rockcliff Cogents are staying in town. We would be hunted down mercilessly.

The people in this city are truly a different breed. They look rough, and are cautious of everyone. I suppose it makes sense, though. There's no telling who you're going to get out here. There's a reason Sincliff is nicknamed the city of outlaws. Makes me wonder why they ever thought it fit to station my mother here.

"Bianca, we should reach out to the local Church of the Giver for shelter. Then we can go looking for some information."

She looks at me with a bit of concern. I don't think she's in love with the church like Katelynn was. I've never asked why, but I get the feeling from time to time that maybe she believes them to be too independent from the will of Rockcliff.

Inside the church, a peculiar and familiar nun named Miss Kelly greets us. If I remember correctly, she was here when I was little. I'm surprised she's still around. What's more impressive is how she thinks that black hair dye is fooling anyone.

"Miss Kelly welcomes you to the Church of our Giver of Life. Do you two kids seek the Giver's holy blessing of matrimony? If you do, simply start by calling upon the Giver of Life and ask his blessing. This is what Miss Kelly believes."

"No. That's not why we are here," I say, stepping forward to lead the conversation. I fear if Bianca speaks, she'll be found out in a minute as not a firm believer. "We are refugees from Rockcliff seeking shelter. Do you have a place for us to stay, by any chance?"

Miss Kelly bows. "Why, of course. The Giver of Life always provides to those who seek him."

She takes us through the empty church and out a back door. We cross a small alleyway and enter another building the church appears to own. It seems they have some farmland on the edge of town, probably to feed the hungry here.

Upon opening the door, we are met with an astonishing revelation. It appears many refugees have taken shelter here. They line the walls and crowd in groups, but there's no doubt they are from Rockcliff.

"We've had several in need as of late. Seems something is going on again. You two make yourselves at home. I'll get some more blankets so you don't catch a cold. Miss Kelly wouldn't want that."

Bianca and I begin slowly walking toward an open spot at the other end of the room. It's incredibly quiet in here for how many people there are. We receive suspicious glares as they try to determine if they've seen us before or not. They can't possibly recognize us without our auras. To their knowledge, it's impossible.

"Lucas?" someone asks behind me. "Lucas, is that you?"

The voice seems like it should be familiar, but it's not. I cautiously turn around, only to be stunned by the last person I expected to find here.

"Justin, is that—"

"It is you, isn't it, Lucas!" he says with excitement.

I want to shake my head and deny it, but I can't hide. With my aura gone, he reaches out for a hug and before I can stop him, his hands are wrapped around me. "Lucas, I missed you."

I'm at a loss for words. "You're not dead?" I ask as he releases me.

"No. But I almost was."

"I mean . . ." I was thinking of just now, when he hugged me, but he's thinking of the attack. "I'm sorry, Justin. It's good to see you. Are you okay?"

149

He nods. "I am now. Say, why aren't you—"

"I am," I say, silencing his final words.

"But—"

"I know, it's a lot to explain. Consider us hidden."

He nods. "That explains why you're so warm."

"I appreciate you keeping this to yourself. So, how has it been since . . . How is everyone else? And Miss Caroline?"

Justin looks to the ground and scratches his short, curly black hair. "I don't know. When the city was attacked, Miss Caroline left us. She was supposed to watch over us, and she left us without hesitation. As the oldest, I tried to get help, but as I left, a Sinder soldier caught me. They lined us up and dragged us off."

"How did you get free?" I ask.

He smiles, recalling the moment. "The Princess Cogent. She came down from the heavens and saved me. She brought me out of that hell."

Bianca and I look at each other and say the name "Princess Cogent," until we both laugh, realizing he's talking about Brooke. Who knew all those skirts she wears over her pants would earn her the title?

"That's the one," he says. "She set me free, and I followed some of the people here to this place."

"When was this?" I ask.

"Yesterday," he answers.

"Was there anyone else with them?" Bianca cuts in.

"I don't know. Everything was so crazy—I only saw her."

I turn toward Bianca. Clearly, we're both wondering if Brooke and the others are still out there.

"There could still be others fighting out there like us. We might not be alone after all," I say.

The smell of burning flesh snaps me from thought. I turn around to see the old nun's hand gripping my bare arm rather tightly.

"Oh my goodness, you're very warm. I brought you these blankets, but it looks like you don't need them. Are you catching a cold or something? Miss Kelly wouldn't want that," she says.

"Eh, yeah . . . something like that. Thanks again for giving us a place to stay."

"The Giver of Life has provided this place for you. No need to thank Miss Kelly," she says with a smile.

"It's a little crowded," Bianca points out, sounding uncomfortable.

150

"Well, you two can stay here, or if you prefer, in the barn outside. It's not much, but it's a roof, and Miss Kelly cares about your safety."

"We'll stay in the barn," Bianca volunteers.

I nod in agreement. "You're too kind," I say to the woman.

"Nonsense. We humans have to look out for each other. I'll go grab you a fresh pair of clothes. Yours seem to be absolutely shredded. Miss Kelly will take good care of you two. Yes, she will."

"Thank you," I say.

As soon as Miss Kelly walks away, Bianca confesses, "She's too friendly . . . and I hate that she says her own name so much. It's creepy. And she didn't even flinch after touching you."

"I know. It's a little odd, but she's allowed to be friendly. We shouldn't judge her—she works tirelessly to provide for people," I remind her.

Bianca raises her eyebrows as if she's not buying it, even if I'm the one saying it. "Lucas, I may not be the most social, but there is one thing I know, and that's strength. That nun has lived out here for years in this place. She isn't still alive by accident."

I can see the concern in Bianca's face, but she doesn't know what genuine compassion looks like anymore. It must be hard for her to see the Mover's goodness as a nonbeliever. Someday she'll see the grace of the Giver of Life. I know I need it now more than ever, for Katelynn.

"If you're not careful, we'll both end up on a lab table tomorrow," she says before storming off toward the barn.

Now that Justin and I are alone, I feel like it's as good a time as any to catch up with him. We reminisce about when we were kids, an escape from the nightmares of today. "Do you remember that game we would play?" he asks. "You clearly couldn't beat me without cheating."

"I don't remember it that way. I seem to recall there being nothing in the rules about what I would do."

"Typical Lucas, always finding a way to win even when you shouldn't. As long as you knew that I was always better."

"Better at losing," I say, laughing with him.

He's right, though. He was always better at every game we would play at the orphanage. The natural talent he possessed was something I always admired about him. In order to beat him, I wouldn't say I was cheating, but I would get lucky often. Or graced, maybe. Miss Caroline might even have thrown an advantageous nod toward where he was hiding a time or two. It wasn't my fault, though. I couldn't stop her from helping me.

151

"Well, it was good to see you Lucas," he says. "Just remember, I got your back. Now go do what you came here to do. I'll be here when you're done, and we can talk more."

I want to hug him again and tell him thank you. Thank you for being my childhood friend. But I'm afraid this time would be different. I'm not sure how much my suppressed aura lowers my intensity. I'm still Cogent, but he didn't scream in agony upon hugging me. "I'll see you around, brother."

Outside, I look for the big red barn Miss Kelly spoke of. Inside, it shouldn't come as a surprise to find Bianca doing one exercise after the next. "Your aura is still hidden," I commend her.

"It's taken some time, but I think I can hold this for a while now. Maybe even all day."

"You don't have to train right now, you know."

She throws a series of punches and kicks in my direction, as if I'm supposed to step in and spar with her. "You know I do," she says, spinning around and doing another combo.

As she approaches me once more, I decide to jump in, catching her strike. She stops abruptly and stares at me. We've been here a hundred times this year, locked in combat, and each time we are, I feel like I learn something new about her.

"Did you know you close your left eye a little when you spin?"

"Are you making fun of me?" she asks.

"Only for not taking a break. We've done enough fighting."

Her training so much indicates to me that she's worried. I've come to know that about her. She struggles to speak about what bothers her and takes it out in activities.

Finally, she pauses. "I don't know how to say it."

"Ahem." Miss Kelly clears her throat. "Here you are. I told you Miss Kelly would provide clothing, didn't I?"

She places a neatly folded stack of garments on top of a crate nearby. It reminds me of when Miss Caroline would bring me fresh clothes back at the orphanage, and the feelings I get with Miss Kelly seem to be just as conflicting. I was a bit shocked when Justin said Miss Caroline up and abandoned them during the attack. I know she lied to me about becoming a Cogent, but I've always hoped she had a good reason. But what she did to everyone at the orphanage is unforgivable.

"Was there something else Miss Kelly could do for you?" she asks, snapping me from my thoughts.

"No. Thank you again," I say with a fake smile.

"Now don't mind me. Miss Kelly must go into town for some supplies for a bit before it gets too late. We've had a lot of guests these past few days. Be good little kids."

She waves, and just like that, the nice old nun is off to the markets. Bianca paces for a moment before quietly leaving the barn. She stops at a fence, leaning in and letting out a sigh. I join her, gazing into the fields at two spotted cows roaming around near the fence.

"This is exhausting, isn't it?" I ask Bianca.

She agrees but continues to look away. I'm sure she has a million thoughts swirling around in her head, like me. I take a moment to silence some of those. It doesn't help me to think of them all at the same time.

"It's peaceful here," I point out as I watch the two cows slowly chew up some grass. "This place seems unreal, sitting between two superpowers that want to kill each other. Makes me wonder if we could make it out there, you know?"

Bianca sighs. "I couldn't do it. I can't sit by while the Sinder Army plagues our country, destroying humanity one day at a time. The peace these people have is false. It's only achieved by Rockcliff and their efforts. Without them, there would be no humanity left."

I nod my head to reassure her that I understand her feelings. I'd known that was the response I would get, after all. Bianca isn't built to live out her days in peace. She's a fighter at heart. And I have to say, after everything we've been through, and losing Katelynn, I'm starting to understand. She's lost a lot of people she loves too, and wants to face it head on.

"What's wrong?" she asks.

"I . . . I'm not getting her back."

The words I've said aloud hurt more than I thought. It's real now, even though it's been real this whole time. "I've lost her," I say again, with all the pain pushing to the surface. "She's gone. I couldn't . . ."

"Stop. Lucas, this isn't your fault. It's the Sinder Army. They are a parasite in this world. Katelynn fought against them, like us. She wants you to keep fighting today. We don't stop until we make them pay for their crimes."

I appreciate that she's trying to cheer me up, but she didn't really know Katelynn like I did. She opposed the Sinder Army and all they stood for, but she did so out of compassion. She would have wanted to change this world through healing it, not fighting it, but she wasn't given a choice. She was too kind for all this.

"You have to push yourself, Lucas. We must push ourselves past our limits. For them."

With her words, I realize this is how Bianca handles the pain of those lost people in her life. She fights and trains every day so she can feel like she has some control over it. In her mind, it's the only thing left for her to do. She must push forward and fight what took them away. I'm really face-to-face with the same decision—to sit here and hide forever or move on and fight back.

"I understand the feeling of defeat, Lucas. It overwhelms me at times, too. But I know that's when I must do it. I have to dig deep and face that wall that tries to hold me back from the world." She lets out a quick laugh. "My father always used to say, 'Make the world yours. Truly make it yours. Don't be a product of it. Mold the world you want to be in.' I like to think that's what I'm doing today. For him."

"He sounds like a wise man."

"He was," she says with a sense of longing.

"You were close to your dad?" I ask.

She nods and stands up. "Let's go."

"Go? Where?"

"I want a pie," she says firmly.

"A little random, isn't it?" I challenge.

She shakes her head, "No. It's what I want right now from this world. A nice, warm apple pie, crumbly and sweet. Doesn't that sound nice?"

I chuckle for a moment and realize she's serious at the same time. The girl with purple hair who's tough as nails will make this world give her what she wants, and the first thing on that list is pie.

"Well, let's go then. You've convinced me," I say, in full support.

The two of us set off to the market, where we look for quite a long time until we find a small bakery that sells pies. Bianca surprises me when she pulls out some money. She must have picked some up from our assault on the Sinder camp.

The two of us sit down outside at a metal table that looks out over the main road. It's a nice little place where we can enjoy the treat.

"See Lucas, this is what right now is about," she says, smiling from ear to ear, handing me a fork so I can join her.

I take the utensil and scrape up a big bite of the warm, crumbly goodness. It's a pure shock to my system, especially as everything I've experienced physically and emotionally lately has been so dark and bitter. "You're right," I admit. "This is good."

She flings back her purple hair and challenges my fork to the next bite. The two of us have a little miniature sparring session until she cheats by pulling out a second fork and, with mine locked with hers, scoops an unchallenged bite into her mouth.

I look at her in complete disbelief.

She freezes, allowing a piece of pie to come tumbling out of her mouth. "What?"

"I thought you were noble and only fought fair?"

"I'm a dual wielder, didn't you know? This is Devotion, and the one that beat you was Fate. So."

She shrugs her shoulders before she sees me go for a counterattack. I manage to scoop up a large bite of pie, which she quickly swats away with Devotion. "I thought we were sharing?" I question her motives.

"We are," she insists, "but I never said I'd make it easy for you."

I know I'll have to play dirty if I want another delicious bite of this pie. I quickly slide my hand under the table and squeeze her leg. It draws away her focus. With my other hand, I swoop in and snatch a forkful. I manage to get half of the pie in my mouth and the other half on my face.

She giggles at my mistake, slides her finger down my cheek, and plops the pie back into her mouth. "You can't beat me," she says with confidence.

Our food-sparring session lasts until the last bite of pie is gone. Then, with full bellies, we can relax and enjoy each other's company. This has probably been the best moment in my life since the attack, the one time I didn't feel that sadness deep within.

"Do you remember the first time we met, Lucas?"

"I think it was the first day of school," I say.

She nods. "Yeah, you didn't seem like much."

"Well, thank you. I wasn't going for much."

"When I had to fight you, I thought you were some loser who didn't care about anything but himself."

I smile. "Please, keep the compliments coming."

"But then, after our first fight, you surprised me."

"Yeah, sorry about that. I don't know if I ever apologized, but I really didn't mean to grab you—"

"No, that's not what I meant. I was clearly the more skilled fighter, and you found a way to not lose to me."

I smile again. "But I didn't win either."

"No, but you didn't lose, and that's when I knew you had some heart in you somewhere."

"Well, thanks."

I watch her scrape the plate clean with her fork, licking it until the crumbs are gone. Bianca looks genuinely happy now. I think she needed this. To get past what happened, if only for a moment.

"So, now that you've been officially defeated here, what else should we talk about?" she asks playfully.

"Well, I know a lot about you now, but I don't know what you were like as a kid?"

She leans back. "Not much to tell, really. I trained all the time so I would someday be a Cogent. I trained with my brother and dad. My mom died right after I was born, so I don't remember her."

"How did you know all that training would lead to you being a Cogent? I mean, there are a lot of things that go into picking it right. How did you know it would be you?" I ask with genuine curiosity.

"I don't know. I guess I just trusted my dad. He told me one day I would become a Cogent, and I believed him. He served Rockcliff as a Cogent for many years before he was killed. There was never any need for me to question why or how he knew. I miss him. I miss sitting with him in the front yard."

She clears her throat and sits forward a bit to shake herself out of her thoughts. "How about you? It must have been hard growing up with no family at all."

"I lost both of my parents in an attack by Silas's right-hand guard, a Feren Elite. I can recall seeing his serrated blade plunge through my parents as they vanished into nothing. As if they were never there. But I know they were there; I know they were always a part of me. After that, Miss Caroline found me—she too had survived the attack and fled to Rockcliff to start a new life. They accepted her as head of the orphanage, and I was her first kid. She became like a mother to me."

"I've seen her before," Bianca says. "From time to time, I would see her meet with my father. I don't know why, but I knew who she was."

"I used to think we were close, but ever since the selection, something has been different. Miss Caroline's not the same person I knew her to be. And now Justin says she even abandoned him and all her other children. I don't get it—I don't get her at all anymore."

Bianca scratches her cheek. "I don't know. I'm sure she had a reason."

I sigh. "I guess. I wish I knew what that was. Now I have no one again."

"Well, you've got me now," she says, catching me off guard.

Normally, Bianca is very tough and distant from her emotions, but she's really opened up to me lately. I guess, under that tough exterior, she's like anyone else.

"We seem to make a good team, don't we?" I admit.

She doesn't respond. Her face doesn't light up like it should. The opposite seems to happen—her eyes go pale white, and her smile turns into a grimace of fear.

"What is it?" I ask, waving my hands in front of her face.

That's when I notice she's looking past me, not at me. I turn my gaze to match hers, only to become instantly immobilized by who I see.

"Commander Silas."

Chapter 17

I can feel it slipping away, all the control I have over myself, my feelings, my thoughts, my body, my aura. My chest tightens as the air leaves my lungs, unable to return. I'm not watching from afar—he's right here in front of me, and this time he's here to kill.

Keep breathing, I remind myself.

Silas stands in the center of the dirt road with six Feren Guards at his side. His soldiers seem to be patrolling around him, looking for signs of Rockcliff survivors. Or maybe they're searching for us? Surely not, though. They shouldn't know anything about us.

We need to go, to flee this place. This isn't a fight we can win. If he notices our auras, we will be dead before we can say a word. My mind works without my body's permission, and I stand up only to be met with unwilling legs as they shake uncontrollably. I stumble, but Bianca catches me and places me back in my chair.

"Careful," she says. "He doesn't know we're here yet."

"We have to go," I say, trying to catch my breath.

"Be calm, Lucas. Your aura. People are starting to look."

I can't, though. I can't snap out of it. If we stay here, we're dead. I need to run. I need to go.

My panic snaps to an abrupt halt as the warm sensation of lips connect with mine. Sweet heat radiates through me in an invigorating way. I welcome the kiss as if more of it will put me at ease. Bianca has taken command over my body, demanding all my focus on her.

I'm unaware if I'm sitting or standing anymore, unable to see Silas. My focus is on her and her warmth alone. I've never felt this before—the sense of joy this brings me as her lips softly touch mine over and over.

"What was that?" I ask.

She doesn't answer, and I don't want her to. It was unexpected in many ways. I think what shocks me the most, though, is how I didn't want it to end. This isn't something you do with your friend. And . . . she's my friend?

"Good. You've calmed down," she says.

Calm. That's right. She was trying to calm me down. This was just to make people look away from us, so they don't see our auras. She was only worried I would get us killed.

"Thank you, Bianca," I say, watching her eyes shift beyond me as she reaches over to hold my hand. I suppose this is how she will convince everyone we're lovers on a date.

Without looking, I'm forced to read her face to understand what's happening behind me. All I want to know is if he's gone or if he's coming, but her face suggests disgust instead. "What is it?" I ask.

"It's the nun."

"Miss Kelly?"

To our surprise, the woman freely approaches Silas. The two share a short conversation before she leads him off in the direction of the church. I doubt this can lead to anything good.

"She ratted us out." Bianca is fuming.

"I'm sorry."

"No time for that," she says, lifting me up from my chair. "Let's go, now."

Bianca stays wrapped around my arm as if we're on a romantic stroll. It will definitely keep the enemy from noticing us. We don't look Cogent, and we're dating. Not exactly what anyone would be looking for.

We make good distance before we hear the screams of civilians. It seems Silas and his men have given up on the peaceful walk they came in with. Now the town descends into a chaos of screams.

"They won't burn it down, right?" I ask Bianca as I recall my last memory here.

"It's a neutral town. They have to get to safety, and they'll be all right," Bianca says. "I knew something was wrong with that woman. Just the way she always said her own name when she spoke. I didn't like her."

She's right, but that changes nothing now. We need to focus on making our way out of the city.

It's the longest five minutes of my life, but finally we're free, outside the town. Then the screams get louder, and the tree line that once looked like a haven becomes a reminder of when I left Katelynn.

I look back at the city, filled with gunshots and explosions now. A billow of smoke rises in the direction of the church. It seems they were the target and not us. At first it's a relief, but then . . .

"Justin."

The dread rises in me. I can't run away again. I can't flee from this fight, even though it's essential. There's no way I can beat Silas, or anyone else. I'm not that soldier. But I can't abandon my friend there.

159

"Bianca, I have to go back. I can't leave him. Please get out of here. I promise I'll come back to you. Go find Brooke."

With my mind made up, I begin my descent back into the city. My blood pumps fully as I allow my aura to shine once more. I calculate the fastest route to the church and begin slamming through every wall in my way. I'll make it to him. I won't let that be the last time I see him. It may be dangerous, but I won't let that stop me. I've made a promise to have his back, and I can't let him down now.

As I'm running through the city, I feel myself being lifted from the ground. My balance shifts rapidly as I stumble through building after building. Once the sensation of spinning stops, I look up at the path of destruction I caused. Did I fall?

I pick myself up out of the rubble and step back onto the street to regain my sense of direction. Then I see that I didn't fall. I was pushed by a soldier in a red jacket. One of the Sinder Army's Feren Guards stands face-to-face with me, his long yellow blade ready to cut me.

Looking back at the smoke, I see I have little time left to strategize a way out. It's too late. He charges at me before I can come up with a plan. The sheer force of his first strike sends me flying back to the ground and into the building.

I know I must act quickly if I want to get out of this. That's when the idea comes to me. Drop the building. I slide from one beam to the next until I take down the whole thing, creating a sort of smoke screen to cover my escape.

My plan should work, but I only make it about ten steps before my head jolts back and my legs fly out from under me. In one swift motion, I'm slammed into the ground, dazed and confused. I try to summon my blade, but I'm too late. The yellow-aura Feren holds his pole-like blade inches from my face.

"So, you're who the commander has been receiving intel about. The bladeless hero who took out two of our outposts. You seem weak, if you ask me."

He stares at me a moment, contemplating how he wants to kill me, no doubt.

"I don't enjoy killing kids," he says, pulling his blade back. "But I still follow orders. At least die on your feet."

It seems I have no choice but to fight. I plant my feet firmly and do my best to fend him off. This likely won't go my way, so my goal is only to hold him off until I come up with an escape.

"You're good," I admit to him. "Much better than the others I've fought."

He pauses, taking interest in my compliment. "What's your name and rank, boy? I'd like to remember the name of the person I've killed today. Out of respect, of course."

Respect is a rare quality to find in a Sinder soldier, but I suppose he could actually be better than the others. He is among their Feren Guard, after all. He doesn't give off the same malicious intent as Hatcher and the others I've come across. This seems like this is just a task he's been given to complete.

"Lucas Conley, First Year Officer."

"And your blade?"

"Lucid."

"It is an honor to fight you, Lucas Conley, and Lucid. I am Ali Mayu, tenth-ranked Lieutenant Feren, and this is my Sasumata."

He seems to repeat my name again quietly to himself as if to commit it to memory. I'm beginning to wonder if the Mover of Life sent this man here to give me a proper send-off. But if that's the case, it will have to wait until I save Justin.

"Please give me everything you've got, Lucas Conley."

Ali changes stances from defense to offense. Sasumata comes swinging by my face as he twirls it around his body in rapid succession. He follows by striking in a series of spear-like thrusts that quickly overwhelm me. I'm only barely able to defend against his attacks, and he knows this.

He strikes my chest with an elbow. I can barely keep up. The air is forced from my body with a rapid series of hand-to-hand blows. I collapse to my knees and scoot backward on my butt. I don't want to die here, but I'm clearly outmatched.

I'm sorry, Justin. I'm sorry Katelynn.

I try to convince myself that this is acceptable. To be beaten by someone far more skilled than me. It has to be. I don't deserve to win—I can't win.

Accepting defeat is hard, but it's something we all must do. Closing my eyes, I wait for the sound of his blade piercing my body. The cut is so quick and smooth I don't feel a thing. I thought it would be more painful, to be honest. The sound of my aura sizzling is the only indication I have that a strike has been made. But something's wrong—I don't feel my aura turning inward on itself. There's no pain. I open my eyes only to be surrounded by a yellow mist erupting.

Bianca walks through the mist holding her blades, then releases them and extends her hand. "Don't ever run off like that again, Lucas! Whatever we do, we have to do it together. Do you understand?"

I nod at the realization that she saved my life. I was a goner. "Thank you."

"Let's go get your friend."

"Brother," I correct her.

Together, we sprint through the city at full speed. Upon closer observation, it's clear the church was set on fire. We look rapidly around the building for survivors and see several that have been recaptured by Silas and his Feren Guards. I don't see Justin, though, which gives me hope.

"He might still be inside," I tell Bianca, trying to devise a plan.

I'm familiar with this tactic by the Sinder Army. They like to set fires and push people into them. It's exactly what they did to me all those years ago. This time will be different, though. I'll get Justin out.

We make our way to the other side of the building and remove a wall, allowing a large group to escape. They'll be free coming out this way, especially since we've taken care of the backup soldier in Ali.

"I've got them," Bianca says. "Go."

With little time left, I burst into the fiery church walls. Smoke blocks my vision, weighing heavily on the room. There's no sign of Justin, or anyone at all, so I continue deeper into the building. For me, the heat is irrelevant, as it can't match the constant state my body is in, but for those trapped inside, it must be unbearable.

I'm inside for at least five minutes, searching. Then I hear his voice call out for me. There's no doubt it's Justin. It sends me barreling through walls to find him. Every second matters. I won't let this Sinder trap claim another person I love.

"Lucas! Lucas!" he calls out to me.

"Justin, I'm here!"

"Help!"

I don't know why I can't find him anywhere; his voice seems to be right next to me, but I don't see him. That's when I realize there's a basement. I draw my blade and cut an opening in the floor to fall through. There, Justin lies pinned to the ground by a beam of fire, his body severely burned.

Chapter 18

I immediately destroy the beam that holds his life. It's too much, though. The fire has already done the damage as I look upon his open wound, a mixture of burned flesh and exposed bone. I drop to his side, knowing there is nothing I can say to fix this. "I'll get you out of here, I promise."

My words and my promise aren't fast enough. Justin reaches up to touch my face, as if he wants to say something to me, but no words are able to come out. His hand drops, lifeless, and his head slumps down. I beg him to wake up, beg him to be sleeping. But I know it's not the truth—he's gone.

The friend I used to play with every day of my life is gone. I shout his name again, begging him to wake up. He's not supposed to go. He's not supposed to leave me so quickly. I didn't get to say goodbye.

"You can't—please wake up," I beg.

With a fiery crash, beams and walls begin to collapse in on us. I stand above him, destroying each one of them. "No. Don't let this happen again," I beg.

But once more, my cries aren't heard by the Giver of Life. It seems maybe there isn't a Giver after all. There's no reason for such pain in my life. My mother, Katelynn, and now Justin. How can this be?

I check again, to be sure he's gone. "We don't have much time," I tell him, hoping to encourage him to wake. "Stop pretending. You've made your point. I'm a bad friend. I should have been there for you."

I hold him gently. "I'll wait—I'll wait for you to come back."

He doesn't, though. He never returns to me. He said my name a moment ago, but now he can't. I hate it. I hate it. I just want to go back. I can save him.

My body slumps by his side, and I begin digging. There's not much time left, but I will give him a proper send-off, a funeral for a brother.

"I'm going to make this right," I tell him. "I'll see you in the end, old friend. By the Mover's hands."

Lowering him into his grave, I push the dirt over his body. Unable to leave his side, I lie next to him and pretend we are in the field behind the orphanage, looking at clouds.

"What do you want to do next, Justin?"

"Do you think it's a little hot out here?"

"It's so strange, the clouds seem red today."

"Hey, look at that bird."

"What do you think Miss Caroline will make for dinner tonight?"

"I hope it's potatoes . . ."

"Do you ever think we'll see our parents again?"

"I hope so . . ."

"I don't know how to do this, you know?"

When I saw him, I thought I would somehow come out of this. That things could return to the way they were. How much will they take from my life before they have enough? My hatred for the Sinder Army is all I have now. My parents, Katelynn, and Justin. I want to take revenge right here, right now. I want to show them that this isn't the way it will be anymore. I don't want to be just a person they run into from time to time. I want to be the person they run from.

I grit my teeth with anger, and my chest pounds harder and harder. "Goodbye, Justin. Goodbye, brother."

The flames still rage on, jumping from one spot to another violently. It's never-ending, although I know that's not true. Impossible as it may seem, through all this chaos, this will end. The flames will have consumed everything, eventually destroying themselves as they have nothing left to burn.

That must be where I am now, at the end. After they've consumed everything in my life, they will have killed themselves. A poetic end, I suppose, but an end nonetheless.

"Lucas, stand up," Bianca says, appearing over me with an outstretched hand. "We have to go."

She leads me out. I stumble along behind her, in and out of reality. We clear the fire, which has grown so big and wide it's consumed the buildings near it as well.

"Let's go this way," she says.

I look back in Justin's direction, knowing I can no longer see his face. He will never come back. The only thing I have left now are my memories of him. He deserved better than what I could give him. He deserved a better friend than me. I left him all alone, and I can't stop thinking about that.

Bianca leads me to an empty enemy vehicle, and I climb in. Heaviness engulfs me as I sink into the seat. I stare out the window, wondering how long it will take to burn the image of his face into my memory. I'm afraid I might forget him, and I don't want to.

I try to recall every little detail I can remember about him. He was always short and stocky. Wide, broad shoulders that made him look strong. His dark brown eyes almost matched his skin. I remember he smiled a lot. He loved to play games and win. The talent he had was unmatched in the orphanage. He was always a real friend to me, even when I wasn't to him. I'll always appreciate that about him.

Justin would always find a way, and now that's what I will do. I must go on. Even if I have to force myself. Like Bianca said, I must make this world what I want it to be. So, I straighten myself out and give myself a few slaps on the cheeks so I can feel alive again.

"Brooke could be alive based on what Justin said. If we go to the camp they recently attacked, we can find a clue as to where they went next. If there are more people out there than her, there is a chance for us. Maybe we can do something about Silas, about the Sinder Army, about our home."

I must finish this somehow, for Katelynn, Justin, Marcus, and everyone else. Brooke is our last hope. All we can do now is pray to the Mover that she is brought to us.

I rest my head against the thick, bulletproof glass, and I pray. "Mover, are you there? Have you abandoned me? I'm still here. I need you to push me through. I can't do this alone. I need your help. Please remember my loved ones, and don't let me ever forget. Oh Mover, be with me."

Even though Bianca doesn't speak during our ride, I know she's there, supporting me the entire time. Death is something we've both seen too much of lately. We both understand the pain it causes and how sometimes you just need a moment to process it.

After about an hour, we arrive at the north Sinder outpost. From a distance, we see a Cogent with a red aura standing in front of the gate. As we approach, we confirm it's not Brooke as we had hoped, but instead Ryan, of all people. His blade isn't drawn, so to be cautious, we stop the vehicle some fifteen feet away before getting out. I'm not sure how this conversation will go, but if he tries to hurt Bianca, I'll kill him.

"Ryan," I say through my teeth.

"What are you guys doing here?"

Bianca takes a step forward, showing she's not afraid. "What do you care? Traitor."

"We're fighting back," I say.

He huffs. "Doesn't look like it to me."

Bianca summons Fate and Devotion. "I should kill you right here."

"Rockcliff is gone. There's no one left. You should join us, not fight us," he says.

"Are you stupid? What makes you think we would ever join you?"

"Didn't you hear me? Because there's nothing left to go back to!"

"And who made sure of that?" Bianca says with a burning intensity. "We've heard there are others out there."

To our surprise, Ryan turns his back, leaving himself open to being cut down in an instant. "Look, there's no way you walk out of this alive. You're only going to get yourselves killed. If you let me take you in, I can guarantee your safety."

Bianca snaps, "Like you guaranteed Cameer's?"

Ryan shakes his head, and his aura flickers violently. "You don't even know what you're talking about."

"Please explain, then. Explain to us how killing everyone from Rockcliff was good for us," she says.

I can see the frustration building up inside of him. It would be easier to fight us at this point. Bianca isn't going to back down, and I'm not going to either. We should kill him where he stands, but I'm also a little curious what he has to say.

"I did it!" he shouts at the top of his lungs. "I did what no one has done since this stupid war began. I gave Marcus a chance to kill Silas and put an end to this war. But he couldn't do it, he was too weak to pull it off. Hero of Humanity my butt. Everyone sang his praises about how great he was, but what was he really? A loser. A dead loser. He forced me to do it, too. Now I'm stuck having to do what I must, to survive. So you can blame me, but you should blame yourselves, you should blame Rockcliff. I chose to live a free man."

Bianca's had enough words; she dashes forward and swings rapidly at him. He evades each swipe using only his body. She goes for his head several times, but he counters with his hands with perfect precision. Before I can jump in, he places a kick in her chest, creating some distance.

A loud buzz echoes from his uniform, pausing the fight. Hatcher comes over the radio. "Ryan, what's going on over there? Are they here?"

His eyes fall on Bianca as he lifts his radio to respond. It's over now. We will have to fight here. It will be tough to win a battle like this. I need

167

to think of a plan to get Bianca to safety in case this goes bad. I can't lose her too. I'll have to hold Ryan off for her as she runs for the truck or maybe the tree line.

"That's just me," he says into the radio. "I'm practicing a new move."

"Well, quit fooling around and stay alert. We got intel they were at Sincliff recently."

"Yeah, yeah."

Ryan's radio clicks off, and he stands there, awaiting our next move. Bianca could attack again any moment, but she holds off, knowing it will raise suspicion.

"This is the last time I will do anything for you," he says.

I get it, in some strange way. I get where he's coming from. He's not evil, he's stupid and selfish. His goal wasn't to end Rockcliff, but to end a war that has been going on since the day he was born. When he couldn't kill Silas with Marcus, he decided to kill Marcus instead and switch sides. It's messed up, but I think I understand.

"Thank you, Ryan," I say, pulling Bianca back. "Let's go."

She pulls away, upset with my gratitude. We get only a few steps before we hear him again. "I don't know how many, but I think they went north on foot," he says.

North is nothing but trees and rocks. They didn't go by vehicle from here. This may be exactly what we need. We aren't alone, and maybe if we can find them, no one else will have to die.

Where are you, Brooke?

Part III

Chapter 19

At first, I believe Bianca and I could take the Sinder Army on ourselves. But now I don't think that's possible. We have to believe that Brooke is out there somewhere, fighting back. Waiting for us to find her and join her.

We've been heading north for about twenty minutes when I realize I never doubted Ryan's information. He easily could have been lying to us. I'm such an idiot, but maybe I have no choice other than to believe him. Why would he lie, after all? Though I'm sure Bianca could list like eight reasons immediately.

While her concerns would be valid, I must let go of them. I know he killed Marcus and basically Cameer, and I hate him for that. But at the same time, I find myself having a bit of sympathy for him.

I can see his logic, as flawed as it is. Everything he did was an attempt to end this war; he couldn't have known it would end up this bad. He never attacked me, and I suppose I should be grateful for that.

"Rockcliff Northern Farm isn't too far," I tell Bianca. "Do you think she'll really be there?"

"She better be," she says, swinging her blade through the thick forest.

Bianca's stomach lets out a loud grumble, and she pauses, as if to reflect on the pie we both wish we could have again.

"We need to find water and some food," I say.

She agrees, and the two of us decide to find water first. This way, if Ryan was lying, we will still be strong enough to fight whatever we face. I only hope we make it in time.

"Wasn't there a stream nearby?" she asks.

I pull open the map and confirm, "Yeah, a little toward the enemy, but not too far. About a mile east."

The mile seems to take forever. I suppose it's just the anticipation and overly anxious thoughts. But we finally make it, and it's beautiful. The sun reflects of the water like stars at night.

"I'll race you there," she says, sprinting ahead.

I try to keep up for a moment, but then I tell myself I can wait. It's not like she can finish it on her own. It will still be there when she's done. "Don't drink it all," I tease her.

"No promises," she says, finding a good open spot.

Without hesitation, she dunks her head underwater as if we're back in our training room. Gulp after gulp, she drinks her fill until she's engorged. Then, once she's satisfied, she rips her head back up.

"Drink too much?" I joke.

She doesn't laugh. Her hands reach up, scratching at her throat, and her eyes go red. She takes one step and collapses back into the stream. Something's wrong. Something's very wrong.

"Bianca!" I scream. "What is it?" I lift her from the water.

My eyes search for some sort of clue, coming up empty every time. She gasps. "I . . ."

"What is it? What's wrong? I don't see anything."

She struggles, wheezing. "Don't drink the water."

I lift her up and place her on the shore. She begins breathing slowly, with the occasional cough. I need to know what we're dealing with, so I look back between the rocks for any clues. It's hard, but when the light hits the right spot, I can see it. A faint trail of a foreign substance running through the stream.

"Poison."

She reaches for her throat and scrunches her nose. "I'll be all right," she says, struggling, but trying to put me at ease.

"I'll get you help," I say, thinking about how far we are from the next town.

"No, I'll be fine. I just need to rest," she rasps. "It tasted awful." The last part comes out as an attempt at a joke.

"Stop," I tell her before lifting her to her feet and throwing her on my back. "I'll find something."

I can't treat her here, so no matter what I do, I'm going to have to keep walking. I squeeze her hand as she rests her head on my shoulder. "Stay with me," I remind her. "Brooke is not too far away."

"I'm not going anywhere," she mumbles, dazed by the poison's effects.

We don't make it as far as I'd like in an hour. And somehow, sunset seems to be coming for us again. We need to gain a lot of ground, and quickly, if we want to make it to the Northern Farm. I wish I had a way of making this easier. At this rate, she'll pass out.

"How are you doing, Bianca?"

With no answer, I set her down and rest her against a fallen tree. She still has a pulse, which makes me feel better. At the same time, the poison has produced a fever, and I'm not sure how a Cogent handles being sick. Her aura could burn it off like it was nothing, or it could go nuclear and kill her. No one's ever said anything about this.

"Bianca?" I try to snap her out of her dazed state. "I'm going to have to leave you here."

"No!" she says with as much strength as she can muster. "Don't leave me, please."

"I have to. I have to get you help."

"No, please. I just need to rest. I'll be better in the morning. I just have to fight this off."

"Don't be stubborn," I say firmly.

"I'm not stubborn, I just don't want to be alone."

It looks like she's trying her best to open her eyes, but they close under their own weight.

"Okay. I'll make us a shelter, but if you're not better by the morning, I'm going to get help. Promise me you're okay?"

She nods. "I'm talking, aren't I? I'm just a little tired."

I chop down a few more trees and stack them up around us to give us some shelter. From a distance, I try to make it look as natural as possible while still covering us from any enemy search parties.

Her head falls to her shoulder as she loses the energy to keep it up. I do my best to prop her in a position where she can sleep safely while I look for things around us. "You have to pull through, Bianca."

In and out, she replies, "I will. But just in case I don't."

"In case you don't! Don't talk like that. You're all I have left. Don't joke like that."

She grins and then whispers to me, "So you need me, huh? I thought I was a bit too controlling and demanding?"

"You are," I say, trying to make her smile.

"If I die, I will have died for our country," she says confidently.

"Stop!" I say, leaning in for a kiss.

Much like she did for me in the market, I need to bring her back to reality. I know no one is watching us this time. But I still think it could work. That's when I notice her lips aren't as warm as they were before. I begin to worry, pulling away.

173

"I'm sorry. I just wanted you to snap out of it. I want you to be okay."

"I'm cold—start a fire," she says, ignoring the kiss.

Cold. I quickly gather up some of the branches and stack them into a pile near her, lighting it with my aura. I'm worried about her, more than before. She shouldn't feel cold. That's not normal for a Cogent. Something's very wrong, and I fear if I don't do something soon, I'll lose her forever.

She needs me, like really needs me. I slide behind and wrap my arms around her, raising the intensity of my aura to provide warmth. My heart races with anxiety as I squeeze her tight.

"Is this helping?" I ask.

She nods her head. "Thank you, Lucas—for not leaving me."

"I'm worried about you," I say, rubbing her arm with my hand.

I'm a little nervous about being so close to her, but at the same time, I'm comfortable. Bianca has been with me since the beginning of school. She's been hard on me, but that's just a part of who she is. She's hard on herself, and she's also a blunt person. She's not like Katelynn at all. Katelynn was sweet and tough, and I . . .

"Do you think we'll find Brooke and the others tomorrow?" she asks.

"Yeah, I hope so. Now get some rest."

I hold her as she recovers. Tomorrow, I hope we do find Brooke. But right now, I just hope Bianca is okay. I can feel her body struggling against the poison. I recall my several trips to the hospital and the time I was bitten by snakes. If this poison is anything like that, she'll need an antidote. Her aura only helps protect her outside—it doesn't do anything about her insides.

I can't leave her, though. I promised. For now, I'll just hold her tight as she fights this battle. She's protected me so much these past few days. It's the least I can do.

"You're pretty tough, you know that, Bianca? You've pushed through so much day after day, and now this. Poisoned, and you keep fighting. I wish I were like you. I wish I had your strength to just keep going. I don't know how you do it. Will you tell me someday?"

I wait for her answer, but it never comes. Out cold. I sit up just slightly, causing her hair to fall onto her cheek. The warm light from the fire illuminates her as she slowly breathes. She's calm and asleep.

"Keep fighting, Bianca. I need you to fight for me now. We're a team, after all."

Chapter 20

I wake in the morning, my hands empty, making my heart skip a beat. Where is she? Did her aura take her in the night while I was asleep? No. She must be somewhere nearby—she has to be.

Jumping to my feet, I begin my search. Surely, they didn't come for her in the night. My eyes settle on a handprint burned into a nearby tree. She must have gone this way. I draw my weapon and set out in that direction.

"Bianca!" I scream at the top of my lungs.

She doesn't answer. I'm left disoriented as the surrounding trees begin to close in on me. Every direction I look feels the same. "Bianca!" I shout again.

Off in the distance, a faint unnatural blue shines through the bushes. I rush to it, sliding down the hill and checking immediately to see if she's breathing. It doesn't look like it. She's in bad shape.

Just as I'm about to perform mouth to mouth, her eyes spring to life. "What are you doing?"

"What am I doing? I woke up, and you were gone. Why are you out here?"

She takes a moment to gather herself together. "I was feeling better for a moment, but I was hungry. So, I thought I'd look for something to eat. But my legs gave out, and I fell. Then I just fell asleep here."

"You scared me. Just wake me up next time." I shake my head. "Come on. Let's get back." Picking her up, I bring her back to my tree refuge. "I'll search the area for something to eat. You stay here and rest."

She nods, and I begin my search. I'm fortunate it doesn't take long. I believe I'm blessed by the Mover this morning, as I find a pear tree not too far from us. They're rare out here. I haven't had a pear since I was a kid.

"Look what I found," I say, holding out my shirt, full of fruit. "Just over the hill."

I drop the pile near her feet and carefully hold one up for her to take a bite of. She's lethargic, barely able to comprehend what's happening. Fortunately, her instincts kick in, and she devours the pears one after the other.

They seem to bring some stability back to her as she's finally able to open her eyes. It seems they're slowly returning to the deep brown color I've known them to be. I'm grateful. "How was that?" I ask her.

"I'm sorry. I didn't mean to eat them all," she says.

"Are you kidding? You don't have to be sorry. I know where the tree is. I'll go back and get some more for myself in a minute. I wanted to make sure you're okay. Don't scare me like that."

"Sorry," she says, closing her eyes. "I'm just going to rest again."

I agree with her request; rest sounds nice. I don't know why, but I'm so exhausted. Maybe it's all the action this morning. If she can recover properly now that she's eaten, maybe we can make it to the farm this afternoon. I don't want to wait too long, or we might miss them, but I know I can't force her to walk if she's not ready.

"Thank you," Bianca says. "For a moment there, I really thought I could do it."

"Don't push yourself so much," I remind her. "We'll set out in a few hours."

"Habit," she says.

"I still think you need some medicine, Bianca. If you're not better soon we could have a real problem."

"Okay. I'll get better. Just don't leave me. I'll be able to walk soon, I promise. I just need a minute to catch my legs and rest my breath. Like five."

"You're not making sense. Five minutes? Let me carry you."

She shakes her head. "I'll walk. You'll have to go slower, but it will be faster than you can carry me."

"Always so stubborn."

If she could walk, it would be faster, but it's important that she doesn't overdo it. This poison seems to be slow but effective. She hasn't recovered despite what she wants to be true.

"Just let me know when you're ready for me to carry you."

"I will," she says, dropping her head on my shoulder.

"Hey Lucas, can you tell me about an amazing day in your life? Something happy and uplifting. Something pure. I could use a good story right now."

I scratch the underside of my face and let a bit of a sigh out. Something pure that makes me happy. I comb through all the memories I can muster that aren't overwhelmed by our current situation. I need to tell her something, something that she can feel inspired by.

"My mother was a soldier, you know. I remember everyone looking up to her when I was a child, not just me. People came to her for advice and

176

felt protected because she was there in the town. She had a smile that put people at ease and commanded respect all at the same time. She was loyal to Rockcliff, and wore her uniform proudly."

"She sounds like an exceptional woman."

"She was. But here's the real story. My mom worked hard. Harder than anyone probably could in town. Because of that, I didn't see her a lot and ended up being watched by different women who lived close by. One day, after she dropped me off, she came back immediately. She picked me up and took me to the market during the middle of the day. She told me I could have whatever I wanted, whatever toy, whatever to eat—anything she could get me, she would.

"It was an amazing day, to say the least. I got my favorite action figure of Marcus, of all people. I still can't believe we were trained by the Hero of Humanity. We ate my favorite food from the pizza shop in town. It was run by this chubby guy with a big beard. He always had a smile when I came around. After lunch, we played every game I could come up with in my head, just the two of us. Hide and seek, statue or soldier, skip rock— we played it all. She didn't leave my side all day long. Eventually, I fell asleep in her arms, listening to her reading her favorite book.

"I remember that day like it was yesterday. It's clear and has a special place in my heart. My mother simply loved me that day and wanted me to know it. I think we have so many days where we are so involved in doing something that we almost never get a whole day of love. And it wasn't a moment too soon. I lost her later that year."

"That sounds like something I can look forward to," Bianca says, flashing me a smile. "It sounds really nice. I hope someday I can do that for my kid."

"You, a mother?" I say in shock. "Never imagined you as the mom type."

She raises her eyebrows, pondering how hard to hit me, I'm sure. "Don't be stupid. There's a lot you don't know about me. I'll be a mother someday, when all this fighting is over and this world is a safe place again."

"Well, I hope someday I can make that a reality for you. You deserve it," I say.

"Let's get going." She lifts herself to her feet. "Brooke is waiting for us."

We begin our trek onward to Rockcliff's farm town, the source of our corn. If Brooke is truly there with more soldiers, we might have a future. So I'll keep on hoping.

Walking with Bianca helps me appreciate the little things about her. She pushes through no matter what, even against her own limits. They just don't exist to her. My mom was like that. She knew what she wanted in the world and always went for her dreams. I feel obligated to help her achieve those dreams, for my mom's sake and for hers.

"Do you think Brooke will still be wearing a skirt when we find her?" Bianca asks playfully.

"Yeah, I hope so. I hope it's the most colorful thing I've ever seen. So bright it hurts my eyes."

We laugh for a moment, losing balance on the steep hill. "I got you," I tell her. "I won't let you fall."

Bracing herself against me, she assures me she's getting better. I want to believe her, and for the most part she's convincing, but it's when she's not paying attention that I see the real pain she's in.

"You know, I think you're pretty tough, Bianca."

She glances at me, uncertain. "Is that genuine?"

"Yeah. Why else would I say it?"

"Oh, I don't know. Maybe because you think you could finally beat me if we sparred right now? Trying to make a name for yourself with my defenses down?"

She has a hard time accepting compliments from anyone. "I just meant you can rely on me sometimes. I know how strong you are."

"Okay," she says, sounding reserved. "Can we stop for a few minutes?"

"Of course."

These breaks she takes last for a few minutes at a time, but the farther we go, the more frequent they become, and the less playful her voice is. It's almost as if she's running out of power. Her throat becomes hoarse again. Seems like the pears are wearing off.

"Here, take this," I say, pulling two small pears from my pocket. "They'll give you some more energy. I've been saving these for you."

Her face lights up with hope for a second, and she drops to the ground, devouring the fruit before resting on a large rock nearby. This is the eleventh time we've stopped, and by far the worst. Maybe I should have given those to her earlier, but I was hoping to make them last a while.

"Don't worry about me. I just need to rest for a bit longer."

Her eyes close, and she passes out. I know she needs help, and she needs it now. We've made a lot of progress, but we're still too far away for me to carry her. I'm worried for her. And I'm worried that if there are troops there and I have her like this, I won't be able to defend her.

"I have to go," I say to an unconscious Bianca. "You need water. You need an antidote. And if I don't go and I lose you without trying, I'll never forgive myself. I want to see you as a mom someday. You'll have the toughest kids. You'll shape the future, and that's why I have to go. I hope you understand."

Chapter 21

Before I leave her behind, I make sure to mark her location. Something only I would know. I stage our cover with fallen trees, but make it appear as if they landed there naturally. Then I check on her again. I remind her I'm coming back and hope she hears me in her dreams. Then, with a kiss on the cheek, I set out toward the farm.

During the first few minutes of my journey, I remind myself that there's no other choice. I fear the worst will happen if I stay. I can only have hope if I go, and go quickly. I need to trust that the Mover of Life is taking me in the right direction.

The forest becomes a blur to me as I stay locked inside my head. I imagine what Katelynn might think of my kiss with Bianca back in Sincliff, whether she would be happy for me or hate me. It hasn't been that long since she passed, but at the same time, so much has changed in my life. I can't help but feel a sense of guilt for my feelings toward Bianca.

This pain of love lost and found plagues me until I finally arrive at the edge of town. The crops—corn and wheat—are tall, consuming the land for miles. It's time to jump out of my head and focus on the task at hand.

I keep my distance, walking along the edge, searching for signs of soldiers, friend or foe. If Sinder holds it, they would be patrolling like they do their camps. But there's no sign of life anywhere—not even the animals are around. If anyone from Rockcliff is still here, they may be hiding.

Excited, I dash toward the center of town, only slowing at the realization this could be a trap. It's hard to be patient when Bianca's life is on the line, but if the enemy is here, then I need to be quiet, and if Brooke is here, I need to find her.

The sun is getting real low in the sky now. If I'm going to do something, I should do it now. I've waited long enough. I mask my aura on the off chance I could use that to my advantage if I run into the wrong person.

Doing my best to avoid detection, I move through the small town from building to building. Seems their medical division is in the center of town—a dusty, single-story house with a medical sign on it.

I'm about ten feet away when I hear a loud crash on my right. I take cover behind a nearby building.

"Brooke?" I whisper before creeping around the house. Two barrels are rolling around on the ground. Seems the wind must have knocked them over. I tell myself to quit being scared—I am a Cogent, after all. If someone were here, they'd likely be scared of me.

"No one is here," I remind myself.

With my newfound confidence, I rush toward the door of the medical center, darting down each row without wasting time. Thanks to Katelynn and all the medicine I would have to get for the orphanage, I have a good understanding of where everything is kept. They like to keep things sorted by type, so antidotes are all together.

Got it!

Even though Brooke doesn't appear to be here, this is a good sign. At the door, I realize I should bring back more than the antidote. Bianca will still need to recover. Food and water are just as important right now. Quickly, I grab a bag and fill it with water, dried meats, and canned foods. Instinctively, I chug every extra bottle of water I can't carry.

Now to get to Bianca.

I plant my feet and head out the door at full sprint. A bright orange spot like the sun comes swinging at my face. With little time to spare, I tilt back, barely missing the blade that almost removed my head.

My body crashes through the wooden porch of the medical center, and I roll out quickly, avoiding subsequent attacks. I suppose I'm fortunate that I learned to dodge so many pillows back at the orphanage. It just saved my life.

Gaining the distance I need, I finally turn around to confront my assailant. *Hatcher.*

Without a word, he moves in for the kill once more. I stumble back, trying not to lose the bag of food. Leaping up and down only stalls him for a minute before his blade opens a gash in my shoulder that sends blood gushing out before it burns off. I drop the bag, its contents spilling all over the ground. I summon my own weapon to defend myself, but I'm too late. Hatcher's blade bounces off mine and slices into my other shoulder. I flail in agony, swinging Lucid wildly, hoping to keep him off. I know it won't hold him, though—he slams me into the ground, pinning me with his knees.

No, I think. This can't be it. My eyes fall on the medicine, now feet away from me. Bianca needs it. She needs me. I can't die here.

"I thought I would find you here," Hatcher says, grinning. "You didn't forget me, did you?"

"How could I forget? You killed Cameer."

"Who? Sorry, doesn't ring any bells."

"And now I'm going to kill you," I say, struggling to break free.

"Sure you are, kid. You ran away from our fight last time. Then you somehow managed to kill my friends."

He plays with me, sliding his blade across my cheek just deep enough to make me shout in pain. He means to enjoy this. However he found me, he's been waiting for this.

"You know, kid, you've Ryan to thank. He said you would be here. I almost didn't believe him. It took you so long to get here. Silas is going to be thrilled when he hears I took care of his little pest problem."

I should have known. Ryan sold us out. He never had any good intentions. The next time I see him, I'll make sure to kill him. I should have known he would betray us.

"Where's your girlfriend, the little purple-haired girl you were traveling with? That medicine isn't for her, is it?" He smiles. "Did she drink the water?"

My arms break free, swinging violently at his throat. He pushes back, but not before I land a hard right across his face. It's not enough, but it makes me feel better.

"You're feisty!" he says with glee. "Well, if your girlfriend isn't dead already, I'll make sure she is soon enough. I mean, she can't go far, am I right? The poison has a slow, crippling effect. It will make for an easy sport. Not even a Cogent can withstand it."

The thought of losing Bianca is too much, but I can't get Hatcher off me. He's far too heavy and strong for me.

"I promise this won't be quick," he says. "Bear and Hara would want me to take my time with you."

Then I feel it—my body being torn apart as his blade enters my side. Foreign and unwelcome, it burns with an unrivaled fire. I can't survive this. It's not possible. But he doesn't want me to die. My throat fills with blood until I choke and spit it out.

The pressure of his legs on my arms and stomach vanishes. I brace myself against the ground for a finishing blow, but it never comes. My eyes go in and out of focus, and I roll back and forth, searching for something to dull the pain.

"What are you doing?" I ask between my teeth.

He doesn't say anything. He waits patiently for me to gain a sliver of hope, and then he squashes it with a kick to my face.

Hatcher plays these games several times, until I give up. Then he waits some more. He wants to destroy me, take away my hope. I won't give up, though—I won't give in. I'll find a way through his games right here and now. I'll end him if it's the last thing I do.

"That's the spirit," he says. "Get up. Now we can have that fight you promised me."

My legs are empty and devoid of any power; my arms can barely move. I need my blade, Lucid, right now, more than ever, and I need it with an edge.

I close my eyes, and with every ounce of focus I have, summon Lucid, with the sharpest edge ever made. I hold this focus while my legs carry me toward Hatcher. With all my strength, I lunge at him. It's time he dies, time he pays for everyone he's hurt.

I connect.

But when I open my eyes, I see I haven't done that. There is no edge. Hatcher holds my blade with his hand in joyful celebration, then plunges his blade back into my side, reopening the wound that has just closed.

I can't beat him. I'm a failed Cogent with an edgeless blade. I drop in uncontrollable agony, begging for swift death. I'm ready to go. "I'm ready," I say aloud.

"You know, it took me a lot of practice to find where to stab someone and let them live. It's a lot harder than killing them."

His words mean nothing to me now. My eyes focus on the fields of wheat and corn. Beyond them lies Bianca. I let her down, I know. But I hope she can forgive me in the next life. I wonder, if I'd taken my duty as a Cogent more seriously, like her, maybe I could have lived. Could have protected the people I loved. I see now that running away from it all was never an option. I suppose Miss Caroline knew that too. Perhaps that's why I'm a Cogent at all.

"Where'd that confidence go? You should beg for your life—it's my favorite part." Hatcher kicks me onto my back and kneels on my chest, blade at my neck. "This is my favorite part, but I want to savor it. Struggle some more, please. I can see it in you. There's still a little bit of hope left that somehow you'll make it out of this. So struggle some more for me, won't you."

183

His expression turns to disappointment as he sees he won't get his way anymore, but then disappointment morphs into concern with a loud tear. I follow his eyes as he rapidly searches for the source of pain. From his chest, an oversized red blade is protruding outward.

With a quick jerk of the weapon, Hatcher bursts into a violent orange mist, his aura eating him from the inside.

What's left to be seen through the fumes of a life is Ryan, cold and stern, holding Dissent. He's ready to take my life. But then he looks at me as if he wants to tell me I'm pathetic. That this was his plan all along somehow. He sent Hatcher after us, hoping to get him alone. Then, when he was fully distracted, he could seek out his revenge for Cameer.

I don't want to believe it, but somehow, it's true. I'm certain. I understand why he did it. Why he killed Marcus. Why he killed Hatcher. I understand that I'm not his enemy.

Before I can muster the energy to confront him, he takes his leave. I'm not sure if I should curse him or thank him. I keep my focus on him all the same as his red aura blends together with the sunset until he vanishes over the horizon.

I'm left empty, alone and beaten, but not without hope. Dragging myself to some of the nearby water bottles, I lop off the top of one and drizzle the water into my mouth like heavenly manna.

It's over. I'm alive. Somehow, I have a chance to save Bianca, and I won't let it go to waste. Back on my feet, I again fill the bag with the medicine, water, and food. There's no way I can run with this injury, but I can walk.

My body takes over for my mind, moving me through the fields and into the forest. I'm almost certain I've blacked out several times during the trip back, but I've made it here somehow. It's as if the Mover guided me back to her.

She's still unconscious, her heart barely beating. I fall to her side, quickly rolling her over. First, I give her water, then the antidote. "You're strong," I remind her.

Her lips move, reaching for the bottle, reaching for life. I kiss her and then collapse by her side.

Chapter 22

The crackle of thunder vibrates through the air, gently pulling me back to consciousness. Water trickles graciously down until it fully engulfs us. Reaching for my side, I feel a sharp pain, which tells me I'm alive. Before I realize it, my mouth is open, as if I'm being fed by the Giver of Life.

Bianca's still here, which is all I care about. She's asleep, but the color of her aura seems to suggest she's getting better. That was close.

My eyes return to the sky, fixed on the dark clouds above. They look violent and ominous, destructive even, yet they bring life. It's strange how things change, how their roar is no longer a thing to be concerned about.

"Hey Lucas, how long have I been out?" Bianca asks, slowly sitting up.

"Maybe a day or two," I say. "I'm not really sure. I've been out too."

She lets out a sigh. "I feel better. I think we can go look for Brooke now."

The gentle rain becomes a downpour, aggressively splashing off the rocks and sizzling against our auras. It springs Bianca to life as she opens her mouth toward the sky, drinking and laughing. Her smile brings me so much joy I re-injure myself. Bianca notices and slides over to examine my wound, lifting my shirt. I don't want her to worry, so I smile through the pain as her hands delicately trace the sealed skin.

"What happened?"

"I was going to lose you. So, I had to go to the farm town to get supplies. You weren't responding—you were in terrible shape. When I got there, it seemed empty. I went for the supplies we needed. On my way out, Hatcher was waiting for me."

"He was the one that you fought outside the city that day, right?"

"Yeah, the one that normally was with Bear and Hara. He was the one that poisoned the water. Turns out Ryan put him on our trail."

Her nose curls. "That traitor. I knew I should have killed him."

"I ended up having to fight Hatcher, but he was too strong. He beat me with such ease. He tortured me. I thought I was going to die there. I really did. I hated that I wasn't strong enough, that I abandoned you again. But right before he could give the finishing blow, Ryan showed up and killed him. I don't think he did it for me, though; I get the feeling he did it for Cameer."

Bianca sits back and investigates the sky. "It doesn't look like it's going to stop anytime soon," she says, placing her hand on top of mine. "I'm glad you're okay. And thank you."

Her stomach lets loose a grumble. At once, I reach into the bag next to me and pull out some of the dried meat. Her eyes light up, and she rapidly inhales every bite until she can't eat anymore.

"I'm sorry," she says. "I don't feel like I've ever eaten this much in my entire life."

Somehow, we find ourselves laughing again. Maybe it's the trauma, or maybe the joy of being back next to each other. That joy is somehow stripped away again, though. My mind won't let me forget that most of this is my fault. For so long, I've been trying to avoid life, avoid working hard. If I had just put in some more effort, we might not be here at all.

"Bianca, I need to tell you something. I'm sorry. From day one, I've been running from my problems, my duty. I used to think that if I could avoid everyone, I'd never get hurt. So, I took the easy way out. And it got so many people I cared about killed. I'm such a horrible person."

"Hey, that's not true. You've fought for me. You saved me. You're not horrible," she counters.

"But I didn't, though. At least, I didn't mean to."

Her face is struck with confusion as she waits for an explanation.

I take a deep breath, knowing that what I say next will be like plunging a blade through her heart. I can't take it back, but it needs to be said. She deserves the truth.

"I was looking for Katelynn when I found you."

I can't look at her. I don't want to look at her right now. We are supposed to be partners who look out for each other and who always have each other's backs, but I didn't. She's protected me countless times, all based on that one moment, and that moment has been a lie from the start. I can't lie to her anymore. She deserves better.

"I was looking for Katelynn, and I planned on running away once I found her," I confess.

Bianca gasps as my words pierce her heart. She doesn't deserve this, but I can't lie to her anymore. I've never wanted to be a better person as much as I do now. I can't apologize enough for who I am.

Her voice shakes. "I see. Well, let me be the one to run away then."

She jumps to her feet and rightfully takes off into the trees. I know it's for the best. She has every right to be upset with me. I've never treated her

186

right, from the very beginning. She's always been an afterthought of my true feelings.

I lie back against the rock, feeling an emptiness that not even the sky can fill. I'm a jerk. Bianca deserves better than me, and will be better off without me. I'll only disappoint her in the end.

The rain drowns out her steps as she leaves. There's an emptiness in my stomach again. But this time, it's not because I'm hungry, but because I'm a jerk.

I'm such a coward. I've run away from everyone I've ever loved. I left my mom to fight for herself, my teacher Marcus, my partner, and even my girlfriend. I'm pathetic, and I don't really know how to not be.

Bianca is such a great person—tough, decisive, and pure. I will only bring her down if I stay with her. Even now, I bet she would forgive me for some stupid reason.

That's when it hits me. I'm doing it again. Running away from her. Pushing her away from me because I'm afraid. If she's out there, she's going to be all alone. I'll have run away again. I must be by her side. I must choose to be by her side.

I am choosing to be by her side.

Self-awareness is a cruel mindset. I can't allow myself to do the wrong thing. I need to be a fighter like her. Bianca's never given up on me before, and now I've forced her to. When really, I was giving up on her again.

"Bianca!" I scream at the top of my lungs, hoping to overcome the thunder. "Bianca! Come back!"

I scan the trees, checking furiously for any sign of movement. I beg her to come back. I even beg the Mover of Life to bring her back to me.

"I'm sorry Bianca! I'm sorry, I just—I can't give up on you now."

I look in the direction she went and begin running as fast as I can.

"Stop!" she yells.

Turning around, I see she never left. She appears from behind the other side of the rock I was resting against. My eyes meet hers through the rain splashing down on us like a waterfall.

"I'm sorry," I say. "I'm an idiot."

"That's not true," she replies.

"I'm afraid . . ."

"What are you afraid of?" she asks.

I gulp. "I'm afraid I'm not strong enough to protect you. I'm afraid I won't be the person you deserve."

"And now?"

"Now I'm afraid I'm going to lose you—because I didn't fight for you."

I know at this moment I would cry if I could, but the rain will have to suffice. I try again to tell her how I feel, but the downpour has grown too loud for her to hear me anymore. Before I can get out another word, I find myself rushing to her. She needs to hear me. She needs to hear how I feel. I won't run away anymore.

"I'm not going to leave you. I want to make you believe me," I say.

"Then fight for me."

Words. Words can't tell her how I feel anymore. It's time I show her. My hands reach up to hold her face. My heart races as my thumb sweeps across her cheek. "I'll fight for you."

My aura surges through my body as everything I've wanted is right in front of me. Her lips are warm and soothing. I want this to be clear. I'm not pretending anymore. I do love her. I'm fighting for her.

Over the past few months, our relationship has changed. Our lives have been shaken to the core. We've lost loved ones and faced death hand in hand. And although our relationship started as a friendship, it's developed into something that's hard for me to explain. Maybe this is what love really is. A complex emotion that you can only understand in your heart. And try as I might, I could never really explain it.

Our next step together will be harder. We'll have to rely on each other more than ever. I'm not sure how far the Mover will take us. If I'm alive, I'll continue to fight for our future.

Chapter 23

We pushed back the crops, our eyes set on the town. "This is probably the safest place right now. No one would think to return here. They have a lot of unused resources inside, too. We should take it easy for a bit."

"So, no one is here?" Bianca asks.

"No, and I doubt they'll be back right away. We should take this time to recover."

She sighs, and then I remember her brother was likely here before.

"Don't worry. I'm sure he's okay. He's probably with Brooke out there somewhere."

She nods. "Let's get some rest. It's been a long two days."

"His barracks are here," I say, pointing to the sign.

We follow the road through the small town until we come across the tiny barracks. Military uniforms, guns, and maps clutter the room. It looks like when they left, they left in a hurry. Either they didn't make it, or they took shelter somewhere else.

"I could see myself stationed here someday," Bianca says. She waits patiently for my response.

"Yeah, me too."

I suppose someday, if the war is ever over, living here as a soldier wouldn't be that bad. I bet our day-to-day tasks would be to keep the villagers safe from wild animals and criminals. It would be a nice, quiet life.

Bianca opens the refrigerator and sees a large chicken wrapped and ready to be cooked. She pulls it out and asks if I'm ready for dinner. I suppose it's a little early in the day, but why not? "I definitely could eat. Can you cook?" I ask with a bit of sarcasm.

"Of course," she responds. "Who do you think cooked for my family? It surely wasn't my brother. He tried and ended up serving us ashes. It was comical. Claims it was all a part of his plan to get out of cooking, but me and my dad always knew he was really that bad at it."

I can't help but laugh at the image. "Well, it sounds like you had little competition. How do you know you're even good, then?"

"Challenge accepted," she says with a wink.

I take a seat at the table and watch, mesmerized. She slices and dices a bunch of extra ingredients with Devotion before placing the chicken in the oven. Now we wait. As she takes a seat next to me at the table, I apologize. "I'm taking back what I said a moment ago."

"I thought you already knew I'm the best at everything I do," Bianca says.

"I like this. I think it wouldn't have been that bad to be stationed here with you after graduation," I say.

"What makes you think I would have been stationed with you after graduation?"

She leans over, her warm lips meeting mine, kissing me for no other reason than because she can. "I guess I assumed you would keep me. As a partner, that is."

"I guess it would be nice," she says. "We would have to get a pet, though. I've always wanted one."

"A pet?"

She smiles. "I want a dog, a strong pup that I can take care of. Call it my love of nature. People used to do it all the time before the war, you know. At least that's what my dad said."

I must admit, it sounds nice in theory, but I'm not sure I could pull it off. Seems like a lot of responsibility. I can barely remember to brush my hair from time to time.

"I don't think they let us have pets in the military."

"They'd let me," she says confidently.

I laugh. "What else is in this future of yours?"

"Oh, I don't know. Lots of stuff, I guess. Whatever I decide."

The timer chimes, prompting her to open the oven. With her bare hands, she reaches in and pulls out a delicious roasted chicken.

"I hardly recognize you. Are you sure you're still the same girl who kicked my butt day after day back in school?"

Setting down a plate in front of me, she gives me a grin. "We could always spar to find out if that's still true."

How long has it been, I wonder? I'm guessing about one week since the attack. I badly miss our daily routine. Running and sparring first thing in the morning doesn't seem so bad now. At least at this moment, it kind of feels like we're back there.

"This looks amazing, Bianca." I can barely contain my excitement.

"And you doubted me. See that? That's skill."

We share a laugh, and I'm reminded of Katelynn. I wonder if she's looking down on us now. If she's happy for us. I've been lucky to find a person to love in my life at all, and now to have found a second? It doesn't seem fair.

Maybe it's time I move on. I should allow myself to see a future without her in it. It's bittersweet, though. I loved Katelynn, but I can't ignore what I now feel for Bianca. And now that there could be a future with her, I don't want to mess that up like I did with Katelynn.

Rays of evening sun peer through the window, bouncing off and mixing with Bianca's blue aura. I wonder if this is a sign from the Giver of Life. I feel like I'm on the right path, the one laid out for me despite all that has happened. I feel the Mover working in my life to get me here.

"Lucas," Bianca says quietly. "Do you want some more?"

I extend my plate toward her. "Yes, please."

She fills my plate up one more time. I get the feeling this could be my last meal for some reason, at least for a while. I want to remember it. So, I make a conscious effort to study the savory flavor of the chicken and veggies she cooked. And of course, I want to remember this moment with her—her perfect smile, her smooth brown skin with its soft blue aura, and the unique purple hair that bounces with life.

After finishing her food, Bianca sets her fork to the side and rests. I can tell she's lost in thought, and whatever comes to her causes her smile to disappear.

"We need a plan," Bianca says, ending our enjoyable dinner.

I set my fork down and carefully take a deep breath. "I know, but I don't really have one."

My mind wanders in circles through each possibility. Honestly, I'm not even sure what we should try. I know running away isn't the answer, and that's about it. The only other option is to fight, but how, and who? We can't just take on the whole Sinder Army.

Bianca gets up from the table and walks over to a map hanging on the wall. We look at each of the markings of known camps, bases, towns, and cities. I join her in strategizing where we should fight.

"We have to kill Silas," Bianca says.

My eyes widen as I comprehend what that means. I suppose, in a way, I knew this was the answer. However, to say it out loud sounds crazy. To think we could end this war by killing Silas is a bold statement, even for Bianca. She knows where we stand. Not even Marcus could do it, and we never even beat him in training.

"We have to gain an advantage somehow. So, we have to fight in a place where we can get that," she says.

I scratch my head for a moment, truly thinking through what she's saying. Finally, it hits me. "What if we bring him to us instead of going to him?"

"And how will we do that?" she asks.

With an outstretched hand, my finger lands on the one place we could get him to come back to. "Sincliff. We go back to the neutral town. We know he's not far."

Bianca waits for me to explain in more depth. "We go back there, but this time we don't hide our auras. We claim the city for Rockcliff and send a messenger that this town now belongs to us. If we can get him to think there's still a part of the Rockcliff Army that's big enough and bold enough to take a city so close to him, he would surely try to end it, wouldn't he?"

Bianca looks back at a stack of uniforms in the corner. "If we do this, then let's make it believable," she says.

We'll wear the Rockcliff uniform as a badge of honor, reminding everyone that humanity still has hope as long as we are alive.

"It's settled then," I say. "In the morning, we fight."

Chapter 24

It's hard to sleep, knowing what tomorrow will bring. I find myself awake for hours, twirling Bianca's purple hair as I hold her. She wants to appear tough, but I can tell she's having trouble falling asleep.

Our trip to Sincliff will be different this time, since we don't plan on hiding who we are. We've decided to make a big impact by pulling up in a Rockcliff military vehicle. This will send a clear message that we mean business, which will get the town talking. And surely Silas will catch word of it soon enough.

"I wonder how everyone will react to us?" Bianca asks as we rise the next day. "I hope this works like you think it will."

In the end, we stroll through the front gate like soldiers with a plan. The citizens stop and watch as we make our way inward. Bianca puts the truck in park. It's time we made our intentions clear. Silas is clever, so I'm sure he will want to eliminate us once he hears only two Cogents have taken over the neutral town of Sincliff.

"You're sure this will work, right?"

I give a couple of nods, hoping to convince myself as well. "Let's do this."

Bianca places her hand on the door, and I know there's no going back.

"Wait!" I gasp.

She turns to me, and before I can tell her how I feel, she places her lips on mine once more. She pulls away, but not before I can grab her head and pull her in for just a little longer.

"This can wait," I say, resting my forehead against hers. "You know we don't have to do this."

Bianca smiles and shakes her head. I know we do. I know we do have to do this, but I just wish there was another way. It's best if we don't talk about it anymore. We both know what awaits us, and talking will only make this harder. I want to tell her I love her, but it will have to wait.

Right now, we have to make a grand entrance. Stepping out of the vehicle, I call for the city guard. It's time to make the announcement.

"Sincliff is under Rockcliff control now. By tomorrow, ten thousand Rockcliff soldiers and twenty Cogents will control this territory, in the name of Prime Minister Maxwell and all his loyal followers."

The message is received with curious looks from the citizens. Many times before, this city has been attempted to be conquered by a side. They may not believe us, but that's not what matters. What matters is Silas hears about two Cogents declaring ownership of this place.

"Don't worry, our message will make it to him," Bianca whispers.

I look in the direction she's nodding and see Miss Kelly standing among the crowd of civilians. The old hag still has the guts to show up in front of us, even after her church burned down. No doubt she'll rat us out a second time.

"This is a neutral town!" a man yells from the crowd. "We don't want you here."

Bianca deflects the man's complaint to me, as if I'm some sort of politician that can be reasoned with. Seems she's only tough when it comes to fighting.

"Look, if you don't like it," I say, "I recommend you leave, because tomorrow this town could be a warzone."

The crowd grows restless with my proposition, so Bianca steps forward and summons her blade. "This is your alternative," she says firmly.

A hush comes over the crowd. They know they can't kick us out. They may not like this, and I don't blame them, but right now, this is about finishing the fight. They can come back to what's left of this place after tomorrow.

"With that done, I think it's pie time," Bianca says with a smile.

"Sounds good to me."

The two of us enter the market area and find the pie shop once more. The lady at the counter recognizes us from the other day but is shocked to see us now glowing. She doesn't serve us with a happy smile this time, but instead a fearful and cautious reluctance.

It doesn't matter though. Bianca is with me, and this is what she wants to do. We order two pies, courtesy of the Rockcliff treasury, and sit down to wait.

"Are you ready to fight him?" I ask.

"I'm ready to eat this pie," she says. "I'll be ready when he gets here, but for now, it's this moment I want to live in and the thing I want to do. We aren't hiding. They will show up sooner rather than later. It just depends on how far away he is."

I spar with her once more for the first bite. Her fork dances with mine, back and forth until she gets the upper hand. She scoops it up and redirects it to me. The warm, crumbly apple pie melts in my mouth, fading my worries about tomorrow.

Bianca turns to the owner. "You should leave," she says firmly. "I want you to live."

Hesitantly, the old lady grabs her things and heads out.

"I'm going to need to eat another one of her pies after tomorrow," Bianca says.

I agree with her. These come out perfect every time. It would be a shame for them to disappear. And if I think about it, this is the first date we've had together.

She grins. "You know, when we beat Silas, I think I'll make her head chef of Rockcliff and declare her pies Freedom Pies. I like the sound of that."

The sweet taste lingers in my mouth, and I recall what Brooke told me about there always being time for a snack. I hope she's still out there somewhere.

The two of us return to patrol after our short break. The town will let us know if this is working by the way they respond to us. At least they seem to know something big is about to happen.

Bianca lets out a long sigh as we start our umpteenth pass around the town. The sun is sitting low above the trees now. We stop by the market once more and drink several bottles of water to stay at our best hydration levels. I'm so grateful Bianca is here with me and that I don't have to face Silas alone. I'm sure with the two of us, we can put an end to this.

Silas may be almost as strong as Marcus was, but Bianca and I have grown a lot this past week. We trust each other more than ever. With our skill combined, if we can fight him two on one, we'll have a shot. He can't ignore us anymore. We've killed Hatcher, Hara, and Bear. We've destroyed Silas's camps and freed a lot of our citizens. Ignoring us would be a mistake. We're the last two Cogents that oppose him.

With another pass around town, I start to get nervous. I hum some of the songs I used to listen to with Miss Caroline. It's the only way to keep from driving myself insane with anxiety.

"How long until he shows?" Bianca asks.

"Not much longer, I bet. If he is close, like I suspect, we'll fight tonight. If not, it will be in the morning."

Bianca plays along with my explanation. Neither of us wants to talk about the possibility he doesn't show. It's best we don't overdo it by thinking about it. We both know this fight won't be easy, so there's no point in bringing that up anymore. Instead, I focus on the small things, like straightening out my uniform.

It feels like only yesterday I was selected to be a Cogent. My world was turned upside down with that decision. When I thought things couldn't get worse, I found out Miss Caroline was part of it. This made me question my life. I still don't get it, but at this point it doesn't matter. I suppose in a way I'm glad I became a Cogent. I may not have been able to protect Katelynn, Cameer, or Marcus, but I can avenge them. I have the ability to stand up to the demons in this world, and more importantly, I have the ability to fight alongside Bianca.

Near the edge of town, we stop to observe the sun. If he's coming, I'd prefer to fight him tomorrow. One more night with Bianca before this happens sounds better.

She notices I'm worried. "We've got this, Lucas. The next time we go somewhere, we won't have to look over our shoulder and wonder who's coming for us."

"Absolutely," I say.

The town's eastern gate faces Sinder territory—this is likely where they will be coming from. Mostly, everyone around town has packed up and fled. I have a feeling the fight will happen tonight.

"Maybe he's waiting for us to fall asleep?" Bianca asks.

I straighten out my sleeves once more—I guess it helps me cope with the nerves I'm feeling. Running through all the moves in my mind, I try to think of the best form of attacking Silas. My thoughts go back to fighting Marcus and what might have worked well against him.

"Look Bianca, when he gets here, let me do the talking," I say, trying to take charge.

"You think he wants to talk to us?"

I let out a big huff. "Yeah, I hope so. He doesn't feel threatened by us. How could he? I'm sure he'll talk, like he talked to Marcus."

I'm realizing how dumb this idea is, but I can't say that to her. She's putting all her trust in me. The thing is, this is my first time really planning to fight. From the very beginning, everything I've done up to this point has been impulsive.

The sun is low on the horizon, and the two of us have begun to slow our patrol. It's quiet. A heaviness fills the air. Perhaps it's lingering from the recent storm, or perhaps it's the ominous presence of the one who approaches. Either way, it silences the world around us. Bugs and birds cease to exist, and a gust of wind sweeps through the now empty city.

"He's here."

I had hoped he would be traveling with only a few guards, but hundreds of his soldiers surround him, as if he's attacking Rockcliff once more. And maybe it's my eyes, but it seems like the whole Feren Guard is with him, judging by the red coats and banners.

I'm afraid, but I don't want to show it. I have to be strong for her. For Bianca and everyone who lost their lives.

Chapter 25

Silas. There's no mistaking it. His dark purple aura radiates with an ominous glow. He and his Feren Guards resemble an army of demons ready to take our lives. "He got the message," I say to Bianca.

"Lucas." There's a strain of fear in her voice.

She doesn't have to say the rest. I already know what stands before us is certain death. I won't run, though. I'll gladly die today for the world she wants to see.

Silas holds his position, but I won't go to him. It's safest for me to wait. I may need to use the city as cover in my attack. He's a smart commander, though. He likely knows what I'm up to, and he won't risk it. So now we play a waiting game.

Raising my aura, I step forward, shouting his name and demanding an audience. My hope is to coerce him into coming down and fighting us alone. He doesn't descend, though.

With a blazing horn, two of his Feren Guards march forward from his ranks. It's a smart move, but I challenge him, calling him a coward for not speaking with me directly. Seems he doesn't know we're alone yet.

The first guard is a woman with a green aura, and the second a man with an orange aura. They come to a halt some fifteen feet away. They're maybe ten or fifteen years older than us.

The man leans to look past me. "Where's your army?"

"They're here. Don't you worry."

I worry, though—I know he's not convinced. "Why doesn't your commander come down here himself? Scared maybe?"

The female Feren snickers at me. "So, it's just you two, then?"

I look at Bianca and then at the ground. I'm running out of ideas here, and quickly. "Tell your commander we want to talk," I say.

"I don't think so. Nothing you wild dogs have to say needs to be heard by our commander."

My blood boils with frustration. I need to project confidence if I'm to obtain an audience with him. "Listen, Silas dies here. Tell him to come fight me."

"While I appreciate your enthusiasm, boy, if you need someone to fight, it will be us. I am the seventh Feren, Sloane, and this is the sixth Feren, Lilith, so consider yourselves lucky to die at our hands."

Bianca draws my focus to her. She hasn't said a word, and yet I know what she's thinking and feeling right now. If we want to fight Silas, we will have to kill them to get to him. I nod my head to let her know I understand.

Summoning my blade alongside of Bianca, I listen to them laugh at the mere sight of Lucid. I remind them that even without an edge, we've still managed to kill a lot of their soldiers.

My comment doesn't sit well, and prompts Sloane and Lilith to summon their blades in unison. They approach, swinging at us meticulously as they weave in and out of each other's attacks. Their style is similar to ours, but their blades are unique. Sloane wields a long sword with a thick tip, while Lilith wields a scythe.

"We can't fight like this," I yell to Bianca as we dodge a series of attacks.

It's clear that they're stronger together, much like us. They've obviously trained with each other for many more years. I fear that the only way to beat them is one-on-one. Our next attack needs to be one that separates them, at the very least.

Bianca calls out to take on Lilith, which leaves me with Sloane. I position myself to be forced in between them, pinning us back-to-back.

"Now!" Bianca shouts.

This strategy doesn't seem to bother Lilith and Sloane one bit. They embrace our movement apart from each other, which makes me feel like we messed up somehow.

"We have to win," I remind Bianca.

"Yeah, I know. So, don't give up on me, Lucas."

"Never."

We push off each other and toward our opponents. I slam my Lucid into Sloane's shoulder, and he doesn't even wince. He takes the hit directly, like it's nothing. There's no fear in his eyes at all.

"Did you think this whole time we were worried about you?" he asks.

Grabbing my blade, he throws it to the ground. "You were never the threat; it's always been her. And you just made it easier for us."

Bianca lets out a shriek behind me. She's struggling. I need to rejoin her—I messed this up again. Bianca is the threat, and now she's fighting alone.

Sloane snickers and places his hand on my shoulder before walking past me. "Don't worry buddy, you can watch your little girlfriend here die first. It will be a good show, I promise."

I won't. I can't. I can't allow this to happen. Even if I don't have an edge on my blade. "I won't let you touch her."

With a swing of my fist, I send Sloane back a step. I use this jolt to launch a barrage of every move I can muster as fast as possible. If I can't cut him, I'll beat him to death. Blow after blow and strike after strike. I connect as many as possible until I force him to his knees.

I only take a breath to check on Bianca. Her eyes look at me as if to apologize. She's losing. I want to tell her to hold on, but Sloane chimes in. "You've got some spunk, kid, but you're not even on my level."

If I don't move fast and end this right here and right now, Bianca is dead. I look at my hand as it shakes in frustration. The sound of Bianca crying out in pain sends a shock right through me. Rage consumes me, and I lunge at Sloane.

His body splits in two from the shoulder as my blade moves through him without resistance.

I cut him?

Sloane's body swells from my strike until it rips apart into a cloud of orange. Lilith is in disbelief as she tries to avenge him. I am too, as I examine the thin razor's edge of Lucid.

Confidence fills me as I grip my blade and set my eyes upon Lilith. Bianca steps over to me, not wasting a moment. "This girl is strong, Lucas. Her scythe isn't like anything we've fought before. She has an advantage over me with that range."

"Don't give up. We got this," I remind her.

We move forward in unison, back to our stylistic rotation of paired attacks. One by one, our strikes become stronger. She has to treat this differently, now that I have an edge. They can't take hits from me anymore.

"Try this," I say, taking the lead on strikes. I throw the same diagonal cross strike I used on Sloane. Lilith stops it in seconds with her scythe. My blade shakes with power against hers until I'm able to push through her edge and into her shoulder.

With Lucid lodged in her, she collapses to the ground. I didn't see this before from Sloane. I'm not even sure how to explain it. She doesn't speak, but she knows. We both know this is her last moment here. Lilith's body contorts in agony, and she lets out a lifeless scream as her aura engulfs her body.

I drop to my knees, drained of energy and emotion. Bianca gives me a moment to collect myself. I'm overwhelmed by the realization that I killed them. I know I had to—if I hadn't, they would have killed Bianca. They were bad people, and still I feel sadness.

"Lucas," Bianca says, reaching for my empty hand to calm me. "Thank you."

I grip her tightly. Without killing them, we'd never have had this moment. I have to remind myself of that. But this isn't over—far from it. The hardest is yet to come. "I'll protect you," I reassure her.

I won't die here, and I won't let anyone kill Bianca either. This will stop right here and right now. There's only one enemy we really have to fight, and I hope by now we've gained his attention.

My heart races, raising my aura with it. The glow from my body doubles in size, spiraling and twirling off me in a violent heat.

My words echo over the field. "Get down here!" I demand.

Silas holds his position for a moment, as if considering who he might send next among his several Ferens. I don't care if I have to kill them all. Eventually, he will be next. And it appears he's realized that too, because he finally steps down.

"Let's make this count," Bianca whispers.

His very presence is menacing, moving slowly toward us, his ominous dark purple aura twice the size of mine. I pray the Mover of Life carries us through this fight, to see tomorrow. This won't be easy, but we're ready to face it—together.

A long, dark purple blade springs forth from Silas's hand, and he thrusts it into the ground before him, a display of strength. He's much larger than us. We can't mess up here. This fight will take everything we have. I pray for patience and strength from the Giver of Life.

"Your fight was impressive," he says, breaking his silence. "I would consider this a reward for that fight. I would be sure to tell your teacher how well you fought today, when you see him again on the other side."

"Let's end this, Lucas," Bianca says, charging forward. I pursue, right on her heels. Upon reaching Silas, she springs back for me to make a cross slash; she follows behind, aiming for his legs and in turn his mobility.

"Counter!" she yells, taking the brunt impact of his blade as he strikes back at us. "Counter!"

201

I swing rapidly by her side, jumping back only to give her space and counter his attacks. We have this—we didn't let him bring anyone else down. He will fall here. There is no way he can stop three blades.

"Faster!" she yells.

This doesn't faze him in the slightest. Every cut we land heals rapidly. Bianca staggers back, struggling to breathe. It seems without me noticing he got a few swings in on her while we were focused on his blade. Then I see it—the scar all along the back of Bianca's right leg. It seems Lilith left a going-away present, hindering her ability to move. I need to give her some time to rest.

"Why'd you, do it?" I ask, halting his progression. "Why'd you attack us?"

"Attack you? You attacked us," he says, correcting me. "How long do you think we should let you take stuff from our people? You take our resources, and you take our weapons, and then claim we attacked you when we retaliate. We're building a new world here, and your prime minister is like the cockroach that just won't die no matter how many times you squash him. Do you understand?"

Bianca lashes out, "I understand your nation is evil and wants to destroy humanity."

He snickers as if she told a joke. "So, you're a puppet for Maxwell—I see."

It's disgusting for him to see himself as the hero in all of this. He's no noble leader, bringing in a new world. He is the villain destroying the world we have. I don't care what he thinks. Either way, he will be dead.

"Are you ready?" I ask Bianca.

She bounces back from the pain she's clearly in, and the two of us return to combat. It's clear that Bianca feels inspired to end this as quickly as I do. Silas is very much ready for us this time. He sprints forward at the last second and slams into me, flinging me back into Bianca, who's preparing to strike behind me. He follows behind this attack, cratering the ground with his blade and forcing us to roll to cover.

"We need to slow him down," Bianca says.

Now split apart, with Silas in the center, we charge him from two different angles. If his blade is tied up, his back will be exposed. Bianca makes it to him first, engaging his blade hand and leaving his side open. I take my swing, only to be countered by a new, second blade and pushed off.

"He can dual wield?" I ask her with some concern.

"Don't worry, he won't be able to move quickly with those two, they're too big."

Unsure, I make my approach with her once more. One of Silas's blades comes flying at my head. I evade with just enough time, only allowing it to strike me in the shoulder. I pause my approach, checking on Bianca, who dodged the same attack. I've never seen anyone able to throw their blade such a distance.

Silas is still in control, fully aware of the fight he's in. We have to do something, and quick. The more time we've given him, the worse it's become. Crippling attacks. That will be our next focus. I give Bianca the signal we learned in the Academy and burst forth rapidly, striking for his legs.

Bianca lands a devastating blow behind his knee, causing him to drop while fending us off. We switch to his arms, making lacerations over and over until he drops one of his blades.

"Enough!" he lets out huff, batting us both away and then hastily pursuing me.

I knock away his blade, but he continues with his fist. I endure an onslaught of punches before I lose my ability to stand up. Bianca sees this and leaps onto his back, attempting to stab him, but Silas avoids every move she makes, throwing her wildly back and forth until she's flung to the ground.

My throat tightens, and I can't move. Bianca has me covered, though, and manages to cut his chest. "Not deep enough," she cries in frustration.

She tries again almost immediately. Silas breaks through her assault, forcing her into a defensive position, but she's too late. My world slows, and I feel the pain she must be in as the blade pierces her stomach. She swings at him still, even with the blade fully entering her body. He's forced to kick her away if he doesn't want to die.

Bianca's body goes limp on the ground as she passes out. Her aura flickers for a moment as she clings to Fate and Devotion. "Bianca! Don't go! Stay with me," I shout.

I can't reach her. Silas has made sure to stand in my way. To get to her, I must go through him. My legs move me quickly to his side, removing his focus from Bianca. Finding my opening, I throw Lucid into the ground and spring over it, summoning it again in the air. He counters, forcing me to move wildly against his strikes. I give him everything I've got and then some, but it's not enough. Silas's defense is like an impenetrable barrier.

"My turn," he says gleefully.

His head slams into mine, disorienting me, followed by a piercing feeling in my wrists as he strikes them with the same precision technique Father Jin used. I'm unable to summon my blade anymore. I swing at him violently, but my fists do no damage to his body, and only send a shock down my wrists every time I connect.

In a last-ditch effort, I try to run to Bianca. Perhaps I can carry her away before he kills us. But that's not possible. Instead of making it to her, I'm flung into the air as a kick sweeps across my face.

Flying, my eyes fixate on Bianca's motionless body, only looking away as my body comes to an abrupt stop. My lungs go dry, and I cough up blood. But I can't give up. I know this. Then Silas's blade enters my shoulder, and everything goes quiet.

While I know I've been stabbed, my body is numb to the pain. This isn't like with Hatcher. I feel nothing as my eyes stay focused on Bianca. The force of Silas's attacks hasn't let up, but I find myself fixated on her. I suppose if I am to die, then the last thing I want to see is her face.

Silas lifts me by my blade hand, high in the air in front of him. With his other, he tries to force me to look at him, as if he's insulted. I don't know why I thought we could win. I guess I'd hoped the Mover of Life was on my side, and would carry me through. I felt like that was true. Like this was what I was meant to do. I was a fool to think that, though. To think I'd changed, that I was strong enough.

"Did you really think you would win?" he asks.

I guess I truly didn't. I've known deep down that it's impossible to slay a demon. He's far too ruthless and skilled for me to beat. But I had to try. I had to. I've run away my whole life, and I've watched everyone around me die. I want a future where we don't have to worry about that anymore. A future that's mundane and quiet. Where we have pet dogs and eat apple pie whenever we want. I want the future Bianca was fighting for. The one she believed in.

The pain from Silas's blade comes shooting into my body, as if the volume on a radio has been turned to the max. My aura flickers with instability, and my life begins to flash before my eyes. I will be dead soon. My eyes stay fixed on Bianca as the world becomes distorted in vibrant colors.

"I'm not ready," I say, talking to the Mover of Life. "I'm not ready to go away yet."

Even now, I want to save Bianca, though she's barely conscious—if she is at all. But her hand still grips Fate as if she hasn't given up. So I, too, cannot give up. I beg the Giver of Life to grant me the strength to see this end. *Mover of Life, please find a way to carry me through. Don't stop here. Don't.*

My eyes become heavy, and it's a struggle to breathe. For a moment, I imagine I hear Bianca calling my name. She could still be alive. I need to fight my body for one more chance to save her.

I try with everything I have to command my body to move, but it won't. *MOVE! I demand you to MOVE!* With all the strength I have left, I swing my left fist and connect with Silas's face. I press firmly into his cheek before I realize I've barely touched him. My head jerks to the side, resting on my shoulder. I've lost. My eyes search frantically for Bianca as I embrace my end.

That's when I see it—a figure made of a pure aura of every color. It stands over her. Is it Silas, or another Sinder Cogent, perhaps? No. I'm too far gone. She is too far gone. I get the feeling this is something else, that I'm witnessing a being far beyond this world.

The radiating figure moves in and out of focus. It hovers over Bianca for a few seconds, then picks up Fate and walks toward me. The colors seem to accelerate and change around the being. Features of a face or faces run through it. For a moment, I think I even see myself in there. Is it me? Am I handing myself Bianca's blade?

I must be delusional. I'm dying. Right here. Right now.

The figure's magnificent colors of red, blue, yellow, green, orange, purple, and white surround me, engulfing my vision. I feel at peace, and my body slips into this state of one. One life, one Mover, one Giver.

The answer to my prayers lies in my hand now. Fate, Bianca's elegant blue blade, has found its way to my hand.

I don't have to tell my body to do anything—with the speed of a thought, Silas is already dead.

I'm released from his grip, and my body bounces off the ground, cratering and pulling me under. A sense of joy rings out inside me, knowing that the Mover of Life brought me here to slay the demon. I'm grateful.

But my gratitude is short-lived as the sound of the approaching Sinder Army creeps in. Roars of unrelenting violence descend upon us from outside the city. I promptly push myself out of my crater in search of Bianca. I can only see her faint blue outline off in the distance.

"Bianca!" I shout. "We did it."

I'm almost to her when my arms give out. My mouth fills with dirt as I slam into the ground. The stampede of soldier's footsteps grows louder and louder.

We may have died, but her dream will live.

"We did it," I whisper.

Chapter 26

In the end, there is no white light, only darkness, nothingness, pain. A burning fire that rips through my body. I hear my name over and over, softly. At first, I can't make the voice out.

Then I have it. It's Katelynn's.

I'm drawn to it as it becomes louder and louder, until her voice erupts with a bright white light.

Light is all I see now, unbearable light shifting in and out of focus. "Am I dead?" I ask, as if Katelynn's voice could respond to me.

"Lucas, Lucas, stay with me."

I'm perplexed at her response, which I can now tell is coming from my left. My eyes shift over to see her face. It's her, it's really her. Am I dead?

She shines a flashlight in my eyes. "Can you hear me?"

I want to sit up and talk to her, but my body won't move. The most I can get is maybe one inch of motion. "Katelynn?"

"But you're dead. I found your necklace in a lab. I held your hand. I sent you off."

She clasps her hands over her mouth, and tears roll down her cheek. She wants to speak, to tell me who I sent beyond, but she can't bring herself to say her name.

"It was Niki, wasn't it?"

Her head drops as she quickly wipes away her tears and grits her teeth. "The last time I saw her, I told her the Giver of Life would protect her. She didn't believe me, so I gave her my necklace and told her not to give up.

"I'm sorry. I couldn't save her."

"No. It's okay. You gave her a sendoff. She's with the Mover of Life now."

I try to sit up. To comfort her.

"Sit back, son," someone says from my other side.

Her voice is familiar, and I can't believe it even when I'm looking right at her. "Miss Caroline?"

"I'm here, Lucas."

It's really her, but she has a bright yellow glow around her body, as if she's a Cogent. I can feel a hand squeezing mine, and trace it back to her.

Before I can get out another word, her arms wrap around me. I'm stunned. It's the first hug she's ever given me.

"I'm so glad you're okay," Miss Caroline says. "You nearly died."

I did. And so did Bianca. Saying her name makes me want to fight with everything I have to find her. "Where's Bianca?"

"She's okay, she's safe."

"She was hurt badly. Is she really going to be okay?"

"I told you, she's going to be fine," Miss Caroline says. "Brooke is with her in the other ambulance."

"I need to see her."

"She's okay, Lucas. You're okay—I finally found you," Katelynn says. "I was so worried I had lost you forever. And I know it's hard to believe, but Miss Caroline was a Cogent this whole time. She gathered our army and tirelessly fought back, saving me and so many others. She didn't want to give up on you, and so every time we heard news of what we thought was you, we came rushing. We got the message that you'd taken over Sincliff, and so we came to support you. That's when we found you had killed the commander of the Sinder Army. We got there just in time. I wasn't sure if you'd make it back to me. But the Giver of Life has brought us back together again." She cries tears of joy, but I don't seem to have the same feelings. I'm overjoyed to see her—I am. But I'm not sure what to say. And then there's Miss Caroline, showing up as a real Cogent this whole time? It all makes sense now, why we couldn't hang on her, why she never cried. She's been hiding it this whole time.

My head pounds with pressure from the back to the front as I attempt to lift myself once more. Nothing works, though, and I find myself dropping back down to relieve the tension in my neck. My tongue feels brittle as it sticks to the roof of my mouth. "Can I have something to drink?"

Katelynn hands me fresh water, sending a sizzle of pain through my stomach. Nothing feels right—It's as if my body is rejecting the water. I must have been close to death. Against the pain, I grab the bottle, taking another chug. I need to make it, to see this through, to see Bianca again.

Recovering, my eyes become focused on the mirror at the top of the vehicle. My reflection shows me the degree to which I barely escaped death. Bruises, scars, and my large wound are all reminders of how close I really was.

"Miss Caroline, where are we going?"

"Home," she responds.

Home.

I'd like to be home again, but I don't think I can get there. It doesn't seem like a real place anymore. Am I really going back? To Rockcliff? I allow myself to relax for a moment, dreaming about being back home in bed. Strangely, I dream of the day I became a Cogent. Lying there, fearing what would come—and now I know. I suppose I should give thanks to the Mover of Life.

"Miss Caroline, have you really been a Cogent this whole time?" I ask, studying the soft tint of yellow in her curls.

She sighs. "Yes, Lucas. I'm sorry I didn't tell you about this earlier. I wanted to, but for your protection, I wasn't allowed. And there's something else you should know now—before your mom died, I was her teacher."

"You knew my mom?" I ask, trying to sit up again.

Her hand forces me back down. "I trained her alongside several Cogents, including Marcus. I was among the first Cogents ever made. I had a duty to raise the protectors of humanity, but I failed them. I failed your mother. I failed you."

"My mother was a Cogent?"

She nods. And suddenly, it all makes sense. That's why Miss Caroline was the only one who survived the attack. And because my mother was a Cogent, she knew I would share the same genetics and be selected for the Cogent program. That's why she trained us in sword fighting.

"I'm sorry, Lucas," she says, trembling with real pain. The kind of hurt you can only see from a mother. This has weighed on her for some time. I can't imagine what she's seen. She's been through the fall of humanity and has tried to protect us ever since.

I want to tell her I forgive her, but she's hugging me before I can get the words out. I'm so happy to see her again. Truly. I'm grateful she's watched over me for so long and never given up on me, even when I was being stupid.

"We're almost there, Lucas," Katelynn says, giving me some more water.

"Thank you."

Her hand lingers on the bottle for a moment, as if she's trying to rekindle what we had before the attack. Unsure how to respond, I comment on her uniform. "You've been fighting this whole time. For everyone."

"For you."

Her words make me happy. To be loved by her is something else. But where do I begin to tell her about Bianca and me? After everything we've been through, how do I tell the girl that I love that I now love someone else?

I can't—and I won't. At least not yet. I need more energy for that conversation, and I'm having enough trouble even focusing on the roof of this ambulance. When I do this, I'm going to need to do this right.

When the low hum of the ambulance comes to a stop, anxiety fills me as I look at the doors. Soldiers open them, and the morning sun pours in. They roll me out, and I stand for the first time, looking for Bianca's ambulance, but I can't see her through the crowd of people.

Katelynn directs me to a wheelchair and leans down to tell me again how happy she is that she found me, then hastily places a kiss on my lips, staying through the burn.

I finally see Bianca standing with her arm around Brooke at the back of the ambulance, her face emotionless at what she's just seen. I want to call out to her, to tell her it was nothing, but I can't. They whisk her away before I can explain.

No one will let me talk to her—they mean to keep me from her for some reason. I wish they knew I only want to be with her right now.

"Okay, Lucas. Let's get you taken care of."

Katelynn takes me to the hospital's underground level, probably the only one left. The place kind of gives me the creeps. It smells like death and rusty metal down here.

"Where are we going?" I ask.

"The recovery pool," she says.

Once the words are out, I can see it exactly in my head. Inside, it's a shallow pool, still and untouched. What surprises me the most is that she asks me to take off my clothes. I try to delay this, thinking she'll leave, but she doesn't.

"I—uh. I can't move well," I confess to her.

Katelynn smiles and walks over to a small metal tray table, picking up a pair of scissors. Carefully, she trims my clothes off my body. I try to joke to her that if I had my energy back, I could burn them off in a second. A neat party trick. She doesn't laugh, though; she continues on with a delicate hand until I'm completely naked.

"You need to lie here for a few hours. I'll be outside," she says.

I enter the pool and fall to my back, sending waves crashing over the edge and onto the floor. The metal door clanks shut, and I settle down as the water warms up. It seems they've done something to this pool, though—the water never boils, which makes me assume they're rapidly changing it out so that it stays cool. Yet it only mildly rotates around my body in a slow current. It takes some getting used to, but once the water cuts off my hearing and the lights dim, I feel like I'm floating in the vat I was created in again, with nothing but my aura.

With my body floating, my mind wanders. I fought and killed Commander Silas; I can't believe it. Katelynn and Bianca are both still alive. We have Rockcliff back. Miss Caroline is a Cogent. She trained my mom. It looks like Brooke and the others are okay. I'm grateful and sad at the same time—sad for the people we lost, but hopeful for our future.

And right now, I need to recover—so I can see Bianca and tell her how I feel.

Chapter 27

The lights illuminate the stage and the anthem booms as I'm brought to the same place where it was announced I would be a Cogent. The crowd is overjoyed, and I wish I could be too, but I struggle to celebrate. Bianca is kept at the other end from me. Liam jabs at Brock, eating up the praise from the crowd. Brooke has decided to wear a wonderful dress instead of her uniform, and Jean is showing her off. I'm so glad they made it out alive. When I get a chance, I'll be thanking Brooke for saving Justin. Seeing him once more meant the world to me.

The room comes to a halt after the anthem. The lights shift to center stage, and Prime Minister Maxwell walks out, triumphant. The crowd goes wild with support, as if he'd slayed Silas himself. He has trouble quieting the room. He speaks of the night Rockcliff was attacked. His recollection starts out slow, with death and destruction, but then he jumps to extreme excitement as he praises us for saving the city.

Deafening cheers fill the room as the prime minister salutes us once more. Bianca looks as though she's recovered well, which makes me feel better. Her face is clean and full of life once again. I still want to kiss her and tell her it's over between me and Katelynn, but I can't.

Much like I was forced to be a Cogent on this stage, I'm forced now to receive their praise. I feel like a fraud again looking into the room of faceless people. This becomes especially hard as I listen to the prime minister give his detailed recap of what happened. He makes it sound as if it was all under control from the beginning, as if Marcus's death was a mild setback and not the reason we lost the city.

Once the city has fallen in his story, he describes Miss Caroline as a strategic genius. He talks of how she helped reclaim Rockcliff and plan out the rescue of our people. Brock and Liam worked alongside her to secure a safe route back, and Brooke led a small disruptive force with Jean and a handful of humans. She successfully liberated people using distance strikes and smoke screens. Stepping up with the beauty of a princess, Brooke extends out a fold of her dress and takes a bow.

When he makes it to us in the story, Maxwell talks as if my absence from the group was a planned rogue op to assassinate Commander Silas. As if I hadn't found Bianca almost dead, and we somehow easily hunted him down. There is no mention of my cowardice. No mention of all the people who died because I was unable to save them. No mention of Justin or any of the countless others I let down.

Next, the prime minister calls for Bianca and me to step forward. He seems pleased with us and stirs up the crowd for a new round of applause. He paints a picture of our final battle, which he didn't see, making us sound almost invincible when fighting Silas.

This is getting uncomfortable. Standing next to her, I check to make sure she's all right. But she doesn't answer. The prime minister places a gold medallion over her head and thanks her for her resilience in battle.

And then it comes to me. I can hear the audience hush for a moment, anticipating the buildup the Prime Minister has orchestrated.

"There is someone on this stage right now. Someone that deserves praise for his sacrifice. Deserves praise for his bravery. Remember his name. He has been chosen by the Giver of Life to defend Humanity. I give you Lucas Conley, our new Hero of Humanity."

Thunderous applause reach a deafening roar. They love me. They truly love me. But they don't know so much of what really happened. Of why I did what I did. And what I didn't do at all. The fact I can stand here now is a miracle. I may be favored, but I'm no Hero of Humanity.

He salutes, and with the anthem playing again, we are rushed off the stage in celebration. I've somehow become a replacement for Marcus, a symbol for humanity, a fraud with a gold medal. I want to tell everyone I'm not the hero they believe me to be, but they've taken away my ability to speak. They'll never know I'm a coward who ran away from fight after fight and was only able to do anything because of the girl standing next to me.

After the award ceremony, Bianca and I are escorted to the prime minister's mansion at the edge of the campus for a victory feast. They claim it's for us, but it seems to be for the wealthy in the city. We are merely a trophy to be paraded about by Maxwell. I do my best to play along, laughing and thanking everyone for the kind words.

As soon as I think we'll get a free moment to talk, a strange old couple approaches and corners us. They look to be of the highest wealth in the community, and explain how they have no doubt humanity will win the war with the two of us leading. Bianca corrects them. "We've won the war. Silas is dead," she says, and I echo her.

The man lets out a creepy chuckle. "Yes, yes, Commander Silas is dead, but his father, Prime Minister Silas, is still very much alive. He will be furious at his son's death, as he should be. But not to worry—he will be next, am I right? Great job, my boy. To our future."

I'm not sure I heard him right. Prime Minister Silas and Commander Silas are not the same person? I stumble backward in confusion, only to be caught by Miss Caroline. "I'm sorry Lucas, I wanted to tell you. But I just didn't know when. I didn't want you to worry while you were recovering."

Under attack once more, I check my side to make sure I haven't really been stabbed. I know Miss Caroline has been a leader of sorts this whole time, but surely they don't expect me to assassinate the prime minister of Sinder. This was supposed to be over.

Bianca has left my sight. Frantically, I search with my eyes until I find her glowing blue aura fading through the crowd. She heard it too—there are two Silases. The prime minister, and his son the commander—who I killed.

I sink to the ground, realizing that Bianca and I are in more danger than ever. We will never be safe. We haven't ended the war as we thought—we've only escalated it. But I can't do this all over again. And I can't let her do this alone.

As I make my way through the crowd of people, Katelynn stops me. She's concerned, asking why I seem distant. It's only been a minute or two; I can catch up to Bianca if I go now. "I'm sorry, I just have to go. We'll talk later, I promise." I know she only means to help me, but she can't right now.

I don't make it five more feet through the crowd before two soldiers approach me and ask me to meet with Prime Minister Maxwell. I tell them I'll be right there and then continue off to the side, trying to avoid the large group that keeps trying to stop me. My movement seems to be monitored, by our own soldiers, and I'm forced to walk through the minister's decorative hedges to escape.

Bianca is my only priority right now; Maxwell will have to wait. My first thought is to check the barracks for her, but when I arrive, it's empty. I don't know why I would think to find her there. She only ever does one thing, and that's train.

Reasonably, I find her at the training room.

I pause to watch her through the windows. Blow after blow, she gives it her all, even when fighting against no one. In my head, I practice what I will say, but I can never seem to get it right. She needs to know how I feel, but I haven't broken it off with Katelynn yet. It wouldn't be right. Either way, I feel like I'm lying to someone who loves and trusts me.

When I open the gym door, Bianca ignores me like she has since we got back. I think she's mad at me, mad that Katelynn is alive. Her face suggests she hasn't left our last battle. It's almost as if she's recreating that fight and trying to improve. Watching from the side, I wait patiently for her to stop, but she never does. She's fighting the demons in her mind, repeatedly and without rest.

"Bianca, I . . ."

She turns her body to avoid any eye contact with me. I'm not going to back down, though. I came here to say something, so I'm going to do just that. Jumping into the ring, I position myself directly in front of her.

"I'm sorry," I say, becoming her opponent.

Her blade connects with mine, inches away from removing my head. "Do you think I want an apology?" she asks, sounding confused.

She swings at me again, this time harder. It's clear she's mad at me. "I'm sorry okay. I'm sorry Katelynn is still alive. I'm sorry she kissed me."

She prepares a volley of attacks, landing with our blades locked against each other. "You don't have to be sorry for that, Lucas. You saved my life. I care about you—and I think you care about me too?"

"I do." She's not wrong. I just don't know how to fix this without hurting someone.

"So, what is there to figure out?" she asks, pushing me away.

I'm not running away. I just need some time. Time to set things right with Katelynn. She doesn't deserve this either. She wasn't there—she doesn't know what happened between Bianca and me.

Bianca's blades fall to her side, her whole being exhausted. She turns around, unable to look me in the eye. "Well, let me know when you figure it out."

"Can you give me some time?"

Angry and frustrated, her glossy brown eyes meet mine. She summons her blade and lunges at me. I parry her swing and continue to follow as she recreates our first fight. With the final attack, however, she beats me to the punch and spins me to the ground, pinning me to the ring.

I'm once again entangled in her beauty.

"Just one more?" she asks, pressing her lips to mine. The warmth from her kiss spreads through my aura, and I pull her a little closer, dreading the moment I'll have to let her go.

215

END OF BOOK ONE

Acknowledgments

It took over a decade to put this together. This story has lived in me this whole time. There are a lot of great people to recognize for helping me along the way. First, a big thank you to my wife, Lauren, who has been there for me all these years. I'm lucky to have such a person that supports and believes in me every day without request, a person in my corner always. Thank you to my children, as they bring joy to my every day. My brother Reuben who helped me flesh out concepts in the early days. My best friend Tommy who gave me quality advice all along the way. My Grandma Sally who encouraged me on a regular basis with excitement. My mother, Juli, who read the whole book in one day. My father, Marty who's always been there for me. My in-laws Brad and Debbie thank you for supporting my family and printing my first draft of my book. My brother and sister in-law Kayla and Rahme for discussing the book with me. My brother-in-law Russ for supporting me. Thanks to the rest of my family: Megan, Micah, Joshua, Reuben, Rachel, Sarah, and Hannah for putting up with me year after year. And a special thanks for my **editor, Dylan Garity,** and my **book cover designer, Alfie Obare**. You two helped bring my book to life, and I'll be forever grateful for that. Thank you.

About the Author

Photo Credit Marie Brock Photography

Jacob lives in North Texas with his wife Lauren and three children. Cogent is his first novel. He is hard at work on his second.

cogentbook@gmail.com
Facebook: Cogent Book @AuthorJacobMaxon
Tik Tok: COGENT_BOOK
Instagram: COGENT_BOOK

Made in the USA
Middletown, DE
17 December 2022

18997580R00135